BRANDILYN COLLINS

bestselling author

DECEIT

A Novel

ZONDERVAN.com/
AUTHORTRACKER
follow your favorite authors

ZONDERVAN

Deceit

This title is also available as a Zondervan ebook.
Visit www.zondervan.com/ebooks.

This title is also available in a Zondervan audio edition.
Visit www.zondervan.fm.

Requests for information should be addressed to:

Zondervan, *Grand Rapids, Michigan 49530*

Library of Congress Cataloging-in-Publication Data

Collins, Brandilyn.-
Deceit / Brandilyn Collins.
p. cm.
ISBN 978-0-310-27644-9 (softcover)
1. Missing persons—Investigation—Fiction. I. Title..
PS3553.O4747815D45 2010
813'.54—dc22 2009053275

Published in association with the literary agency of Alive Communications, Inc., 7680 Goddard Street, Suite 200, Colorado Springs, CO 80920. www.alivecommunications.com

Cover design: Curt Diepenhorst
Cover photography: Shutterstock®
Interior design: Michelle Espinoza

Printed in the United States of America

---

10 11 12 13 14 15 /DCI/ 21 20 19 18 17 16 15 14 13 12 11 10 9 8 7 6 5 4 3 2 1

For Sarah Collins,
my beautiful daughter-in-law.

WANT TO DISCUSS *DECEIT* WITH YOUR BOOK CLUB?

Insightful questions about this story and how it applies to your life can be found on my website at: www.brandilyncollins.com

"Would it turn out well if [God] examined you?
Could you deceive him as you might deceive men?"

Job 13:9 (NIV)

“God sees not as man sees,
For man looks at the outward appearance,
But the Lord looks at the heart.”

1 Samuel 16:7 (NASB)

DECEIT

ONE

FEBRUARY 2010

Some evil shouts from rooftops, some scuttles in the dark. The greatest evil tips its face toward light with shining innocence.

Baxter Jackson shone with the worst of them.

In my sister's kitchen I focused out the sliding glass door to her backyard. Relentless rain pummeled the night. The weather matched my mood. The *Vonita Times*, our town's weekly paper, lay on the square wooden table across from me. Its front-page headline glared: *Skip Tracer Accuses Police Chief of Shirking Duty.*

My sister followed my gaze. "Maybe it really was an accident, Joanne."

I shot her a look of accusation and hurt. "You too?" As if the rest of the town weren't enough. "I thought you agreed with me."

She drew a long breath. "I don't know what to think. Two wives gone does look suspicious, but there's no proof Baxter did anything. Once Cherisse's death was ruled an accident— "

"How many people fall down stairs and die, Dineen, even if they are hardwood? That only happens in old movies."

"But that's what the coroner *said*."

"And he's up for reelection next year, and who do you suppose gave the most to his last campaign?"

"I know, but I just can't believe any coroner would find signs of a murder and look the other way, especially this man. I mean, I *know* Bud Gidst. So do you."

I pushed back my chair, picked up my plate, and stacked hers on top. Marched them over to the sink and set them down none too gently. I loved my sister like crazy, always had. She was twelve years younger, and I'd always looked after her. I steered her clear of bratty, bully girls in grade school, the wrong guys in high school. I urged her to fight her self-serving ex in court until he paid the two years' worth of child support he owed for Jimmy. But the fact was, Dineen had always been too trusting. She just couldn't believe anything bad about anybody until it hit her in the face.

"Sometimes people don't want to see the truth, Dineen." I rinsed the plates, the water hissing. "Autopsy findings are open to interpretation. To say all those bruises and contusions on Cherisse's head didn't match a fall down the stairs would be calling Baxter Jackson a liar. Maybe Bud didn't want to believe that."

Or maybe his ruling was far more sinister. Baxter Jackson was the richest man in Vonita and practically ran the town. He sponsored a Little League baseball team and personally paid for Vonita's Fourth of July fireworks. He was everybody's best friend. Nobody in the county ever spoke against Baxter.

Except me.

I turned off the water. If only I could wring that eavesdropping reporter's neck. My argument with the chief of police had not been intended for the public's ear.

"Yeah, maybe." My sister sounded only half convinced. She pushed a lock of dark hair behind her ears, then hugged herself.

Voices from the TV drifted in from the den. Nine-year-old Jimmy was watching some reality cop show. My head hurt. I walked back to my chair and slumped into it, suddenly feeling old at fifty-two. Dineen pressed her lips together and regarded me with a beleaguered expression. Her hazel eyes held concern. "I'm just sorry you've gotten yourself mixed up in this."

Thursday's newspaper headline fairly shouted at me. I reached out and flipped it over. "I know." I gave her a wan smile. "But I shouldn't be worrying you about it. You've got enough to deal with right now, given your stress at work."

Dineen shrugged. "It's not that bad. Things are just crazy because Doug's so wrapped up in the lawsuit. It's almost over. He'll win, as usual, and he and his client will walk away with lots of cash. Everybody will be happy again."

Everyone except the San Jose hospital he was suing.

I made a face. "Including you, I hope. Happy, as in getting a big honking present for all the abuse you've taken." Dineen answered phones at Doug Brewer's firm, nothing more. She wasn't a law clerk. She didn't deserve his snapping temper. But when Doug was fighting a big case, *everyone* around him bore the brunt of his impatience.

"Were things any different for you on Friday, after that came out?" I gestured with my chin toward the newspaper. Doug and Baxter were good friends. I didn't want my sister taking any heat for me.

My sister fiddled with her hair. "Not really."

"What does 'not really' mean, Dineen?"

She tilted her head. "A few people did ask me what you were thinking. I didn't even see Doug. He went straight to court."

Yeah, what *was* I thinking? Who was I to go up against Baxter Jackson?

"Know what?" I sounded sorry for myself, and I hated it. My nerves were just too worn to care. "Right now you and Jimmy are about my only friends in town."

"Come on, that's not true."

"It *is*, Dineen. You should see the looks I've gotten the last few days. The disgusted whispers." Sudden tears bit my eyes. I looked at the table.

Dineen made an empathic sound in her throat. "What about all your friends at church? You'll see them tomorrow."

Her words pierced. I shook my head. "I can't go back there, not now. With Baxter as head elder? Which side do you think would win? And anyway, I don't want those dear people taking sides. I can't put them in that position. They loved Cherisse, and Linda before that." My voice tightened. "They're like family to Baxter. They're grieving along with him."

Cherisse had died only two weeks ago. I could imagine church members' reactions as they read that newspaper article. Even though they loved me. Even though I'd attended that church for fifteen years, long before my husband, Tom, died of a heart attack. I was the one who always got things done. Led committees, rallied the troops for fund-raisers, taught Sunday school. They knew my heart for helping others. But how *dare* I talk against Baxter Jackson—especially as he mourned the death of his second wife? How could I be so cruel?

Dineen laid a hand on my arm. "I'm sorry. I know how much you miss Linda."

Yes, I did miss her. Terribly. Linda, the irrepressible woman who encouraged everyone around her. Even in those moments when some inner pain she refused to share fleeted across her face, she would shake it off, flash that dazzling smile of hers. Now, six years later, Linda's disappearance still haunted me. Baxter claimed she'd left the house one night and never returned. A few days later her car was found some twenty miles away, smears of her blood on the front seat. Her body was never recovered. I didn't believe Baxter's story about my best friend—not after what she'd told me. And she hadn't been herself for weeks before her disappearance, would barely even return my calls.

But Chief Eddington hadn't listened to me then either.

Indignation bubbled inside me once more. I raised my eyes. "Two wives in six years, Dineen." One unsolved murder and one *accident*. "A total of one million dollars' life insurance. *One million*. Why would he even take out policies on his wives in the first place, when neither of them worked?" Linda's policy had taken three years to come through. The courts had to declare her dead first, aided by the fact that her credit cards, bank account, nothing had been touched since the night of her disappearance. Even so, I wouldn't be surprised if Baxter's influence swayed that legal process as well.

Dineen lifted a shoulder. There was nothing in this argument we hadn't covered a dozen times before.

Sometimes I wished I could be more like her. More of an accepter, less of a fighter. Life would be so much easier. But I just hadn't been wired that way.

I leaned back and pressed my hands to my temples.

"Another headache?" Dineen asked.

I nodded.

Dineen rose and walked to the cabinet by her refrigerator, where she pulled out a bottle of heavy-duty aspirin. She shook out two and handed them to me. "Here."

"Thanks." I swallowed them with the last gulp of water from my glass. A gust of wind pelted rain against the sliding door. It was nasty out there. February in Vonita, California, forty miles south of San Jose, was balmy compared to some parts of the country. The current temperature hovered in the low forties. But the dampness made it feel so much colder. I hated winter rain. It reminded me of death and despair. Five years ago I'd buried my husband on a day like this.

I pushed from my chair. "Better go."

"Want a Jelly Belly hit?" Dineen gestured toward my favorite cabinet.

"Always." I managed a smile. "Especially if you've got Grape Jelly or Watermelon. They're my headache flavors."

Dineen fetched a large glass bowl from the cabinet. "I don't know what's what in here. You figure it out."

I leaned over the bowl, moving the candies around with a finger. Grape Jelly ones are dark purple. Watermelon are green. I found a few of each and popped them in my mouth one by one, relishing each bite. Nothing in this world beat Jelly Belly jelly beans. Particularly on a night like this.

In the den I leaned over the couch to brush my fingers against Jimmy's cheek. He was recovering from a nasty bout of flu. Jimmy looked pale and tired, but he smiled at me all the same. His brown hair stuck out in all directions—a casualty of lying against all the gathered throw pillows. "G'night, Aunt Joanne."

"Good night, favorite nephew."

"I'm your only nephew."

"Well, if I had a hundred, you'd still be my favorite."

At the front door I pulled on a raincoat and picked up my umbrella. Dineen hugged me hard. "This mess will all blow over, you'll see. Chief Eddington can't stay mad at you forever."

"Sure." I slid my purse over my arm. No point in disagreeing, even though I knew better. Wayne Eddington and Baxter Jackson went way back. "Thanks for dinner, as always."

Dineen nodded. "See ya next Saturday."

"You bet."

She opened the door, and the monster wind blew its clammy breath over us. I stuck my umbrella outside, hit the button on its handle, and hurried down the porch steps to my Toyota 4Runner. By the time I slid into the car my ankles were wet and chilled.

The loud battering on the roof turned up my headache. Gritting my teeth, I started the car. The digital clock read 8:33 p.m.

My house lay about five miles from Dineen's on Stillton, a rural road at the edge of town. I drove stiff-backed, fat raindrops cascading through my headlights and bouncing off the pavement like spilled popcorn. My thoughts eddied with increasing frustration. In my own business as a skip tracer I spent my workdays hunting down people, many of them criminals. I'd built a good reputation for finding my skips. Now I had a possible double murderer in my sites, one of his victims my best friend. A friend I could have saved, if I'd only pushed harder.

And now I couldn't do a thing about my suspicions.

I passed through the last stoplight on Elmer and turned left onto Stillton. Two miles of narrow road and curves, and I'd reach my warm, dry house. I turned up the heat in the car. Eyes narrowed, I drove slowly, frowning at the headlights of an oncoming vehicle until it swished by. My windshield wipers drummed a furious beat.

"*Why* didn't you investigate Cherisse's death?" I'd demanded of Chief Eddington four days ago. We stood in his office at the station, the door open. I tried to keep my voice low.

The chief's face reddened. He planted both hands on his thick hips. "So now you're going to rag me about *this* case for the next six years? They're *over*, Joanne. Both Jackson cases are closed."

"And you're happy about that, aren't you? Now life can just go on, and Baxter remains your favorite pal."

The rest of our heated argument ran through my head. I'd never even seen reporter Andy Wangler in the station, much less in proximity to hear us. He must have salivated all over his notepad.

My last bend before home approached. I eased off the accelerator.

A hooded figure darted into the road.

I gasped and punched the brake. The anti-lock system shuddered. The figure jerked its head half toward me, one side of a man's face lit skeletal white. A rivulet of blood jagged down his bony cheek. The eye on the shadowed half of his face shrunk as black and deep as an empty socket.

He raised his arms.

My car slid toward him.

I whipped the steering wheel left. The figure jumped backward.

Too late.

I heard a sickening *bump* on my right fender. In peripheral vision I glimpsed the body knocked aside. My Toyota kicked into a spiral over slickened asphalt. The world dizzied as I spun, my widened eyes taking in a dancing fence on the road's left side ... the curve I'd already traveled ... a gnarled oak straight ahead ... a crumpled figure on the ground. My wet tires sang and sizzled, the smell of my own sweat acrid in my nostrils.

A hysterical thought flashed in my brain: *I hit the Grim Reaper.*

With a final nauseating jolt my SUV carved to a stop in the middle of the dark and rain-pelted road.

TWO

Sounds hit first — the beating rain, the squall of my heart. I slumped forward, unable to move. Breath shuddered down my throat, my fingers glued hooks on the steering wheel.

An eternal moment passed ... two.

The hard fist of reality punched me in the face. I'd hit a man. What if I killed him?

I lifted my head. Where was the man's body? I could barely see the pavement, much less the field beyond it. My car hulked astride both lanes, canted toward the left side of the road.

I straightened. My shaking left hand found the door handle, wrapped around it. The door opened with a sodden click. With a grunt I shoved open the door and half fell from the car. Despite my coat, snarling rain soaked me within seconds. It dripped into my eyes, trailed corpselike fingers down the back of my shirt. I swung my pounding head right, left, seeking my bearings.

During the spin I'd glimpsed the man on the right.

Hunched over, I fought my way to the front of the car, around its hood. Squinting, I searched the road's edge for the man. My car's headlights, pointed in the opposite direction, were no help.

There. Not far from the oak tree. He lay on one side, his back to me, unmoving. No Grim Reaper after all. He wore not a cloak, but black jeans and sneakers, a black hooded jacket. He looked average in build and height.

I surged over to the man and sank down on one knee. With tentative hands I reached out and brushed the back of his slick jacket hood. I couldn't see his face. Should I turn him over, check for a pulse? What if he was alive and the forced movement made his injuries worse?

I placed my fingers on the man's shoulder. He groaned. Startled, I snatched my hand away.

Only then did I think of my cell phone. I should have called 911 before leaving my car. Time was ticking and every second may be valuable to the man's life. Yet a voice deep within me whispered a vague warning. Something about this whole thing was off. Besides, I hadn't been going fast at all.

"C-can you hear me?" I forced the words out, loud enough to survive the hammer of the rain.

The man rolled away from me onto his stomach.

"Sir? Let me help you."

"No."

The word came raw and muffled. Had I heard it at all?

"Are you hurt? Do you want me to call for help?"

"No. Just listen to me."

"But— "

"Listen."

Nonplused, I watched the man gather both arms close to his chest, pull his legs up. Palms flat to ground, he pushed himself to a trembling crouch and hung there, head down. Rain streamed off the tip of his hood. I could see nothing of his face.

"Please let me help you up. I can take you to the hospital. Or call 911."

His body tensed, shoulders arching like a wounded animal rising. "I'm just shaken." His voice growled, menacing enough to make me draw away. "I'm fine."

"You don't look it."

"I'm *fine.*" Fury pulsed in his tone. He pushed up further on his haunches, face still hidden, then unfolded his body until he stood. I jumped up and took two steps back. For a moment the man wavered. He stepped one foot forward, found his balance.

The rain sizzled and bounced and pounded. I would go mad with it. "At least let me take you somewhere. Where's your car? Where did you come fr—?"

"You want Baxter Jackson?"

My mouth snapped shut.

Slowly the hooded head turned toward me until one eye glared in my direction. The cheek below it looked waxen, the blood thick.

A mask. He was wearing a mask.

What kind of man *was* this?

Intensity vibrated from his blackened stare. I tried to turn, flee, but my legs rooted to the road.

"*Do* you?"

"Who are you?"

"Joanne, *do you* want to see Baxter Jackson pay for Linda's death?"

My eyes widened. "I—yes."

"Find Melissa. She knows what happened."

Melissa.

Understanding leapt into my head, dark and gleaming. My knees nearly gave way. I was *right.* I'd been right all along.

"You're telling me Baxter killed Linda."

"Melissa saw it."

The words stunned me. Fierce questions crowded my tongue. "Does she have proof?"

"She knows where the body is."

A body. Grief singed my lungs. I'd known Linda was dead. The courts had ruled she was. But without remains, a stubborn ray of hope for life always shines.

Hooded Man seemed to swell in size. The rain and darkness beat down on me, drowning out rational thought. My mind screamed to escape this surreal and throbbing scene. I backed away—and a steely hand clamped on my arm.

"Wait."

I froze, gaze fastened upon my still-running car, its windshield wipers in frantic swipe. The SUV sang of warmth and safety. Suddenly it seemed so far away, as if I'd fallen into a Stygian painting and looked back upon my world, eternally lost.

The fingers tightened around my arm. "*Don't* tell the police."

A shudder racked between my shoulder blades. "I won't."

"Don't tell *anyone*."

"Okay."

"Jackson will kill you if he finds out. Understand?"

"Yes."

The cold fingers fell away. "Go."

Without a backward glance I ran to my car, around the hood. Flung open the driver's door. I fell inside and slammed the door shut. Dry air closed in, the pounding now in stereo upon every inch of the roof. I pulled the SUV's gearshift from Park to Drive, turned the wheel right to straighten out the car.

My headlights stabbed the road. I threw a glance toward where the man had stood.

He was gone, swallowed into darkness.

THREE

Melissa saw it.

As my foot hit the accelerator, sickening regret washed through me. I eased off, ready to brake. In that split second I saw myself jumping out of the car, yelling for the man, begging him to come back. Why hadn't I pressed him for more information? Why had I allowed panic to overtake me?

New fear surged. How could I even think of looking for a strange man in a mask after dark? All alone out here?

I pressed on the gas. My car engine gunned. Immediately I slowed, afraid to go too fast in the downpour.

My house lay close, just around the next bend. It seemed as if I'd been gone for hours.

The inside of the 4Runner began to fog. I turned up the dashboard fan.

She knows where the body is.

Melissa Harkoff—the sixteen-year-old foster girl Linda and Baxter had taken in during that summer of Linda's disappearance. Someone from social services had arrived at the Jackson house to pick Melissa up the day Linda's blood-smeared car was discovered. A few weeks later Baxter announced in church that he'd heard Melissa had run away from her new foster home. He'd led us all in a special prayer for her safety.

I'd always felt sorry for Melissa. She'd arrived at the Jacksons a frightened teenager, trying with all her might to look strong, hardened. I sensed that Melissa watched every word she said, wanting to fit in, seeking Linda's approval. I know she came to love living with the Jacksons. And she'd been so grieved at Linda's disappearance. To think that Melissa witnessed Linda's murder. How terrified she must have been. Baxter probably threatened *her* life if she told.

Questions in my head whirled and eddied. The Hooded Man—who was he? How did he know Melissa saw Baxter kill Linda?

When the police had questioned Melissa she gave them the same story as Baxter did. No one ever suspected she knew anything different. *I* hadn't even suspected that. Melissa had seemed to think the world of Baxter.

I rounded the curve. The lights of my house glowed into view, a welcoming beacon. Never had my small home, its front porch with white square pillars, looked like such a haven. I turned right into my driveway, hit the garage remote, and slipped inside as soon as the door opened.

The sudden cessation of rain on my car roof rang in my ears. I turned off the engine and tried to breathe. Wet cold bit into my muscles until my whole body shook.

"Don't tell the police."

I should, though. Not about what the man had said, but that I'd hit him. What if he turned against me and reported a hit-and-run?

But why would he do that, after the warnings he'd given? And with no victim, what would I tell the police? That I'd hit an unknown masked man who'd materialized from the night, then vanished like a specter? The Vonita police would surely be all ears. They were so attuned to listening to me these days.

Did I know this man? I hadn't recognized his voice. But he'd spoken in such a gravelly tone.

On purpose?

I pushed the button to close my garage door, grabbed my purse, and got out of the car. My feet squished as I crossed to the door that led into my kitchen. I placed my hand on the knob—

Wait.

I pulled up short.

Why had the man been out on that road? Where had he come from, where was he going? He'd been so close to my house. What if he meant to harm me? What if he'd been *here* while I was gone? It was no secret I went to my sister's for dinner every Saturday night.

Water dripped from every inch of me, puddling at my feet. I shivered.

If the man wanted to harm me, why hadn't he taken his chance when he had me alone on the road, not another car in sight?

Maybe because the accident had hurt him just enough ...

I lifted my hand from the knob and stared at the door, afraid of what I might find on the other side. I shook all over, miserably cold. Logic wormed its way into my brain once more—the man hadn't hurt me, far from it. He'd given me incredible information. Melissa *knew* what had happened.

But how could I trust this man when he hadn't even been willing to show his face?

Fine, Joanne—and if you don't walk through your own door right now, just what do *you plan to do?*

A violent shudder possessed my limbs. I could barely feel my fingers and toes. I needed a hot shower. Warm, dry clothes. I needed to think this through.

The SUV's engine ticked. I looked back at the car. Water plinked from it onto the garage's concrete floor.

I could get back inside the car, return to my sister's house.

Then what?

I faced the door, heart stuttering. Another hard shiver wracked my body. I craved heat. Needed it, *now.*

Breathing a prayer, I opened the door and ventured into the house.

FOUR

JUNE 2004

Wow. Sixteen-year-old Melissa Harkoff's jaw hinged loose. The house was *crazy*.

She gaped through the back window of the Jacksons' fancy car. A Mercedes. That should have given her a clue. But nothing could have prepared her for this *mansion*. Two-story, with big gray stones around the front door, and chimneys on each end. The driveway circled in front, a long sidewalk sweeping up to three wide steps of the porch. Green, thick bushes lined the sidewalk, and big pots of flowers sat on the porch. The windows were large and clean. And the house went on for ... like forever.

How many rooms did a house like that hold? Twenty? Fifty? Each one must be as long as a yacht.

And one of them was for her. A bedroom. With a sturdy door she could close.

Tears welled in Melissa's eyes. This couldn't be happening. Any minute now she'd wake up back in her mother's filthy trailer. She'd open her eyes to a stained, saggy ceiling. Hear her mother's hack and cough, the clink of the first bottle she'd pulled from a paint-peeling cabinet. Gin. The whiskey would come later. Melissa would smell the trailer's stale mustiness of dirt and despair. A life going nowhere. She'd pull on old clothes and slip out the door to school before taking a true, deep breath.

Melissa blinked back the tears. She never cried in front of anybody, much less people she hardly knew.

She looked down at her lap, taking in the new designer jeans Linda had just bought for her. The pink, crisp top. Matching sandals. They'd stopped at a big mall before coming here. Mr. Jackson—Baxter, he told her to call him—had waited patiently while she tried on a bunch of stuff. He told Melissa she looked "very nice" when she came out to show Linda the jeans and top she liked best. He was holding Linda's hand, and they smiled at each other like they shared a fun secret.

Baxter wasn't hot-looking at all. He had a boyish face, kind of round, with thick, dark hair parted on the side. The hair looked totally eighties. He had brown eyes, and his jawline was a little soft. Sort of looked like a grown-up choirboy. But there was something about him. He wasn't that tall, but he seemed to tower over Melissa, as if some power vibrated from his body. She'd found herself eyeing him, trying to figure him out. He was nothing but kind to her. Not coming on to her in any way. But what *was* it about him? In a huge party, you'd know when this guy entered the room. You'd *feel* it, as if the air changed. *Magnetism*, that was the word. He oozed it.

Melissa's hands trembled. She stuffed them between her knees. This day was too much already. Had to be a dream. One wrong move with these people, and she'd find herself back in the system tomorrow, praying for another foster home.

The last one hadn't turned out so great.

"You like the house?" Linda asked from the front seat. Her voice was light, sort of chirpy. As if she was talking to a child. She half turned around, part of her face in view. She was pretty, with smooth skin and gray-blue eyes. Her makeup looked stunning. She'd done the model thing with eye shadow, darker at the corners, and colored liner smudged just right underneath. Melissa wanted to learn how to do that. Probably needed expensive makeup, not the cheap stuff she'd managed to buy for herself. Or steal.

"Yeah." Melissa affected a shrugging tone. "It's nice."

Linda smiled. "Good. I hope you like your room. We can change anything you don't like."

"Are the walls all gray stained?"

Linda made an empathetic noise in her throat. "No."

"Does it smell like old socks and stale cigarette smoke?"

"No."

"We don't smoke," Baxter said. "Nasty habit."

Tell me about it. "Then I'll like it."

Baxter pulled the Mercedes into a three-car garage. In the space next to them sat a blue BMW. And on the other side of that, a red Corvette.

Melissa thrust her jaw forward, studying the vehicles. Why have three cars when you didn't even have kids? Mrs. Campbell, her social worker, had told Melissa the Jacksons couldn't have children. Maybe they planned to bring a bunch more foster kids home. Maybe Melissa would end up babysitting a bunch of little brats. Or cleaning out the fireplaces like Cinderella. *Something* had to go wrong here. This was looking too perfect.

Baxter turned off the engine and caught Melissa's eye through the rearview mirror. "Welcome home, Melissa."

Home. Not "welcome to our house." Welcome *home.*

Melissa stared back at him. She wanted to say something, but her throat felt too tight. She nodded.

Linda turned around again, and Melissa's gaze wandered to her face. She studied Melissa with a mixture of sadness and hope. "We know you've had a hard time, honey." Linda's voice was soft. "But everything's going to be fine now. We'll all work together to *make* it fine."

"Better than that." Baxter patted his wife's arm. "We'll make it great."

FIVE

FEBRUARY 2010

In the kitchen I flipped on the fluorescent light, the door to my garage closing behind me. My gaze cruised the room. The porcelain sink lay clean and empty, a glass to its right on the counter. The beige cabinets and drawers were all closed. The floor, except the spot I stood upon, was dry. Nothing looked out of place.

My eyes fixed upon the sliding glass door that led to my small backyard patio. Locked.

I took off my dripping coat and laid it on the counter. Set my purse on the table. The sounds of my movements seemed so loud. For a moment I stood, breathing. Feeling the house. Had that man been here, done something?

Why would he?

My feet took me through the kitchen and into the living room, in the front part of the house. I lingered just inside the doorway, looking at my brown suede couch and matching armchair, the women's magazines scattered on the long wooden coffee table. My TV and stereo and tall, slim cabinet of CDs—most of them classic rock. All appeared normal.

"Melissa saw it." The man's voice echoed in my head.

I crossed the living room to check the locks on the front windows. In place.

Next I walked straight across the entry hall and into the second bedroom used as an office. My desk and computer sat as I'd left them, the screen saver randomly sifting through pictures. A photo of me and Tom filled the monitor. I stared at it remembering the day five years ago, only three months before his fatal heart attack. Tom had been an outdoorsman, rugged in his way, yet gentle and kind. Laid back. He'd been a counterbalance to my fighter personality. "Just calm down, Joanne," he'd told me more than once. "Think twice before you rush into things."

If only I could hear his wisdom on this night.

The picture faded, and a shot of Linda materialized. She was sitting on my back patio, laughing, head thrown back, and perfectly made-up eyes half-closed. One hand in her fashionably blonde-streaked hair. Her nose was scrunched. I could almost hear that laughter now—boisterous and full, with a note of sheer abandonment. Nobody laughed like Linda.

The scene poofed away.

My head pounded.

I touched my mouse, and the file I'd been working on before leaving for Dineen's blipped onto the monitor. The Bruce Whittley case. A month ago Whittley had skipped out on his wife and two children in Burbank, California, leaving them with a mountain of credit card debt and an overdrawn bank account. His wife's incensed parents had hired me to find him.

Now I needed to find Melissa.

That might not be so easy. A trail six years cold, maybe a new last name from marriage. And after seeing Baxter kill Linda, being tracked down as a legal witness would be the last thing Melissa would want. She'd be at least a medium-level "fresh" skip. Maybe even a hardcore skip by now if she'd spent those six years running up bills she couldn't pay. Even if I did find her, she could refuse to talk.

My gaze rose to the wooden clock on the wall. Its gold hands read 8:48. I'd left my sister's house just fifteen minutes ago.

How could that be?

A shiver racked me from shoulders to toes. Something inside me whispered that my life had changed in those fifteen minutes. As if I'd entered a malevolent cave and did not know what lay before me. In the last few days, I'd already become a pariah in this town. Hooded Man's stunning information now shoved me into a far darker place—Baxter Jackson's greatest enemy. Because if anyone could find the runaway teenager after six years, I could.

"If he finds out, he'll kill you."

I closed Bruce Whittley's file on the computer.

Rubbing my arms, I turned aside and focused on the window behind and to the right of my desk. The blinds were drawn. I always shut them after dark. I leaned over the desk, lifted the bottom of the blinds, and peered at the lock. In place.

Did Hooded Man stand alone, a single person who wanted to bring Jackson to justice? Or was he one of a group?

Whatever the answer, he was a coward. Knowing the truth, yet saying nothing all these years. Leaving me to ferret it out alone.

Fine. If I had to go this alone, so be it. When it was all over, everyone would know the truth. This time I wouldn't let Linda down.

I left the office through its second exit, into the hallway stretching to the master bedroom on the end. High on the wall to my left, just outside the kitchen, Billy Bass the Singing Fish stretched motionless upon his wooden mount. He faced the kitchen and the door leading to the garage, his tail toward me.

I moved to stand before him. "You see anything, Billy?"

His cold glass eyes revealed nothing.

Dineen had given Billy Bass to Tom on what turned out to be my husband's final Christmas. The thing nearly drove me crazy, but Tom loved it. Billy Bass had a motion-sensor switch. If anyone walked past him, he'd burst into the stupid song "Don't Worry, Be Happy," flipping his tail and raising his head to look you in the eye. Three-year-old Jimmy and Tom had played it over and over that Christmas, laughing for hours. I swore I never wanted to hear the song again.

Once Tom died I couldn't bear to take Billy Bass off the wall. Once in a while I even turned it on just to hear it sing. It always made me think of Tom. But by now the batteries had died.

Oh, Tom, I need you now.

Turning away from Billy Bass, I walked down the hall to peek into the laundry room, then the second bath on my left. I saw nothing askew. All the same I stepped inside each room to inspect the window locks.

My bedroom remained. I entered the room, which ran the length of the house from front to back. The bed was still neatly made, its magenta comforter meeting a matching dust ruffle. The drawers of my two dressers were shut, scattered framed pictures of me and Tom untouched. Near the window facing the front yard sat an armchair—my favorite place for reading. The novel I was halfway through sat on the chair. A romance.

Why did I torture myself like that?

More important questions nagged me. Once I found Melissa—then what? How to convince her to come forward now, after six years of hiding such a terrible secret?

I checked all my bedroom windows. Still locked.

On dark impulse, I picked up the phone on the nightstand by my bed. Pushed *talk*. The dial tone hummed in my ear.

The beige-tiled master bathroom looked normal. I lifted aside a window curtain and pressed my face to the glass, peering into the backyard. My two gnarled oak trees bent beneath the deluge like wizened old men. I could barely make out the black wood fence at the rear of my property.

If someone had wanted to approach my house unseen, this was the night to do it. But no way could Hooded Man have come inside without leaving footprints, a trail of water.

Which he easily could have cleaned up.

Another violent shudder possessed my body—both of fear and penetrating cold. I should take a hot shower. But stepping under that nozzle would place me in such a vulnerable position. Naked. Running water masking other sounds.

Time to install a burglar alarm. In the quiet town of Vonita, I'd never before felt unsafe.

As I pulled back from the window I caught sight of my reflection in the glass—a pitiful sight. My chin-length brown hair was plastered to my head, my face looking white and clammy. My dark, frightened eyes appeared sunken, and the lines running from my nose to mouth cut deep. Age fifty-two, nothing. I could have been sixty-five.

I dropped the curtain into place, a needle of despair piercing deep. Linda's disappearance had been terrible. Tom's death one year later had aged me. We'd never been able to have children—a crucial loss Linda and I had in common. I'd felt so alone since Tom's passing. Now this. Suddenly a part of me didn't want to find Melissa at all. I was just too tired.

Maybe I should move away from this town, start a new life. I could live anywhere in the country, since my work was done from home.

But I'd have to leave Dineen and Jimmy—my only family. And how could I ever live with myself, knowing Baxter Jackson still walked the streets? Linda deserved justice. And if Cherisse had been murdered, so did she. If I did manage to present the Vonita police with evidence of Baxter's guilt regarding Linda, they'd likely take a second look into Cherisse's death.

My teeth chattered. I *had* to warm up. In a flurry of motion I peeled off my clothes and turned on the shower to hot.

As I stepped into the tub, a frisson shook my shoulders. I swiveled my head, focused with sharp eyes on the bathroom door. My bedroom and the whole empty house loomed in my mind, full of shadowed corners and unknowns. I hadn't checked closets.

Where had Hooded Man gone after he'd disappeared? Where was he now?

"Jackson will kill you if he finds out."

My jaw tightened. I didn't want to give in to fears. Hooded Man had relayed his information and was now long gone.

Stubborn imaginings chewed my mind.

Unclothed, skin still wet from the rain, I battled cold worse than ever.

Exhaling aloud, I wrapped myself in a towel and traversed the chilly bathroom tile in my bare feet. I walked out into my bedroom, crossed the room, peered down the hallway. Nothing. Just my house. Lit. Safe.

Why couldn't I believe that?

With a firm hand I shut my bedroom door. Locked it. No harm in being cautious.

Back in the bathroom, I locked its door also.

The shower pelted hot water, steam rising from the tub. My soaked skin couldn't bear another minute of cold. I hurried over to the tub and stepped inside. Yanked the shower curtain shut. Eyes closed, heart thumping, I surrendered myself to blessed heat.

SIX

Hot water never felt so good.

I stepped out of the tub, body red and muscles throbbing with heat. The long shower had beat my headache back to a dull pinch. My thoughts had settled into grim determination. I would find Melissa Harkoff. And I would start tonight.

Bruce Whittley and the other skips I was being paid to find would, by necessity, still claim my work days. So what if I lost a little sleep working on Melissa's case after hours? And for the moment I still had the rest of the weekend.

My fingers itched to get started.

Quickly I dressed in a sweat suit and super-warm socks and blow-dried my hair to keep my head warm. A new and volatile wind moaned around the back corner of my house. It taunted that I would never find Melissa. That she'd made herself as invisible as the brazen air that formed its groaning.

When I shoved those thoughts aside, questions about Hooded Man nibbled my mind. Had he driven out to Stillton and waited to flag me down as I returned from Dineen's house? If so he'd stashed his car on some turn-off. Or had someone dropped him there, prepared to pick him up after the message was delivered?

A bloody-cheeked mask. Why had he chosen that? Didn't he know such a visage on a wild-weather night would be frightening? Why not wear a clown mask, or a Richard Nixon, for that matter?

Right, Joanne. As if those would be any less scary.

Whatever the reason, Hooded Man had obviously gone to great lengths to hide his identity. A telephone call would have been so much easier. But he was no doubt paranoid about the number being recorded. Maybe he knew just enough about skip tracing to think I had super capabilities on both of my phone lines. I didn't. My home line would record a number just like anyone else's — if the ID wasn't blocked. But I did also have a "trapline" using an 877 toll-free number, which recorded all incoming numbers whether the ID was blocked or not. Traplines are one of my many crafty tools.

In a skewed sort of way Hooded Man's paranoia bound us together. We were both scared of what Baxter Jackson would do if he discovered my mission.

I sat down before my office computer. The clock read 9:18 p.m. Outside, the rain clawed my windows like some monster come to beg.

A shudder kicked across my shoulders.

It could be a late night, depending on how long it took until I exhausted my online tricks. This wasn't exactly the time of day I could pick up the phone to verify information I unearthed. I'd need two things to get me through: Jelly Bellies and music.

In my bottom drawer, I consulted my Jelly Belly stash. All fifty flavors were there, each labeled in its own plastic zip bag. I pulled out Sizzling Cinnamon — my flavor for mad. Cappuccino for raw determination. Green Apple for sassiness. The last one was a lie, but I needed all the encouragement I could get. I ate two of those green babies, one after the other.

From my iTunes I selected my huge playlist of classic rock and clicked *shuffle*. Chicago flicked on — "Baby, What a Big Surprise."

Apropos.

Pumped up and ready, I opened a new file, then hesitated in naming it. If the worst happened and Baxter somehow discovered what I was doing, I didn't want Melissa's information easily found on my computer.

My fingers typed in "HM" for Hooded Man.

The familiar thrill skidded down my spine. The hunt had begun.

SEVEN

JUNE 2004

Melissa stumbles up the hall from her tiny bedroom, arms against the thin walls for balance. The smelly trailer lists to one side, as if it's about to fall over. Melissa's feet slide and drag, the hallway never-ending. She's heard a noise and needs to see what has happened. It's something terrible. Now it's so eerily quiet, not a peep from her mother. "Mom!" Melissa calls, but the only response is the echo of her own frightened voice. She tries to move faster, but her muscles feel like they're weighted with lead.

The trailer stretches, stretches, until it's as long as a football field. Chill bumps pop out on Melissa's arms. Way at the end she can see the back of their ragged couch, the metal frame around the front door. Beyond the living area lies the tiny, crusted kitchen. No movement there. No stream of mumbled cussing. Where *is her mother?*

Cigarette smoke thickens the air. Melissa sucks the biting odor into her lungs with every panted breath. Fear and rage swirl in her head until she can't tell one from the other.

The trailer shifts. Suddenly she's in the living room. She focuses across the small area, over the stained carpet onto broken linoleum at the kitchen's edge.

Sticking out from behind a cabinet is a bare, yellow-toenailed foot.

A squeak pushes up Melissa's throat. She runs around the couch, cuts left toward the kitchen. She jumps past the cabinets—and sees the blood.

Her mother lies on the floor, face up, eyes open and glazed. A shocked expression wrenches her hardened face, as if she's just stared into hell. A gash digs into her forehead, blood smeared down her temple, into her ratty fake red hair. One hand lies on her motionless chest, fingers spread. The other is fisted upon her hip. A foot away lies a bottle, half its contents spilled on the linoleum. The sharp-sweet smell of whiskey clogs Melissa's nose.

Whiskey—this early in the day?

A strangled cry dies on Melissa's tongue. Her feet cement to the floor. She stares at her dead mother, disgust and anger and panic squeezing her lungs. Thoughts hit her so fast and hard she staggers beneath their blows. Her despicable mother is gone. Melissa is alone. *What will she do now? Where will she go?*

Melissa moans aloud and drops to her knees. This can't be. She wants her mother. She never hated the woman, not really. "Come back, Mom. Come back!" She buries her face in both hands and sobs. And the next thing she knows, her mother's blood has flowed across the floor, up her legs to her arms. She pulls her hands away and stares at them, at the red ooze in the lines of her palms.

Melissa's jaw unhinges. She tilts her head toward the ceiling and screams—

A grating whir in her throat jerked Melissa awake. Her eyes popped open, sleepy gaze fixing upon a pale blue wall. She lay on her side, right hand scrunching the flowered coverlet on her queen-size bed. Morning sun filtered between drawn curtains at one of the large windows in her bedroom.

The Jacksons' house.

Warm relief flushed limpness through Melissa's body. The air smelled faintly of the vanilla-scented candle she'd lit on her dresser the previous night.

Her fourth day in paradise. Sort of. If she'd let it be. Everything still seemed amazing—the house, the way Linda and Baxter treated her. It's just that Melissa wasn't used to things being so right. When you'd lived your whole life with a drunk for a mother, who'd just as easily slap you as look at you, it was hard to relax. Melissa's muscles still quivered at sudden sounds—the phone ringing, a pot banging.

She rolled on her back and stared at the high, perfectly painted ceiling. The dream flashed in her head. Melissa closed her eyes. Wasn't the first time she'd had it—in some form. Details tended to change. Weird how dreams of a real event could mix truth and fiction. Like blood flowing from the floor up to her palms.

Five months ago when she'd called 911, back turned against the sight of her dead mother, she'd had no blood on her hands. But there was a lot of it on the floor.

Later, after the autopsy, the detective said her mother had been drunk. *Yeah*, Melissa thought, *tell me something I don't know*. Her mom probably blacked out, stumbled and fell, he said. She hit her head on the counter, split her forehead open. She was only thirty-eight years old, but her liver was "damaged beyond repair" by cirrhosis. That by itself would have killed her soon anyway.

One of life's little ironies.

A knock sounded on Melissa's door. She jumped, then rose up on her elbows. "Yeah?"

"It's Linda. Can I come in?"

Melissa had never heard that question in the trailer. Her mother had always just barreled into her tiny bedroom. "Sure."

The door opened and Linda stuck her head inside. She wore no makeup yet, but she was still pretty. "Time to get up for church. We leave in an hour."

Church. Melissa blinked at her. Was it Sunday already? "Oh."

Melissa hated church. Not that she'd ever been, but she'd heard about it plenty. Full of hypocritical people. They'd probably all look down their noses at her.

Linda smiled. "Don't look so forlorn. It won't be bad. Really. And it'll give you a chance to meet some girls your age."

Who probably wouldn't want a thing to do with her.

Melissa's mouth tightened. "What am I supposed to wear?"

"Any of the jeans and tops I bought you. The service is casual. You want some breakfast?"

"No. Thanks. I'll eat later."

Linda nodded, smiled again, and closed the door. She sure did smile a lot.

For some time Melissa lay in bed, arguing with herself. She didn't have to go to church. Nobody could make her. She'd never liked being told what to do.

Yeah, and she could also get kicked out of this nice house in a hurry. That didn't fit into Melissa's plans. She'd already grown used to her large, beautiful bedroom.

She huffed at the ceiling. Life was full of compromises. An hour of church, even with stuck-up people, was worth a week of living here.

Melissa got out of bed.

She threw open the door to her walk-in closet and studied the five pairs of designer jeans and two dressier slacks hanging neatly in a row. Maybe she should wear the white slacks. But if all the girls were dressed in jeans she'd feel weird.

What did she care what they thought of her?

Melissa took another five minutes deciding. With an animated shrug she pulled on a pair of True Religions and a short-sleeve blue top. In the bathroom she carefully applied the new makeup Linda had bought her. Then she stood before the full-length mirror, turning back to front. She looked *good.* Designer jeans were amazing.

"Morning, Melissa." Baxter shot her a broad smile when she

walked into the kitchen. He was dressed in a suit and tie, looking out at the backyard and drinking from a mug. The aroma of coffee filled the room. Linda wasn't around. "You look great."

Melissa eyed him warily. Four days here and she still hadn't figured this guy out. He acted so nice. And normal. But no man living in a house like this could be normal. Besides, males usually wanted something. Her stepdad sure had, and she'd only been eleven at the time. Melissa's mom hadn't been around to stop it. The men who lived with them after that had been no better.

Melissa looked at the floor. "Thanks."

Baxter walked to the sink and set his cup down with a faint *click*. "You want coffee?"

"No thanks."

He turned toward her. "Anything to eat?"

She shook her head.

Baxter regarded her for a moment, concern in his expression. Melissa forced herself to stare back. *Where* was Linda?

"Do you like living here, Melissa?" he asked.

"Yes."

His face softened. "Good. I want you to be comfortable. I hope in time you'll see you can trust us. You don't have to be on your guard here."

Melissa felt herself go numb. No response, not a single word would form on her tongue. How did he see her so clearly? And who talked like that anyway—just saying something right out? Words were meant to be shields. Words were meant to be dances.

She lifted a shoulder. "I'm just fine."

He opened his mouth as if to say more, then nodded.

Linda saved the moment by entering the kitchen. "Hey there, Melissa, you look terrific." She was rubbing lotion on her hands. Melissa smelled roses. Linda wore cream slacks and a green silk blouse. She looked perfect. Melissa's heart swelled. Why couldn't somebody like this woman have been her mother? Why had God given Linda no children and let Melissa be born to a ratty alcoholic?

Baxter crossed to his wife and drew a finger down her cheek. "And so do you."

Linda swiped her hand through the air. "Oh, you say that to all your wives." She turned and grinned at Melissa. "Okay, let's go!"

On the way to church Linda babbled about the girls Melissa would meet. Heather and Christy and Belle and Nicole. Other names Melissa couldn't begin to remember. "They're really looking forward to meeting you."

Melissa stiffened. "They know I'm coming?"

Baxter glanced at her in the rearview mirror. "Sure they do. Last Sunday we told everyone we'd be picking you up in a few days. LInda was too excited to keep quiet."

Only Linda was excited?

The thought plucked at her. Melissa pushed it away.

Terrific, she told herself. A whole church just waiting to see what she looked like. Probably been talking about her all week.

By the time she, Linda, and Baxter slid out of the Mercedes, Melissa had checked the wall around her heart for loose bricks. She'd be polite to the adults and grimace later. As for girls her age, she didn't need them. Friends wanted to know things about you. Friends could hurt you.

No one who knew the real Melissa Harkoff, who knew the slummy life she'd come from and the things she'd done, would ever want to be her friend.

EIGHT

FEBRUARY 2010

Fifteen years ago I'd forged my way into skip tracing while working in a private investigator's office in San Jose. The work is exciting. But unlike the portrayal on trumped-up TV shows, most skip tracing is done online. I could stay warm and dry in my house while I chased Melissa through the teeming, winding halls of cyberspace. Sitting at a computer may not translate well into television, but I find it as exhilarating as a street car chase. It *is* all about the hunt. The rush of stalking down pieces of the puzzle, the adrenaline surge of closing in on the skip. Mere fingers on keys, hunched shoulders, and eyes glued to the screen can't begin to portray the real-life drama that hinges on the outcome of a search. A skip located can completely change lives. It means a criminal apprehended, a child reunited with birth parents, the recipient of a surprise inheritance, money for the impoverished children of a deadbeat dad. It forges justice, dredges tears, spews anger, builds hope.

My first task in finding Melissa: list the few pieces of information I knew about her. Name: Melissa Harkoff. I didn't know her middle name. Age: twenty-two. That was it. No Social Security number. No last known phone number or address. I didn't even know if she was still in California.

Social Security numbers are important to garner the most reliable information. More than one person might be named Melissa Harkoff. I needed to hunt for her SSN by running her through credit headers—information from credit reports that includes name, past and perhaps current addresses, SSN, and date of birth. The actual credit information is not included. Credit headers are my most important source of data, and they aren't openly available online. Skip tracers and others who qualify can buy restricted-access commercial data services, which are the source of these credit headers. I subscribed to two such services.

I opened Skiptrace One and typed in Melissa's name and assumed state—California. Hit enter.

My window rattled. I jumped and jerked my head toward the sound.

A second rattle.

Just the wind.

I took a hard breath, willed my nerves to settle. Ate a Sizzling Cinnamon Jelly Belly, followed by a Cappuccino.

When I looked again at my monitor, fourteen results filled the screen.

Three different Melissa Harkoffs. One date of birth was too long ago. Surprisingly, the other two were 01/27/1988 and 09/13/1987. I leaned back in my chair, trying to remember if Melissa's birthday had already occurred in June of 2004. No way to know. Either birth date might be hers.

This complicated things. I'd have to run down both birth dates, and even when I established a current address and phone for each, I wouldn't know which was the right Melissa. If I got lucky I might find the two women's photos online through a simple Google search. Or I may have to watch the residences and see for myself who lived there.

For all I knew neither date of birth was my Melissa because she'd married two years ago and now had a new last name.

I cut and pasted the fourteen address results in my HM file, lining through the four listings for the birth date I'd thrown out.

In skip tracing I'm like a hungry cat.

You've seen the stomach-to-the-ground pursuit of a feline with a bird in its sights. It plays out each cunning move, now creeping forward, now poising to pounce. If the prey flutters to safety the cat returns to where it started, hiding in the grass, seeking the next victim.

But my usual logical pattern wouldn't work tonight. I'd have to hunt both Melissas at once.

My HM file would keep track of every step so I wouldn't lose my place. I would rely on my memory for nothing. You never know when an unexpected event will pull you away from the computer, erasing the next intended move from your brain.

A fierce gale spit raindrops through its teeth. They hit the window like shells breaking.

Chicago sang "Chasin' the Wind" as I typed the Social Security number of 01/27/1988 into Skiptrace One's search by SSN page. Three addresses popped up. The most recent was in San Jose, but the report date read 11/09/2006. Over three years old.

Melissa, is this you?

The lack of a fresh address on a skip can mean two things. One, the person has ruined her credit and just isn't using it, waiting out the seven-year period until delinquent accounts fall off the report. In that case Melissa could have moved in with a boyfriend and her current address wouldn't show up on the credit header. Two, the skip does live at the most recently listed address and simply hasn't applied for any new credit in the past few years.

Or this most recent listed address could be plain inaccurate. Wrong addresses end up on credit headers more often than you'd think. Maybe Melissa intentionally gave a false address to a creditor. Maybe she bought a used car and the salesman made a mistake in writing down her address. Or a data entry error could have been made at some credit bureau.

I noted the three addresses in my HM file.

Backing up, I sent the Social Security number of 09/13/1987 through Skiptrace One's search by SSN page. Four addresses appeared on my screen, the most recent dated just six months ago in Gilroy, "Garlic Capitol of the World." Gilroy was only about fifteen minutes away, up Route 101.

Would Melissa stay that close to Vonita? She'd been a runaway from the social services system. To my knowledge she had no relatives in the area to whom she could run. You'd think she'd leave the area to make a new life. Maybe even the state.

But people can surprise you.

I now had a Melissa Harkoff in San Jose and one in Gilroy. Time for a Google search. If I got real lucky I'd find a picture, perhaps attached to a wedding announcement or business or church. I'd also check social sites like MySpace and Facebook.

The wind groaned like a wounded beast. Rain smashed against my house.

Just a winter storm. Nothing to fear. But my nerves zinged.

I turned up the volume on Aerosmith's "Dream On," shoved two Sizzling Cinnamon Jelly Bellies into my mouth.

At Google I typed in "Melissa Harkoff" + Gilroy. Hit enter—

The electricity smacked off, and my world plunged into darkness.

Somewhere in the distance a door slammed.

NINE

For a long piercing second I froze in the darkness, my fingers clawed above the keyboard.

The garage. That muted slam had come from the garage—the door leading to the backyard.

I pushed back my chair, heart in my throat. My mind spun through a terrifying scenario. Hooded Man was in my house.

Where was my cell phone?

My landlines wouldn't work because they were on plug-in phone systems. My cell phone was ... in my purse. On the kitchen table. Near the door an intruder would sneak through from the garage.

Rain and wind lashed the house. Their noise was loud enough to mask cautious footsteps, the easing open of a door. Even so, I cocked my head toward the kitchen and listened for a swish of clothes, a whisper of breath.

Nothing.

I stood up, eyes straining to see. Stillton is a rural road, no streetlights. When electricity goes at night, the house caves in on itself, hording the blackness. Usually the moon can lighten my way, the pinpricked stars. But they'd fled the broken sky long ago.

In the kitchen in a drawer lay Tom's powerful flashlight—the kind he'd carry when we went camping. And candles and matches.

Had someone cut my electricity? Or had the wind knocked a tree into a power line?

Breath on hold, socked feet moving like an inward sigh, I crept from my desk and to the hall. At the threshold I placed a palm against the doorjamb and leaned my head forward, tilted toward the kitchen. In my mind I saw Hooded Man's waxen cheek, the jagged blood. Heard his raw-toned voice. *"Baxter Jackson will kill you if he finds out."*

The darkness was too thick to make out any movement.

I eased into the hallway, one hand trailing along the wall. My muscles balled up, ready to spring my body away, fight back. My ripping heart pulsed at odd points in my body. An ankle, the back of one knee, my left shoulder—as if my ribcage couldn't contain it. I could *taste* my terror, a bitter sludge at the top of my throat.

I'd checked every door when I got home. Dripping wet and chilled to the marrow, I'd *checked.* Windows too.

One foot lifted, I then stepped toward the kitchen. I managed a second step.

Was Hooded Man there, smugly watching the hulk of my shape walk right into his grasp?

I pushed myself forward, chanting a mantra that I was being foolish. A power line was down, and wind had slammed my back door.

My *locked* back door.

A vision of myself flashed into my head—getting out of the car earlier that evening, carrying my purse. I'd headed straight for the entrance to the kitchen. Hovered my hand at the knob, too afraid to turn it.

I *hadn't* checked that rear garage door. Of all stupid things. I hadn't even thought of it.

Maybe I'd left it slightly ajar. The wind hadn't been howling when I arrived home. When it rushed from its lair in anger, it had seized the door, swung it open, then slammed it shut.

The kitchen was five steps away. My legs shook, both lungs burning for air. I arched my shoulders back, giving myself breathing room. The wind bulleted rain against the kitchen windows and sliding door. Almost as if it were following me. Minutes before it had been attacking the front of the house.

I reached the threshold of the kitchen. My right hand trailed high on the wall—across Billy Bass.

I squinted into the maw of the kitchen. The flashlight drawer was straight across the room on my left. Heat singed my nerves. Every second was agony. I couldn't stand to inch across the floor, waiting for arms to grab me.

My toes hit linoleum. A firework burst in my chest, and I stumbled as fast as I could toward the drawer, left hand skidding across cabinets.

A handle bumped my fingers.

I whirled left, yanking at the top drawer, no longer caring how much sound I made. The contents rattled and rolled. If Hooded Man had come, he knew where I stood. He was toying with me. If he came at me I'd rip off that mask, shine the flashlight into his face.

My hands scrabbled in the drawer, seeking the chunky feel of cool metal. I found it, and a small cry escaped my throat. I jerked out the flashlight, pushed the *on* button. A large, beautiful beam rent the blackness.

I turned, swinging the beam around the kitchen. It lit up the refrigerator, the sink, cabinets, the table, my purse. No Hooded Man. No Baxter. I yanked it toward the base of the door leading into the garage, checking the floor for footprints and water.

Clean.

I lurched toward my purse, pulled out my cell phone. It was still on. My hand clutched it, thumb arching in to hit 2, the speed dial number for Dineen. Not until the phone began to ring did I realize she was probably asleep. Dineen always went to bed early.

The phone rang twice. Three times.

"Joanne?" My sister's voice sounded thick.

"Is your electricity off?"

She hesitated, as if her mind couldn't catch this sudden conversation. "No. Is yours?"

"How do you know? Aren't your lights all turned off?"

"My phone's working."

Oh. Stupid me.

She made a sound in her throat. "Besides, I see streetlights."

"Mine's off."

"Oh. Probably the wind."

"What if it's not? What if somebody's *here*?"

Sheets rustled over the line. I could visualize her bed, her room. So close-sounding over the telephone, yet so very far away. I wanted to crawl through the wire, come out in her house. I wanted to hide there from Vonita, the world. I hadn't meant for the whole town to hear my accusations against Chief Eddington. And as much as I wanted Baxter Jackson caught, I hadn't asked for a scarifying Hooded Man to leap in front of my car. I just wanted it all to go away.

But something told me it had barely started.

"Why would somebody be in your house, Joanne?"

"I don't ... the door slammed. In the garage. I thought it was locked."

"Have you checked out there?"

"No, I just now grabbed a flashlight."

"Well, go. I'll hang on the line."

I know what she thought. It's the wind. Just like she thought Baxter could be innocent. My generous sister—never wanting to believe the worst.

"Okay." I set the phone down on the table, aimed the beam toward the garage, and opened the door. Light split across to the far wall and its window. I moved the flashlight around. Saw no one.

With one foot I forced down the door stop. Stretched to the table to pick up my phone. "Okay. I'm going into the garage." I stepped over the threshold. The air chilled considerably. Heat didn't run out there. The walls seemed so thin, as if they were mere cardboard against the storm.

I aimed the flashlight at my car. No one there. I searched the achingly empty other side, where Tom's car used to sit. Ran the beam over the furnace and water heater, the garbage cans. No Hooded Man. No Baxter. Just suspicious-minded me, unable to imagine the length of this night.

"Joanne?"

"The garage looks fine. Checking the door."

I edged over to it, shone the beam on its knob. Unlocked. I checked the bolt. Also unlocked.

I had not left the door that way. I *hadn't.* It had been pouring when I left the house for Dineen's. Why would I go outside?

"Is it open?" Dineen asked.

"Unlocked, if that's what you mean. Both the knob and the bolt."

"See? The wind probably just slammed it."

Of course. No doubt.

I clicked both locks into place.

"You want to spend the night here, Joanne? It might take the power company awhile to fix broken lines in this storm. Maybe a whole grid's out."

What I wanted was to know if my house was the only one without electricity.

"Maybe. I'll call you back."

"Well, do it soon, okay? I'm ready to go to sleep."

How easy for her.

My mouth opened to spill the whole story. Hooded Man on the road, his stunning words about Baxter. I was Dineen's older, always-stable sister, for heaven's sake. Didn't it occur to her I might have a *reason* to be paranoid?

The words stuck in my throat.

"Sure. Thanks."

I clicked off the phone, shivering. Too cold out here. Too close to the rain. I turned to head back into the kitchen, call 411 for the power company's number. The flashlight beam raked over the width of the garage, bouncing against the double doors on the other side, hitting my car. The concrete floor nearby glistened beneath the light.

My hand halted. I aimed the beam downward.

Water droplets lit up like tiny stars.

I stared, moving the flashlight toward the front of the car … to the back. Water lined the floor. I jerked the ray down farther, tracing the concrete from the car to where I stood. More dribbled water. I jumped aside, checked by the door. Wet.

That last part was to be expected. If the door had blown open, rain surely whooshed in. But the trail leading across the garage …

I eased toward the door to the kitchen, heart thudding. Followed the telltale path with the light once more, from rear door to car. That dripped water couldn't have come from me when I arrived home. The trail I'd left then, not yet dried, went from my car to the kitchen door. I hadn't gone anywhere near the backyard door.

Someone *had* been here. Had come through that rear door. Which I'd left *locked.*

What did he want in my car? Did he think I'd leave my purse in there?

Maybe I'd surprised him when I came into the garage. That was it. He'd run behind the SUV to hide.

Which meant he was crouching there *right now.*

I whirled and jumped through the threshold into the kitchen. Kicked up the bronze stop and shoved the door closed. Locked it.

Panic peeled away the layers of my mind. What to do? Reason had fled. Like a trapped animal, I pressed against the wall, trying to think. I couldn't jump in my car to flee to my sister's. But what if he *wasn't* out there; what if he was in *here*? I'd just barricaded myself in a dark house with an intruder.

Palms sweating, I aimed the flashlight at my cell phone and dialed 911.

TEN

JUNE 2004

Baxter walked into the Vonita True Life Church like he owned the place.

The sanctuary had two long rows of pews with one central aisle. Purple and red carpet. A large cross on the back wall. A podium on the stage, and off to the side, instruments. A drum set, guitars, a keyboard. Melissa eyed them in surprise.

After crossing the threshold Melissa hung back behind Linda, suddenly shy and hating herself for it. What was the big deal? She could take care of herself just fine. Hadn't she done that all her life? No need to care what the people in this church thought of her. As long as the Jacksons believed she was okay, she'd keep that beautiful big roof over her head.

"Come on, Melissa, it'll be fine." Linda extended an arm, ushering her inside the door. Her crooked smile mixed sadness and purpose, as if with this one church service she was determined to erase all the hurts of Melissa's sixteen years.

Lots of luck.

"Barry. Steve." Baxter shook hands with two men, then walked farther down the church aisle toward others. They all responded with overlarge nods and smiles, followed by gazes wandering toward Melissa. Linda placed a gentle hand against Melissa's back and guided her toward the wives. "Sarah, Eileen, Sandy—this is Melissa."

Melissa's mouth curved up like some puppet who'd had its string pulled.

The women all made a big deal over her, smiling and saying how pretty she was, complimenting her on the clothes. "Linda's been so looking forward to having you," the one named Sarah said. She was a tall woman with short brown hair and small green eyes. Her eyes crinkled when she smiled.

"Oh. Yeah," Melissa managed.

"You enjoying living in that amazing house with these amazing people?" one of the other women asked. Eileen, maybe.

"Yes."

They all surveyed her, as if waiting for more.

The third woman smiled grandly. "Well, that's great. I know you'll enjoy it there. And in this town too. Everybody knows Baxter and Linda. Won't take long before you see just how fortunate you are."

More people came through the door, men and women and kids, everybody wanting to meet Melissa. Three of the girls Linda had mentioned—Heather, Belle, and Nicole—arrived together, chatting away as if they'd just come from some party. Melissa's mouth went dry. Linda waved them over. Melissa straightened her back and watched them approach with a cool expression. Heather was blonde, with a sweet, round face. She shot Melissa a sparkling smile, as if she really meant it. "Hi. Nice to meet you. Last week Linda was real excited that you'd be here today." Belle and Nicole nodded. Belle was a little overweight, with gorgeous long black hair. She looked ... something. Maybe half Chinese?

"Thanks." Melissa managed a smile. A hint of warmth touched her chest.

Nicole was short and tiny, like a bubbly cheerleader. "Isn't it incredible, living with Baxter and Linda?" Her voice sounded almost tinkly, like she'd burst into laughter any minute.

"Yeah. Their house is beautiful."

Nicole tilted her head. "Oh, I know. But I wasn't thinking that. I'd live with them in a shack. Everybody in town loves them, you'll see. This town wouldn't have half the things it does if it wasn't for Baxter."

Melissa could think of no response. She tucked the information away in her mind.

"You want to sit with us?" Nicole asked.

Melissa's eyes cut to Linda, who stood halfway across the sanctuary, watching like an anxious mother. Nicole followed Melissa's gaze and raised her voice toward Linda. "Can she sit with us?"

Linda nodded, giving Melissa a reassuring look. "It's fine if you want."

A long second stretched out. Melissa eyed the girls, calculating. Would Linda be more disappointed if she said yes or no? Melissa's mind flashed to the beautifully painted walls of her new bedroom, the designer clothes in her closet. The quietness and peace in the Jackson house. She couldn't lose all that. She couldn't.

"Thanks." She gave the girls a winning smile. "Maybe next week. For my first time here I'd like to stick with Linda."

The girls murmured their understanding. Melissa eased away and walked to Linda, noting the softened expression on her face.

Score one for Melissa.

A few minutes later the service started. Melissa didn't know what to make of it. Guys in jeans played the instruments, a group of four guys and girls singing. A screen up front showed words to the songs. People sang and clapped their hands. Melissa stood by Linda, watching the words flip by on the screen, wishing she could melt into the floor. It was all so strange. Melissa hadn't expected to participate in anything. She'd thought she could just stare at some preacher, pretending to listen. For her first week, maybe the second, she could get by with just standing there. But in time Linda and

Baxter would expect her to join in. They'd probably expect her to believe just the way they did.

Melissa's fingers curled around the pew in front of her. She could do that. She could pretend anything they wanted. As long as they kept being so nice to her. As long as they didn't turn out to be something totally different than what they seemed.

ELEVEN

FEBRUARY 2010

My wait for the police to arrive unwound in an endless spool, teeming with imagined noises. I huddled in the corner chair at my kitchen table, the end of the flashlight pressed against my chest. Its strong beam penetrated the viscous air, daring some malicious form to appear. The 911 dispatcher had told me electricity was off in over half the town.

Small comfort now.

She wanted me to stay on the line, but my trembling fingers hit the wrong button and cut us off. Immediately the phone rang. It was Dineen.

I told her the police were on their way. That someone must have jimmied the lock on my rear door.

"You're kidding." Her tone collapsed, as if reality had just slapped her with the fact she'd been nonchalant while her sister faced danger.

I didn't want to tell her I may have surprised the intruder in the garage. Couldn't find the energy to launch into the grimness of Hooded Man. I simply breathed into the phone, gripping my flashlight like a fatal weapon.

"Maybe I should call 911 back."

"No, stay with me until they arrive," Dineen declared. "Then you're coming over here."

Fine with me. No way could I imagine staying in this house alone all night. "Hey, I'm the big sister. I'm supposed to give *you* orders."

"Now you see what the other side's like."

The wind's fitful dirge lowered a key, although not from losing power. It was merely changing tactics. Like the big bad wolf, it wanted nothing more than to blow this house down.

"You need some Cream Soda Jelly Bellies, Dineen. Help you chill out."

My imagination wanted to bounce off the darkling walls. I clutched the phone, pushing my thoughts back to skip tracing.

Where had I left off with Melissa? Two Melissa Harkoffs with different birthdays, that much I remembered, although I couldn't recall the dates. I was just about to google them to search for photos when my computer blipped off. Had I failed to note anything in my file? If so that data would be lost. I'd have to reconstruct it.

"Joanne?"

"I'm here, Dineen."

Where were the policemen? Were they taking their time responding because of that article in the newspaper? Surely their loyalties lay with Chief Eddington. Were they driving over here in shared smugness—*that woman deserves any trouble she gets*?

I couldn't see a front window from where I sat. I should move into the living room or my office—areas now unchecked. From there I could watch for police lights. Even though I didn't believe anyone was in those black rooms, the mere thought of entering either one sizzled my skin.

"Dineen, I'm going to move where I can watch—"

The doorbell rang. I jumped so hard my veins rattled.

"They're here." I shoved from the chair. "Call you back."

I tossed down the phone and made for the front door, my blessed ray of light cutting a swath through the darkness. In the hallway I could see red flashing lights through my living room windows, pulsing the furniture like a macabre disco. I threw back the door. Two policemen stood on my covered porch, hulking wet shapes against the raging night. Both of them carried flashlights.

"Thank you for coming." I stepped aside, let them in. The door banged closed behind the last one.

"Sorry," he said, and I thought of my garage rear door, how it could have slipped from someone's hand …

Water dripped from the men onto the floor. My overworked mind blipped the surreal thought that the rain was winning. It wanted nothing more than to overtake my house, drive me crazy.

The officers' badges read Mike Trent and Ron Blasco. They shone their flashlights around the hall, their faces looking bloated and shadowy in the umbra of beams. Trent looked in his late twenties. I'd never seen him before. Blasco, a father in his early forties, used to attend my church, although I hadn't seen him there in months. He'd known Tom. Even fished with him on occasion.

"Mrs. Weeks." He nodded. "We hear you may have had a break-in."

I spilled my story, one hand at my neck. I told them nothing of Hooded Man. Only of the garage door slamming, the trail of water across the floor.

"Okay," Blasco said. "Stay right here. We need to clear the house."

They pulled their guns, aimed and ready. Together they entered the living room in the steely half crouch I'd seen so often on TV. Now it was real. Now it was my life.

The throbbing red from the patrol car outside beat against their bodies, purpled their uniforms. The light reflected the rain running down my windows, pulsing the officers' faces with translucent rivulets of blood. I pressed against the front door, shoulders taut, and prayed. I'd prayed countless times for comfort when Linda disappeared, countless more for strength when Tom died. I believed in Jesus my Savior. I believed in prayer.

I also knew being a Christian didn't always keep you out of trouble. Look at Linda. Now look at me.

The officers directed their beams around the room, searching beyond the couch, behind the TV. All clear.

They brushed by me into my office. Beyond that, they would search the bedrooms and baths, the laundry room. I couldn't see them anymore, but I heard closet doors opening, the ripping back of a shower curtain. I hung on to their every sound, hugging them to my chest as reminders these men could save me. My muscles tensed into rocks, each cringing second drawing out ... out ... as I braced for noises I didn't want to hear. A long squeal of car brakes too often leads to the crunch of metal. Here it would be a sudden shout, the *blam*, *blam* of bullets.

The policemen ventured back up the hall, intact, whole. I drank in their vague shapes as they passed by toward the kitchen.

One of them gasped. Feet shuffled. Flashlight beams swung.

My fingers clutched each other.

"Oh, man." Blasco's voice. "It's a fish."

"Yeah." Trent. "My light caught those eyes."

Billy Bass. I let out a breath.

I heard the policemen move forward.

The kitchen had to be safe. I'd just been there.

Only one place left in the house.

"Watch out in the garage!" I called. "He could have been hiding behind the car."

He *had* been there, hadn't he? Whoever *he* was. (Hooded Man? A burglar?) Rational thinking insisted he would be long gone. But fear drowned out its voice.

The door into the garage opened. Closed with a *click.*

I waited, heart tripping. The storm raged at my back, separated by a mere piece of wood that had never seemed so flimsy. In my mind's eye I pictured the garage. My car, the furnace, water heater. So few places a man could hide. But enough. My fingers gripped the flashlight until they cramped.

No shots. No shouts.

The garage door opened again. Footsteps approached. Ron Blasco appeared in the entryway, the beam of my flashlight at his waist level. Mike Trent pulled up beside him.

"All clear, Mrs. Weeks." Blasco gestured with his head. "We checked everywhere inside."

I tried to swallow the stone in my throat. "Did you see the rain trail, how it led from the back door down to the car?"

"Yes. And we checked that rear door. It's locked and bolted."

"Like I told you, *I* did that. I found it open."

"Understood. We saw no signs of forced entry."

I knew that already.

"What do you think about the water trail?" I pressed.

The officers exchanged glances. Mike Trent spoke up. "We can see why you were suspicious. But it's also very possible that the door was left unlocked and not quite latched. The wind forced it open and blew in rain, right in that line you saw."

Yes, that was possible. Probable, even, if it hadn't been on *this* night, after a hooded and masked stranger nearly caused me to wreck on the road. But I couldn't tell them that.

Could I?

I surveyed the officers, Hooded Man's warning in my head. How to tell them I'd been stopped on the road without telling them why? And without the *why* I would just sound paranoid.

"Yes," my mouth said. "I suppose that's possible."

Blasco cleared his throat. "We're going to check outside around the perimeter. If you'll just wait here another moment."

I moved away from the door. They stepped outside and down my two porch steps into the blistering rain. I stood in the doorway, the squall wrapping me in a cold drool. I couldn't stand it. When the officers disappeared from sight, I shut the door, shivering.

A few minutes later they were back, freshly soaked.

Ron Blasco shook his head. "We saw no footprints, no signs of disturbance around your house. Granted, on a night like this ..." He raised a hand, palm up. "Still, we're satisfied that all's clear."

I nodded, numb. "You'll make a report, though—that you came out? It'll include what I told you?"

"Absolutely."

I bit the inside of my lip. What more could I do? "Thank you for coming."

"No problem." Mike Trent offered a quick smile. "Don't hesitate to call again if you need us."

From the doorway I watched them trot to their car and slide inside. The flashing lights cut off. They drove away from the house, onto their next mission. Or maybe back to the station. For their sakes I hoped it had electricity.

I stepped inside, closed the door, and locked it. Checked the bolt twice. A third time. The black stillness of the house hovered over me, disaster waiting to strike.

Could my back door have just blown open? *Could* I have carelessly left it unlocked when I went to Dineen's for dinner? Try as I might, I couldn't believe that now, not after seeing that trail of water.

A shiver zigzagged down my back. The policemen had been nice enough. Diligent. But what were they saying about me now? Joanne Weeks, crazy lady, full of conspiracy theories. Thinks the chief of police is helping Baxter Jackson cover up two murders. Now claims a phantom broke into her home.

Bearing my flashlight I eased back into the kitchen, body still atingle. Yes, my dark house had been cleared, but try telling my nerves that. At the kitchen table I picked up my cell phone and dialed Dineen. She answered on the first ring.

"What happened?"

"Nothing. Except I'm at your house in ten minutes."

"Okay." Her voice read she wanted more but would wait until I got there.

If only I were with her already. Getting there meant going back out in the storm. Heading down Stillton's curves. I wondered if I'd ever be able to drive that road with nonchalance again.

I shivered inside and out. My system desperately needed calming. Cream Soda flavor wouldn't do the job. "You got any Strawberry Daiquiris in that paltry Jelly Belly stash of yours?"

"Joanne, one day your teeth are going to fall out from all that sugar."

"*Do* you?"

"I have no idea."

"Fine. I'll bring my own."

TWELVE

His special cell phone rang—the one not registered in his name. He jumped at the sound. Only one person had the number. He answered before the second ring, nerves zinging. "I'm here."

"It's done."

"Really."

"Yeah."

He closed his eyes. "How'd she react?"

"Scared. Surprised." The caller's voice hitched. "I think she's in."

"We don't have time to 'think.'"

Another catch in the voice. "She's in."

"What's the matter with you?"

"Nothin'. It's just wet out there."

Sounded like more than that. He couldn't afford to have anything go wrong. His stomach was already tied in knots. "Something not go right?"

"I told you—it went fine."

He turned the words over in his mind. It had *better* be fine. "Okay. Keep on it. And keep me informed."

"Yeah."

He clicked off the line and stared at the phone, calculations churning through his mind.

THIRTEEN

Dineen and I stayed up past 2:00 a.m., talking and listening to the wind howl. Rain arrowed against her windows, refusing to quell. Noah must have felt like this.

The lights in the house were the warmest and loveliest I'd ever seen.

I sat against one end of my sister's couch, legs drawn up and covered with a throw blanket. A small bowl on my lap held a dwindling supply of Strawberry Daiquiri Jelly Bellies. I'd had the sense to bring my bag of Orange Sherbets as well. They were number two on my list for calming nerves.

Dineen had settled at the other side of the sofa, bed-headed and clad in blue pajamas. She listened with ever-widening eyes as I related my insane story. *Don't tell anyone* didn't apply to my sister. God knew I needed *somebody*.

When I finished she stared at her light brown carpet, frowning. I knew the gears were turning in her head. Dineen liked to process everything before she spoke. I'd learned to wait out the silence.

She refocused on me, circles beneath her eyes. Her mouth held the same tightness as when she'd anguished over fighting her ex-husband in court. Suddenly I was sorry I'd told Dineen. She didn't need more stress in her life. She had Jimmy to raise.

"Joanne. *Do* you think that man was at your house tonight?"

For a moment I wavered toward saying *no*, offering my sister solace. Then I thought of Linda's guarded tone the few times she'd talked to me in the weeks before she died.

"Somebody was. I've thought about it ever since the police left. On the way over here I remembered the last time I'd been through that door. It was yesterday, when I went out back to do some planting. I came in, my hands full of tools and plastic containers to throw away. I leaned against the door with my shoulder until it closed. Later I think I locked it. But even if I didn't—that door was latched. It wouldn't have blown open."

"What would he want in your house?"

"I don't know."

"Maybe it wasn't him at all. Could have been a burglar, and when the door slammed loud enough to alert somebody in the house, it scared him off."

"Yeah, sure. Burglars always pick wet nights like this to go out. Leave less trail in a house that way."

"You watch too much *CSI*."

"I don't watch *any CSI*. I'm a skip tracer, remember? I deal with bad guys all the time. After awhile you get to thinking like they do."

The wind groaned. Dineen shifted her position on the couch. "So are you going to look for Melissa?"

I stared at her. A world of difference hung pendant between my sister and me, as much as we loved each other. She would never understand the guilt I'd felt over Linda's death. If only I'd told the police what I knew of Baxter Jackson *before* she disappeared. If only I could have persuaded her to talk. Once she was gone it had been my story against the world's. By then it was too late.

"I have no choice, Dineen."

She sucked her lower lip between her teeth and looked away. "You do, though," she murmured. "You could just drop it. That man in the road can't do anything to make you. And what courage does he have?" She made a *tsss* sound through her teeth. "Hiding behind a mask while you do the work."

I made no reply. She had a point.

"If you do find Melissa, what then? She's likely to deny knowing anything."

When I find Melissa, not if.

A blaring realization hit me—one I should have thought of before. The idea lifted me off the couch, sent my veins swimming.

It didn't make sense that Hooded Man would come to my house. Why would he? But what if it was *someone else* connected to this case? Someone who'd already found out what Hooded Man had said—and wanted to stop me?

I paced to the television and leaned over, pressing my palms on its top. My head dropped between my arms. "I don't know how to convince her to talk." My tone sounded off-key, distracted. "I'll figure that out when I get there."

I thought of Baxter Jackson, the long arms of the King of Vonita. He palled around with the mayor and city council members, the chief of police, judges, powerful businessmen. Could he have secretly forged ties with the underworld as well? With people soulless enough, money-hungry enough to kill some woman just because he wanted her dead?

A guttural moan escaped me. If Baxter Jackson had sent whoever broke into my house, how could I stay there at all, even in the daytime? Much less for a night. I didn't even own a gun for protection.

"Joanne?" Dineen's voice twisted with worry. "What?"

I was up against a wall. I couldn't rest until this was done. Not until I found Melissa, and she led authorities to Linda's body. Then it would be too late—and too obvious—for Baxter to come after me. But until Linda's body was discovered I wasn't safe at all. Maybe not even here at my sister's house. If someone was after me, this would be the first place he'd look if they didn't find me in my own home.

"Jo-*anne*. Talk to me!"

My eyes pressed shut. How to tell my single-parent sister I may have brought danger to her home—the safe haven she'd created to raise her son?

I pushed away from the TV and faced Dineen, a slow fire spreading beneath my skin. Fear had gripped me in its jaws long enough tonight. Truth was, it would clamp down again if I let it, like the rain outside, chewing the walls to get in.

Forget Strawberry Daiquiris and Orange Sherbets. I'd need a different supply of Jelly Bellies to keep me awake: Café Lattes and Chocolate Puddings. This would not be a night for sleep in my sister's guest bedroom. Not a night for sleep at all.

"Dineen, I need to use your computer."

FOURTEEN

JUNE 2004

Strange, how the sermon in that first church service seemed to be spoken straight to Melissa. She had to fight against squirming in her seat. The preacher, Pastor Steve, was tall and broad-shouldered. Reminded Melissa of a linebacker. He had a deep, penetrating voice, and he roamed the stage while he talked, a mic like singers used hooked to his ear. Pastor Steve spoke of trustworthiness deep inside a person, not on the surface. How God always saw straight to the heart. Linda made agreeing noises in her throat now and then, and Baxter nodded a lot.

Melissa felt herself shrinking.

She didn't fit with these people who were so into God. She didn't fit with Linda and Baxter, who were so picture perfect. Even the teenage girls in this church said how great they were. Give it a few days, maybe a few weeks, and the Jacksons would see right through Melissa. That she was bad to the core.

Maybe they'd taken her on because they already knew that. She was their social project. They were out to change her, raise her out of her miserable life. Sort of like adopting a beaten dog from the pound.

Were they in this because they really cared about her? Or did they just want to make themselves feel good?

Pastor Steve strode to the simple podium and flipped through a Bible. "Psalm 51:6 says about God, 'Surely you desire truth in the inner parts; you teach me wisdom in the inmost place.' This"—he thumped his chest with his forefinger—"is where it counts. Right here. You think you're fooling everyone else? You'll never fool God. And in the end, *he's* the only one who matters."

"Amen," some man across the church said. Melissa's eyes cut in his direction. He looked about fifty, with graying hair and a tanned face, a deep groove down the side of his cheek. He sat close to a woman with shoulder-length brown hair. Her chin tipped up toward the preacher, a slight smile on her lips. Something about these two people pulled at Melissa. They looked like normal folk. Not powerful and engaging like the Jacksons, as if they could take over a room just by entering. But these people seemed ... warm. Real. Like people you'd want to hug, and they'd hug you right back, harder.

Real. Melissa turned away, uneasiness brushing the back of her neck. She focused again on the preacher. Why had she thought that word? As if Baxter and Linda *weren't*? She'd seen them together for four days now. Watched the way they gazed at each other, heard the way they talked. Of course they were real. More important, they were her family now. They *had* to be real.

The picture of Melissa's mother, dead and bleeding on the dirty kitchen floor, flashed into her mind. Melissa pushed the memory into a dark corner.

She tried hard to block out the rest of the sermon. Focusing above the pastor's head, she stared at the wooden cross hanging on the wall. Now and then some of his words slipped through. "A stained life made clean and whole ... a weight off your shoulders ... the burden of dishonesty and sin gone ..." The words made her feel small and cold.

Coming here every Sunday wouldn't be easy. Harder yet—pretending to like it.

After the service everyone gathered their purses and Bibles, then stood around talking. Melissa folded her arms, gaze cruising the room. Her eyes met Nicole's, and the bubbly girl flashed her a smile. Melissa smiled back.

Call you this week. Nicole mouthed the words with animation, miming holding a phone, then pointing to Melissa.

Okay. Melissa nodded.

"Well, here she is." A woman's voice sounded on Melissa's right. "What a beautiful girl you are."

Melissa turned and found herself face-to-face with the woman and man she'd seen across the church.

"Melissa," Linda slipped an arm around her shoulder, "I want you to meet my dearest friend, Joanne Weeks. And this is her husband, Tom."

Dearest friend? Had to be at least ten years between them.

"So glad to meet you, Melissa." Tom Weeks nodded at her, his mouth curving. His nod, the way he looked at her — even his smile seemed so matter-of-fact. As if Melissa Harkoff had every reason to be standing right here in this church. As if she belonged here.

Melissa allowed her face to soften. "Nice to meet you."

"Oh, I'm so glad you're here." Joanne patted her arm. Up close, Melissa could see gold flecks in her brown eyes. "Linda's really been looking forward to you coming." Joanne blinked, as if catching her slip of the tongue. "So has Baxter."

Melissa bit the inside of her cheek. "Thanks."

Her focus trailed past the Weekses to land on Baxter, shaking hands with the pastor some ten feet away. Joanne turned her head, as if following Melissa's gaze. They both looked at Baxter, then at each other. In Joanne's eyes the truth flickered. She didn't care much for Baxter Jackson.

How about that. Not everybody liked the man after all.

Melissa gave her a shy smile and allowed her focus to drift to the floor. Baxter had managed to sidle off when the Weekses approached. Maybe he didn't like Joanne either.

What was that about?

An awkward silence pulsed.

"Your clothes look great on you," Joanne said. "Linda said she was going to take you shopping. She's quite the fashionista."

"Yeah." Melissa looked down at herself. "She helped me choose everything. She was great."

"Well, I don't know much about fashion, but I bet you'd look good in anything. Overalls, even." Tom gave her a grandfatherly wink.

His kindness pierced Melissa. She'd never known her grandparents. Her mother had lived in an alcoholic bubble, floating far and wide from relatives. According to Melissa's mother, her own mother "wasn't worth spittin' on," and her father died young from liver disease — another alcoholic. Standing in the church with Linda and the Weekses, Melissa felt sure they could see the big, black hole of her heart.

Know what — the pastor's sermon was a lie. God *didn't* matter. He wasn't the one who'd put a mansion's roof over her head, bought her new clothes. The Baxters mattered. Tom and Joanne Weeks mattered, being Linda's good friends.

Melissa turned a winning smile on Tom Weeks. "Thanks. Maybe I'll wear overalls next Sunday."

They all laughed.

Linda removed her arm from Melissa's shoulders and leaned conspiratorially toward Joanne. "Hey, did you catch your guy?"

Joanne firmed her mouth in a satisfied expression. "Yup."

"All right!" Linda grinned. "You always — "

"Linda." Baxter called over. "Time to get going."

She waved her hand, as if erasing her thought. "Coming!"

Linda hugged Joanne. "I'll bring Melissa over this week — maybe late some afternoon, when you're done working?"

"You bet; let's do it."

Melissa said good-bye and trailed after Baxter as he headed for the door. Linda followed.

Not until they were nearly home did the question pop from Melissa's mouth. "What did you mean with Joanne—catch your guy?"

Linda half-turned in the front passenger seat. "Oh, I was talking about Joanne's work. She's a skip tracer."

Melissa screwed up her face. "What's a skip tracer?"

"She finds people who are missing. Tracks them down using all sorts of special ways on her computer."

"Oh." Melissa pondered her lap.

"Keep that in mind, Melissa." Baxter flashed her a smile in the rearview mirror. "You don't want to go running off from here—ol' Joanne will hunt you down."

Linda gave him a playful punch in the arm. "She's not 'ol' Joanne.'"

Melissa shook her head. "Don't worry, I'm not going anywhere."

They'd have to chase her out of town before she'd leave this place.

FIFTEEN

FEBRUARY 2010

By 2:20 a.m. I was perched at my sister's unfamiliar computer in her small guest room. My bag of sundry toiletries and a pair of pajamas sat untouched on the quilt-covered bed. The storm had lessened, giving me hope that by dawn it would wear out completely. Dineen had returned to her room to sleep.

In a bowl on my left lay a stash of Café Latte and Chocolate Pudding Jelly Bellies. I'd filled a large glass with water and brought it in as well. A yellow pad of paper and a pen sat on my right. I'd be taking some notes by hand, as well as logging them into a new file.

Before setting to work I'd checked every lock in the house. I'd even crept into Jimmy's room, hearing the soft whoosh of boy-sleep as I tested his windows. Dineen was leaning against the wall in the hallway, arms folded, when I gently closed his door.

"You think you're being followed or something?" She'd rubbed one eye, as if too tired to entertain fright any longer.

"I don't know what to think anymore."

Her computer was taking forever to boot up. I shoved a succession of Chocolate Puddings into my mouth, urging it to *come on* under my breath.

I'd left the bedroom door open. If someone came into this

house, I wanted him finding me before Jimmy or Dineen. *I'd* be the one he was looking for anyway.

Such bravado. Where had it been when I'd been in my house, alone in the dark?

Finally the computer sat ready. I brought up the Internet.

In my mind I'd reconstructed what I could of my search. I'd found two Melissa Harkoffs of the right age. One in San Jose—although that address had been listed four years ago—and a second in Gilroy, with an address listing only six months ago. I didn't have my case file, but I could start over, again finding the two birth dates and their Social Security numbers. And I could log into my commercial data services and software from here.

But first I would start with Google—where I'd been when my electricity cut off. If I could find a picture of my Melissa, I could avoid numerous rabbit trails.

I typed in "Melissa Harkoff" + San Jose. Sixteen hits popped up, most of them apparently connected to a church. I clicked on the first and discovered the newsletter for San Jose Evangelical Fellowship, edited by Melissa Harkoff. Scrolled through it, looking for a photo or anything that might indicate this person's age. No such information. I followed the second hit ... the third and fourth. Different issues of the same newsletter.

The rest of the hits also failed to yield a photo or descriptive information. But the newsletter articles sounded quite dull for a twenty-two-year-old. Would someone that age be interested in writing about such things as a church picnic, volunteer committees, and the need for substitute Sunday School teachers? The photos that I did see contained not one young person.

On my pad of paper I jotted down the church's name and phone number. I also placed it in my new note file. Unless I found my Melissa elsewhere, I may need to conduct a pretext call. A church office should be easy to bluff. I could pose as an attorney, looking for heirs to an estate of a deceased client. The receptionist wouldn't likely give me a telephone number, but she'd pass mine on. That's where my trapline came in. When Melissa called back it would trap her number. From there I could trace the address.

But my phones wouldn't work until my electricity came back on.

I leaned back in my sister's chair, blinking gritty eyes. If only I knew this was my Melissa. I could watch the church entrance tomorrow, stop her on her way out of the service. Then the trick would be to convince her to talk. Would the news of the death of Baxter Jackson's second wife be enough to sway her conscience?

My mouth twisted. If this church-active Melissa was the right one, how could her conscience have allowed her to stand by a lie for six years, knowing Linda's murderer walked the streets? Where was her sense of justice? What kind of Christian was that?

A false one, that's what. Like Baxter, head elder at Vonita True Life Church. Perhaps he had taught our Melissa all too well.

I drank some water, scarfed down some Café Lattes, and googled my second possibility—the one in Gilroy. A few hits blipped on the screen—for Bluefly Flowers & Gifts. I clicked on the link and landed on a basic-looking website for the shop. Owner Melissa Harkoff smiled at me, a bouquet of flowers in her hands. She was gray haired and at least in her mid-fifties.

Not my gal. Not the right age to match the birth date that had led me to a Gilroy address in the first place. Apparently this was the third Melissa Harkoff I'd originally found, the one with a birth date too long ago. But *two* Melissa Harkoffs in such a small town? Surprising. I hadn't considered the name to be all that common.

Could this woman be a relative I hadn't known about? Someone who'd know where my Melissa was? I copied and pasted the number and address of the shop in my computer file and wrote it on my yellow pad. Even so, I doubted it would lead anywhere. Linda Jackson had told me Melissa had no relatives, which is why she'd ended up in foster care.

My mind was growing sluggish. As hard as I typically worked, I wasn't used to staying up all night. I needed some decent music along with my Jelly Bellies to keep me going.

Diminishing the screen, I opened Dineen's iTunes and perused her playlists. Ack. All jazz and pop. I knew my sister had poor taste in music, but this was downright embarrassing. How did a person exist without classic rock?

So much for music. I closed the program.

I stretched my neck right, left. Rubbed a hand across my forehead. Outside the wind had finally ceased its uproar. Fine drops plinked at the window, mere shadows of the night's deluge. By morning, perhaps, all would be quiet.

I listened for telltale sounds in the house. Nothing.

Maybe I *had* been wrong. Maybe I'd left my rear garage door unlatched. That was much easier to believe now that I sat in Dineen's home, enveloped by light. I *wanted* to believe it. Especially as the bed across the room looked more and more inviting . . .

I sat up straighter and pulled in five deep breaths, hoping the oxygen would clear my head.

The computer clock read 3:10 a.m.

My right hand reached for the mouse, my brain ticking through what I had so far. I'd eliminated an older Melissa in Gilroy, but I still hadn't found the one in that town who could match the birth date in '87 or '88. And the San Jose birth date still needed to be run down as well. If only I could remember those exact dates. I could do no more now without finding them again, then rematching them to Social Security numbers. There were still a lot of techniques I could employ once I had those SSNs.

Opening Skiptrace One, I went back to the beginning, typing in Melissa's name and the State of California. Up came the fourteen addresses I'd found, with the two possible birthdates: 01/27/1988 and 09/13/1987. I ran those dates and snagged their Social Security numbers. From there I traced the addresses on each SSN.

Next, phone records.

Using the search-by-address screen, I ran the most recent San Jose address—820 Willmott, a single family residence—through the system's real-time directory assistance. Real-time directories are up-to-date, unlike the stored data on free Internet directory sites, which could be six months old. Regular folks use those sites. Not an experienced skip tracer—except when old data are needed.

The Willmott address yielded no listed number. Melissa might well be there and choosing to guard her anonymity.

If I were Melissa, weighted by a dark secret, I'd certainly have an unlisted number. Once you'd lived through something like that, had seen a man you believed in and respected warp into a monster, whom could you ever trust?

The unlisted number wasn't necessarily a dead end. Skiptrace One provided a data source for such numbers. Unfortunately the data wasn't always complete. Beyond that I could turn to the information broker in Los Angeles I used for finding hard-to-obtain data. Numerous times Jeff Cotton had uncovered information I simply couldn't find. But I hoped not to turn to Jeff here. I didn't want *anyone* else knowing I was searching for Melissa.

I ran 820 Willmott through the unlisted number search, asking God for a little help.

Bingo. A phone number. For a Melissa Harkoff.

I keyed the number into a different kind of search—to see if it was a landline or cell phone. Answer: cell.

Hmm. My Melissa? Sounded promising. These days younger people often used cell phones only, no landlines.

Cell phones were both good and bad news for skip tracers, since people tended to keep their numbers when they moved. If this number was attached to my Melissa, it was probably still accurate. On the other hand, she may no longer be at the address that had led me to the phone.

But I still had other tricks up my sleeve.

Using credit headers instead of directory assistance this time, I ran a reverse address check to see what names came up attached to 820 Willmott. Melissa Harkoff appeared second on the list. First and more recent—only two months ago—was a Tony Whistman. Either Melissa had moved out and Tony had moved in, or they lived together, and Tony had recently done something—bought a car, applied for a new credit card—to activate a report.

I noted my findings in my computer file, then took a little time hunting down information about Tony Whistman. It wasn't hard to find. He was a realtor with RE/MAX in San Jose. He had his own website, which included his photo and a cell number. Tony looked to be in his mid-thirties, gray eyes, light brown hair. Beneath his may-I-help-you smile lay a hungry, intense expression, as if this young man sought to make millions and retire by age fifty. Make that forty-five.

Interesting. He'd be thirteen years older than my Melissa, but these days that meant little. Could they be living together?

I copied Tony's information into my file. Printed out the color picture from his website.

Although I continued searching, I found nothing to definitively tie Tony to the Melissa Harkoff I sought. No blog or pages on his website with personal photos. Neither did I find anything to detract from that possibility, such as a newspaper article about his marriage to someone else.

Turning aside from Willmott and Tony, I ran the older San Jose addresses attached to a Melissa Harkoff through phone-number searches. Each came up with a listed number in someone else's name. If my Melissa had once lived at those addresses, she didn't anymore.

Willmott remained.

Using the Gilroy addresses I repeated the process. The older ones yielded numbers under different names. The most recent came up with a phone number for a Melissa Harkoff. My gal or the florist?

I'd bet on the florist. She had to have a home number somewhere. Likely it was in the same town as her flower shop. But hunches could be wrong. A phone call in the morning should tell me what I needed to know.

Morning. I blinked at the computer clock. Four-fifty. In a few hours it would be light.

I pushed back from the computer, walked through the darkened hallway and into the bathroom. Exiting there a minute later, I found myself skulking through the house, checking locks again, peeking through a curtain to look outside. The rain had stopped. The world, what I could see of it, lay sullen and spent. Small branches and leaves littered Dineen's front lawn and her neighbor's yard across the street.

Where was Hooded Man now?

Who was Hooded Man?

I returned to Dineen's computer, wishing it were my own. I needed to search my photos for a picture of Melissa. I knew I had at least one of her and Linda together. I could picture them now on my back deck, Melissa looking proud and lovely in the new clothes Linda had bought her. She'd been living with the Jacksons less than a week, and I had just met her at church the previous Sunday. Melissa would speak little of her childhood, saying only that she was glad the horrible days following her mother's death were behind her. She seemed so grateful to be living at the Jacksons' home. To her it was a mansion, a new life.

The Café Latte Jelly Bellies were gone. I ate what remained of the Chocolate Puddings. *Rot my teeth with sugar, yeah right, Dineen.* It would never happen. She was just jealous of my hard choppers.

I drank the last of my water and looked over the information in the computer file. Somewhere along the way I'd eased up on my handwritten notes. Not good. Even though I'd ask Dineen for a flash drive to copy the file and take it back to my computer, I still wanted the written backup, just in case.

I stopped to write the notes on the yellow pad.

Finished with that, I sat back, data chugging through my tired brain. I would run other searches while waiting for dawn. Meanwhile the Willmott address held real promise.

A page I had seen on Tony Whistman's website suddenly registered. I blinked. Returned to the site. I found the page ... and in my soggy head a plan began to form.

SIXTEEN

JUNE 2004

The sounds wafted into Melissa's subconscious, chilling hands pulling her from another terrible dream of her mother dead on the kitchen floor.

Melissa's eyes blinked open to focus blearily on the open door of her walk-in closet. She was in the Jacksons' house, not her old trailer. Her new bright and shiny life.

Relief washed through Melissa, aching and cold. She shifted in her grand bed. Cracks of light shone through her closed curtains, promising another sunny day.

In her mind's eye she could still see the broken linoleum of the trailer kitchen. Her mom's bare feet, her body spread on the floor. The whiskey bottle and the blood—

The sounds came again—whatever had awakened Melissa. Now they clarified. Muffled voices in argument. A man's rapid words, pulsing with anger. A woman's retort.

Baxter and Linda.

Melissa raised up on one elbow, head tilted, listening. The voices sounded like they were coming from somewhere on the right side of her bedroom.

How could that be?

She threw back her covers and slipped from bed. Stood still, barely breathing, eyes roaming the room as if ghosts of the Jacksons morphed along the walls.

Maybe she'd imagined the sounds. The Jacksons didn't argue.

"Stop it, Baxter!"

Linda's words filtered sort of thick and tinny, as if from some distance. Melissa's focus jerked toward the ceiling across her room.

The heating vent.

She trotted over to her desk, picked up the chair in front of it, and set it down beneath the vent. Then climbed up on the chair, cocking her ear toward the ceiling.

"How *dare* you talk to me like that in my own home?" Baxter's voice was rough, seething.

"It's *my* home too." Linda's words caught, as if she was about to cry.

"I had this home before you came here, and if you took off tomorrow, I'd still have it. You just happen to live in it."

"I take care of it. I take care of *you*."

Hard footsteps thumped. "*I* take care of me. Not to mention the entire town."

Melissa's muscles tensed. She drew her arms around herself.

"Now you listen to me, Linda. You're going to have that dinner party *this* Saturday. I don't care what else you were planning. You'll invite who I tell you to invite, and they'll sit where I want them to sit. And before you start whining, remember you live in this house because *I* pay for it."

"This isn't about being thankful! I just wanted to do it next weekend so I could take Mel—"

Melissa heard a muffled *smack*. "My clients are more important than that girl."

Melissa's fingers curled into her pajama top. No way. He'd *hit* her.

That girl.

Silence.

"I'm sorry." Linda's voice shook.

"Go make me breakfast. You're making me late for work."

The voices stopped. Melissa craned her neck to one side, concentrating on hearing more.

Nothing.

Shaking, she climbed down from the chair. She slumped into it and leaned forward, staring at her bare feet digging into thick carpet. Wishing like anything she could erase the last sixty seconds.

Baxter had slapped Linda. As much as Melissa didn't want to believe that, she knew the sound. She'd heard it enough against her own cheek.

Maybe it was just a one-time thing. After all, she'd never heard their voices through the vent before. Besides, nice church-going men like Baxter didn't hit their wives. Trailer trash did that, like the kind who'd lived near her and her mom. Melissa could count off ten neighbor men in a heartbeat who'd shoved their wives around.

Yeah, and men who hit their wives didn't do it just once. They lived it.

Melissa raised her head and focused across the room, feeling sick. She'd had such plans for living here. Suddenly they were crumbling. What kind of home had she gotten herself into?

People were no good. No matter where you went, they were all just liars.

Melissa ran a hand across her forehead. She should just go back to sleep. Forget she heard anything. Whatever had happened, it was over. It didn't pose her any threat, none at all.

She pushed to her feet, headed for bed, then found herself veering for the closet. Even as she headed for the walk-in she told herself not to do it. *Just pull a pillow over your head and sleep, Melissa. Just tell yourself everything's going to be okay.*

Melissa crossed the threshold of the closet, trying to think nothing, nothing at all. She pulled a silky summer robe from a hanger and thrust her arms into it. Tied it around her waist. She stepped out of the closet and gazed at her bed, bottom lip sucked between her teeth. This was her last chance to turn away from this.

Her eyes closed in disgust. What a wimp she was. After all she'd handled in her past? After her own mother's death?

Head up, determination pulling back her shoulders, Melissa strode toward her bedroom door.

SEVENTEEN

FEBRUARY 2010

At 7:00 a.m. on Sunday I sat at Dineen's kitchen table, sipping coffee and feeling like the walking dead. A thick lump of tiredness sat in my chest, blood sluggish through my veins. Worse, my brain felt like mush. I had to wake up. Today of all days I needed my wits about me.

No sign of Dineen. I hoped she was sleeping soundly. I'd rummaged in her computer desk drawer and found a flash drive, copied my file onto it. My pages of handwritten notes were in my purse. One more cup of coffee and I was out of here, back to my house. I needed to shower, prepare for the tasks that lay ahead.

I needed electricity.

Wandering into the den, I flipped on Dineen's TV to low volume and searched out local news. The meteorologist was the man of the hour, prognosticating that although the storm of the decade had run its course, more rain could hit as early as this afternoon. A reporter stood in a Vonita neighborhood, indicating downed small trees, a broken mailbox. "A tree on a power line cut electricity to over a hundred homes last night. Repairmen worked into the early hours of the morning to fix the problem. Those Vonita citizens will surely be happy to wake up to restored power this morning."

Thank you, God.

The news sent a spark of energy through me. I drained my coffee and returned to the kitchen. I cleaned up after myself and left a note for Dineen: *Thanks so much. Looks like energy is back on at my house. Will call you later.*

As I pulled away from Dineen's, a dull ache thrummed in my head. Another full-blown headache was on its way. I detoured to stop at the convenience store for some high-powered aspirin.

The sky hung swollen and bruised. Runoff funneled down the side of the curb, the drains unable to keep up. In some places the water swirled into the street. My tires hit the puddles, sending hissing sprays at the gloomy sky. People were in their yards, picking up branches and other debris. A few glanced my way. No one waved. Before the newspaper article, that wouldn't have been the case.

Maybe they hadn't noticed who I was. Maybe I was just being paranoid.

I thought of all my friends at Vonita True Life Church, attending services in a few hours. Would they breathe a sigh of relief when I didn't show up? How many would offer their condolences to Baxter for my harshness?

My headache was quickly growing worse. I pulled into Perry's Corner Store and lugged myself inside.

"Hey, Joanne," Perry Bracowski called from the cash register area. He put the paperback he was reading facedown on the counter and shot me a smile. Perry was never without a detective novel. They filled the long hours at work, he'd once told me. After his wife died a year ago—following a protracted battle with cancer—he admitted to reading all the more. The books didn't fill the empty spaces at home, he said, but at least they were something.

Other than the two of us the store was empty. "What're you doing here on a Sunday morning?" I asked. Hired help usually opened the store. Perry worked the later shift and closed. Plus I knew he typically attended the Baptist church in town.

"Ah." He waved a hand in the air. "Lost my employee. Again. Doggone kids, think they have to go to college."

We smiled at each other.

"Nice night we had, huh?" He raised his bushy eyebrows.

"Stellar." I headed for the first aid section, close to the checkout counter, my rubber-soled shoes squeaking against the floor.

"A CSN night."

CSN—Crosby, Stills and Nash. Perry was playing our name-that-song game. I slowed, trying to think through the pain in my head. " 'Cold Rain.' "

"You got it. The *CSN* album, 1977."

I managed a smile.

"You one of those without electricity?"

"Yup. Went to my sister's for the night. You?"

Perry grunted. "I got lucky."

He folded his arms and watched me pluck a bottle of extra-strength pain reliever from the shelf. Perry is around my age, with an average build but strong, his hair pepper and salt. Dark brown eyes. A bit of a dreamer in a feisty sort of way. Not content, like my Tom. Not nearly as laid back. But I've always liked Perry. Solid—that's the word for him, in body and soul.

Silence descended. Perry's gaze slid to the nearby rack of Vonita's weekly paper, then bounced away. He cleared his throat.

I walked to the checkout and set down the plastic bottle. Perry focused on it, then raised his eyes to mine. "Headache?" His tone revealed more than the question.

"Yeah."

He opened his mouth as if words trembled on his tongue, then shut it.

I suppressed a wince. Perry and I had known each other for years, yet he didn't feel he could say what was on his mind? The subject separated us as tangibly as the slick green counter. Was he judging me for that newspaper article?

He concentrated on working the register, and I paid him. "Want a bag?" he asked.

"No, thanks. I'll just stick it in my purse. After I take some." I opened the top and dry-swallowed two tablets, then dropped the bottle in my handbag. With a nod to Perry I turned to go.

"Joanne?"

"Hmm?"

He shifted on his feet. "For what it's worth, I think it looks fishy too."

The words practically glowed in the air between us, as if Pandora's box had been opened. My eyes locked with Perry's. I wanted to say thank you, squeeze his arm to express how much his statement meant to me. Instead I blurted, "Why?"

His gaze wandered past me. "You know Linda was supposed to be on her way here that night? Baxter said she had a headache and needed some aspirin. Funny, huh. Just like you coming in here right now."

Not so funny. More like prophetic. A link from my best friend on that fatal day to me here, now, pursuing the truth. "I remember that's what Baxter told the police."

Perry focused on me once more. "I always thought that was strange. You know I've owned this place for years, before Linda came along. Not once did she come here that late at night. During the day maybe, but once dinnertime hit ..." He shook his head.

"Maybe a bad headache was enough to change that."

"That's what I told myself. What's kept me quiet all these years. And after all, it's Baxter, so who would doubt him? But then when Cherisse died ..."

"You don't believe that was an accident?"

He smiled wanly and tapped the paperback. Shrugged. "Maybe I read too many of these things."

"Maybe you're listening to your gut when others are refusing to."

"But it's *Baxter*."

I'd had the same reaction on that fateful day when Linda first told me things weren't right in her home. One day during a visit—shortly before Melissa came to live with her and Baxter—Linda had seemed sad, weighted. It was so unlike her. I pressed her to tell me what was the matter. After a succession of feeble claims that she was "fine," she gave in. She lifted up her shirt, showed me a large purple bruise on her back. I gaped at it, my mind refusing to grasp her silent message.

Never would I forget Linda's reaction. Her eyes closed in pain, as if my stunned silence had sealed her fate—who would believe Mrs. Baxter Jackson, if not her best friend? "I didn't get that from walking into a door," she said, her voice bitter and bleak. And she lowered her shirt.

I scrambled to apologize. Tried to explain I'd simply been shocked. I asked questions, begged for more information. How long had this been happening? How often? How could I help? We had to go to the police, our pastor. *Somebody.*

But Linda waved away my *mea culpas* and growing indignation. Before my eyes the victim side of her that I'd never seen, would not have believed existed, pulled back into its shell. Linda's buoyant expression and laugh returned. But after that I saw through them, realized the mask she'd perfected. And I would wonder, *Has Baxter hit her today? What might he do tomorrow?*

If only I'd pushed harder, made Linda go to our pastor. But she wouldn't hear of it. The last few weeks before her disappearance she couldn't even hide the stress in her voice when we talked on the phone. Finally I threatened to go to Pastor Steve without her.

"*No,* Joanne. I'll deny everything."

"But— "

"It's for Melissa. She needs a home. This will all work out. You'll see."

That had been the last time Linda and I spoke.

I blinked away the memories, startled to see Perry's eyes boring into mine as if trying to laser into my thoughts. For a moment I wanted to blurt out everything. About Linda's abuse and Hooded Man, my determined pursuit to finally see justice done. I had to bring Baxter's horrible secrets to light. For Linda. For me. I'd let her down. I'd let her *die*.

The old sickening guilt washed through my stomach.

The moment passed. Perry was still staring at me. I couldn't tell him his suspicions were wrong. Neither could I tell him the whole truth.

My head tilted. "You and I have lived over half a century, Perry. You've never seen anyone who surprised you? Who turned out to be something far different than what they claimed?

He gave a slow nod, as if acknowledging my underlying message. "Yeah. Sure I have. Like the Styx song."

Styx. I thought a moment. " 'The Grand Illusion.' "

" 'The Grand Illusion.' "

"Yeah. Like that."

Perry pulled his head back, his jaw moving to one side as he digested my response. He'd apparently learned plenty from those detective novels, the way he was pulling reactions from me.

He gestured toward the newspaper rack. "That article. It's the first time I heard how much life insurance Baxter had on Cherisse."

"It was a rumor I'd heard." Via Dineen at the law firm where she worked. One of the lawyers there was Baxter's attorney, and somebody leaked the information around the water cooler. "It sounded plausible, since Baxter had the same amount on Linda. But I didn't know for sure until I threw it at Chief Eddington and he didn't deny it."

"Half a million is a lot of money, even for Baxter Jackson. And right now, with real estate in the tank— "

The automatic door whooshed open behind me. I glanced over my shoulder to see a young mother and her little girl hurry into the store, hand in hand. They barely glanced our way and made a beeline for the bread aisle.

I looked back at Perry. "Gotta go."

A crinkly rustle sounded as the mother picked up a package. She swiveled toward the counter, pulling her child along. "Come on."

"Take care, Joanne." Perry gave me a firm nod. "Do what you have to do."

I blinked at him, my mouth opening to ask what he meant, but the mother-daughter duo approached. Perry shot me a meaningful look, then accepted the bread from the young woman. "Good morning. This be all?"

My body turned toward the door, my mind lingering on Perry. As I slid into my car I thought about Hooded Man, his possible cohorts, and wondered if Perry knew far more than he'd let on.

EIGHTEEN

How different my house looked in daylight. Beleaguered and worn from the storm, yes. Some branches were down in my backyard, and water stood in puddles at low points in the grass. But inside the place was warm and lit, void of threat. It was hard to believe I'd sat trembling in the corner kitchen chair last night, waiting for the police.

How shadows horrify a mind.

I set down my purse and overnight bag, retreated into the garage to check the infamous rear door. Still locked and bolted. I opened it and looked outside, scanning the nearby ground for footprints. Nothing.

With the door locked once more I searched the garage for anything out of place. Again nothing.

My nerves bristled. Was it just from the memory of last night? Or a frisson at the thought I was overlooking something?

In the kitchen I pulled two fresh batteries from a drawer and replaced the old ones in Billy Bass. Switched him on to motion sensor. I waved my hand, and he went off, raising from his wood mount and singing. "Don't Worry, Be Happy." A picture of Tom flashed through my head. How he had laughed the first time he turned that thing on.

Stupid, wonderful song.

I took a shower, which helped wake me up. Had a bagel and

cream cheese for breakfast, chased by strong coffee. I ate by rote, my thoughts churning. I needed to find Melissa *today.* Somehow convince her to talk to Chief Eddington. The thought of another long, unknowing night in my house—even *with* lights—made me shiver. After being awake for thirty-six hours by then, I'd need some serious sleep. But how could I close my eyes, knowing last night's intruder might come back?

By 8:30 I was at my computer, copying my notes on the flash drive into the HM file. My fingers itched to call the Melissa Harkoff in Gilroy. She would either be the florist or my Melissa. If the former, I could hone in on the Melissa in San Jose.

It was a little early to call on a Sunday morning. I promised myself I'd wait until 9:00.

My mind flashed on Perry, his parting words to me. What did he know?

I drained another cup of coffee. My nerves had begun to twitch. Too much caffeine on too little sleep. I couldn't even eat Jelly Bellies. The sugar would send me completely over the top. Nor could I listen to music. Sounds were too loud—the ticking of the kitchen clock, a car passing on Stillton. A buzz saw in the distance. Agitation rocked my stomach.

In the kitchen I sliced some cheese, drank a glass of milk for protein. Maybe as it digested I would feel better. At the moment it proved no help. I took a water bottle with me into the office, ducking to avoid setting off Billy Bass.

Back at the computer I ran my two SSNs for Melissa Harkoff through some public records databases on Skiptrace One. Most importantly I wanted to see if either the Gilroy or San Jose Melissa came up in criminal court proceedings or a marriage license. If Melissa had a new last name, I'd have to generate leads all over again. And if she were in jail I'd have a whole new situation on my hands.

Once when I'd just started skip tracing I spent days resulting in dead ends on a skip only to discover he had died. Wouldn't hurt to check death certificates either.

The results came up empty—no court proceedings, marriage, no death.

I ran a few other searches until I was satisfied the two Melissas I was tracking remained the most promising.

Nine o'clock arrived. I ran two pretexts in my mind for the phone call to Melissa in Gilroy. Which scenario I used would depend on the sound of the answering voice. I picked up the phone to dial—and saw my hands shake.

Stupid. I'd done plenty of these calls in the past.

But my own safety had never before depended on finding a skip.

I replaced the phone, took a drink from the water bottle. Massaged my fingers. When I was sure my voice wouldn't tremble, I dialed the number.

The third ring cut off in the middle. "Hello." An older woman, certainly not in her younger twenties.

"Hi, my name is Mary Sawyer. I'm trying to find the florist Melissa Harkoff—who owns Bluefly Flowers and Gifts in Gilroy?"

"Yes, that's me." Her voice sounded pleasant, patient. It fit with the picture on her website. I felt myself relax a little.

"Oh, hi. Sorry to call you at home. I'm in the area and I need a bouquet for an event tomorrow morning. I saw from your website that you open at ten. If I came down then, would I be able to have something made up at your shop right away?"

"Sure. As long as you're a little flexible and I can use things on hand."

"No problem. Thanks so much, I appreciate your time. I'll see you then." I paused, then chuckled. "There's another Melissa Harkoff in San Jose—do you know her? I almost called her first. Glad I didn't."

"Really? No, I don't know her. No relation to me."

Not surprising news. "Well, thanks again."

I hung up and slumped back in my chair with a sigh. My heart beat too hard. But I'd done it. One lead eliminated.

On to the next.

A door slammed outside. I jerked toward the window. In my peripheral vision I caught movement in my driveway. I leaned forward, peering through the blinds.

Baxter Jackson headed toward my front door.

NINETEEN

JUNE 2004

Halfway down the Jacksons' hardwood stairs, Melissa stopped to erase all suspicion and righteous indignation from her face.

From the kitchen wafted sounds of Linda. Making breakfast for her man.

Mouth firmed, Melissa continued on down.

Linda was fork-whipping eggs in a bowl. She stood at the counter by the refrigerator, her back to Melissa. Dressed in designer jeans and a satiny blue top.

Melissa padded up to the counter to stand on her right. "Good morning."

"Oh!" Linda gasped, her fork halting midair. "Melissa. Hi." She did not turn her head. "What are you doing up so early?"

Melissa examined her profile. Linda had already applied makeup for the day. Her one visible cheek looked normal. Melissa shrugged. "Just … couldn't sleep, I guess. You want some help?"

"No, no, I'm fine." Linda sidestepped to her left and placed the fork in the sink. She turned away from Melissa and busied herself at the cabinet beneath the cook-top island. Pans banged. She straightened, a small skillet in hand. With utmost concentration she placed it on a burner and turned on the gas. Reached for a spatula in the island's top drawer and used the utensil to cut a slab of soft butter from a nearby dish. The butter went into the pan. She would not look at Melissa.

The *San Jose Mercury* newspaper had been laid on the kitchen table, front page up. Facing Baxter's chair.

Melissa moved to the cabinet of plates and pulled one out. Selected a fork from the silverware drawer. "Here." She set them on the counter beside the cook top.

Linda glanced her direction. Her eyes looked red. "Thanks."

"Sure." Melissa eased back to lean against the tile. Waiting. When the butter heated up, Linda would have to turn around for the whipped eggs.

Linda moved the butter around with the corner of the spatula. A hand-painted clock on the wall ticked in the silence. Melissa thought of her mother and all the heavy silences that had hung between them. Some angry, some despairing, some so full of Melissa's will to not care that they practically dripped defensiveness on the floor. If you took all those moments and strung them end to end you'd have a lifetime. Melissa's life.

"Hand me that bowl, would you?" Linda's head moved slightly. She shuffled left as if to force Melissa to her right. But Melissa crossed behind to her other side. She set the bowl down, throwing a look at Linda's cheek. Linda raised her hand, pretending to smooth hair away from that side of her face. But too late. Melissa saw reddened skin, in the shape of fingers.

She stepped away, then sauntered toward the table and sprawled into a chair. "So. What're we going to do today?" She glanced at the newspaper, upside down to her.

Linda poured the whipped mixture into her pan. Sizzling arose, and the smell of eggs and butter. "I'm going to plan a dinner party for Saturday night." Her voice lilted, ever so light. "Maybe you can help."

"I thought we were going to see some play on Saturday."

"Oh." Linda raised a shoulder. "I asked some friends about it, and they didn't have very good things to say. I just think you'd be bored."

Melissa ran her tongue across her top lip. "How many people are coming? To your party, I mean."

"I haven't decided that yet."

"Oh. Who are you thinking of inviting?"

"Haven't decided that either. I'll do that today." Linda moved to the refrigerator and pulled out a container of orange juice.

If there had been one thing more prevalent in Melissa's past life than silence, it would be the lies. So many lies. The world was a wretched place to navigate when you didn't know false from real.

Melissa curled her fingers around the edge of the wooden table. "Think maybe the Weekses will come?"

"Probably not." Linda grasped the pan's handle and tipped it one way, then the other.

"I thought Joanne's your best friend."

"She is. But this dinner's more for Baxter's business associates."

"You like doing that? Putting on business dinners for him?"

"Oh, it's great. I love it."

Not once had Linda looked up from her work. In a crazy second Melissa imagined herself stomping over to Linda, pointing at her reddened cheek. Screaming at her to "Stop lying!" Instead she sat in the chair, jaw working back and forth.

One truth about the world? If something looks too good to be true, it probably is. How naive she'd been.

Melissa focused on her pink nails. Linda had taken her to a beauty salon yesterday, and they'd both had manicures. Melissa's nails looked so perfect. Long and painted, with flowers on her ring fingers. But her nails weren't perfect. They were fake.

Linda concentrated on the omelet, carefully folding it over with the spatula. "There." With a satisfied smile she flicked off the gas burner.

As if an omelet would change what had just happened in her bedroom.

Melissa rose and pushed the chair up to the table—just so, like she'd found it. Her eyes burned, but her insides burned more. How bad would this get once the Jacksons got tired of doing their "marriage made in heaven" thing? Would Baxter end up hitting her too?

"I'd live with them in a shack," Nicole had said at church. *"Everybody in town loves them, you'll see."*

Melissa watched as Linda slid the omelet onto its plate, then placed the pan in the sink. Every move she made kept her back or right profile to Melissa.

"How long have you and Baxter been married?" Melissa blurted.

"Seven years." Linda squirted dishwashing liquid into the pan and began to scrub. "Why do you ask?"

Melissa focused on Linda's hands as she cleaned the pan. Linda's nails wouldn't break making any dirty thing shine. They were hard and fake like Melissa's.

"Just wondered."

Baxter entered the kitchen in suit and tie, ready for his work day. He could have been three men entering, for the energy he brought into the room. Melissa straightened. "Well, hi, Melissa. You're up early." His voice sounded as kind and warm as ever. He shot her a winning smile.

Something inside Melissa loosened, even as she knew it shouldn't.

Linda made no comment. She was too busy rinsing the clean pan and reaching for a drying towel.

"Morning." Melissa smiled back. "I just ... woke up early. I'll probably go back to bed."

"Sounds good to me." Baxter gave her a wink. He walked to the counter and picked up his omelet and fork. "Thank you, sweetie." He aimed the words toward Linda. "Looks great."

"You're welcome." Linda dried vigorously. Her reply sounded flat.

Melissa faded away from the table as Baxter approached and took a seat. She needed to get out of the kitchen. The last place she wanted to be right now was between these two. Suddenly all the years of seeing her mom whacked around didn't seem so bad. At least Melissa knew what she was dealing with. At least in the trailer a wolf looked like a wolf.

She faked a yawn. "I'm going back upstairs now. Linda, when I get up I'll be happy to help you plan your dinner party."

Baxter's fork, speared into a large bite of omelet, stopped mid-air. Just for a second. "That's nice of you." He popped the fork into his mouth and chewed, no guile whatsoever in his expression. He drew the newspaper toward him and focused on the front page.

"That'll be great." Linda kept her head down as she turned to replace the pan in the cabinet. "See you in a few hours."

Melissa left the room.

Halfway up the stairs she lingered, leaning over the banister toward the kitchen. But she heard no voices. She imagined Baxter finishing his omelet. Would Linda turn to him, defiantly display her red cheek? Was she whispering a threat to tell?

Not a sound.

Melissa hung there for a moment, staring at nothing, then trudged up the stairs. Who would Linda tell anyway? And *why?* She had everything. A mansion to live in, beautiful clothes, a BMW. All the money she wanted. And she didn't even have to work for it. Who wouldn't put up with some bad stuff for all that?

Who wouldn't lie and pretend everything was A-okay?

Melissa padded down the long hall, reached her bedroom, and shut the door behind her. The sun had risen higher now, the room glowing a warm blue. Her eyes fixed on her desk chair, sitting where she'd left it—under the heater vent. Melissa hurried over to the chair, picked it up, and returned it to its proper place. Then stood in the middle of the room, mind churning. What if Baxter had noticed her open door at this end of the hall? What if he'd come in here, seen the chair? He'd figure out in a heartbeat she'd been listening.

But then, even if he knew, he wasn't about to let on, was he? His knowing would just be one more part of this game.

Melissa thrust her hands into her hair and sank upon her bed. She focused on her knees, pulling her whirling thoughts together. Okay. Fine. So this new reality wasn't quite what she'd dreamed. So what? She could handle it. She'd survived her entire miserable life, hadn't she? Would she rather go back into the system, take a chance on another foster home? It would likely be way worse than this.

She'd just have to be more careful. Watch her back. Make sure she did everything necessary to keep from getting kicked out.

Melissa sat up and raised her gaze toward the heavens. Really, how was this any different than what she'd been doing ever since she'd gotten here—pretending to be what they wanted her to be?

Let Baxter and Linda play their game. She'd beat them both at it.

TWENTY

FEBRUARY 2010

Baxter Jackson. Outside my house.

I shoved from my chair, heart tripping into overdrive. My hand flew up and hit the water bottle. It tipped over, spilling onto the desk, then rolled off and hit the floor with a plastic *glug*. I snatched it up and set it aside. Grabbed the computer mouse and minimized my HM file screen.

Steps sounded outside. And men's voices. Baxter wasn't alone.

The doorbell rang.

I shrank into the middle of the office, away from the window. Looked around wildly.

A knock sounded at the door. "Joanne? You home?"

Pastor Steve's voice.

My hands pressed against my cheeks. Pastor Steve's presence was good news. He'd never want to hurt me. But he and Baxter together here—on a Sunday morning? Steve would be preaching at the church service at 11:00.

What *was* this?

My feet moved me toward the door. Before opening it I shoved back my shoulders, steeled myself. Caffeine and fright zinged through my veins. My face felt hot.

I opened the door and somehow found my voice. "Hi, Steve." My eyes remained on my pastor. "Baxter."

Steve shot me a smile. "Sorry to show up on your doorstep like this, Joanne. Baxter and I met early at church this morning before service to talk over … the issues at hand. After some prayer and discussion we thought it would be a good idea to come see you."

Prayer and discussion? A fly on that wall would have drowned in Baxter's honeyed words.

Baxter spread his hands. "May we come in?"

I dared a look at his face. He surveyed me with his unique mixture of serenity and power. *I'm being a good Christian—or I'd squash you.* Pain edged the expression. His face looked thinner. He'd lost weight since Cherisse's death.

"Sure." I stepped back and ushered them into the hall. Twelve hours ago I'd done the same for two policemen—in the dark. I felt no less shaken now.

I closed the door and faced the two men, my hands laced in front of me. An awkward silence followed. Clearly they expected me to invite them to sit down. I would not.

Baxter glanced into my office at my computer screen. Thank goodness all he could see was the desktop. His eyes flicked away.

Steve cleared his throat. "Baxter, you want to …?"

"Yes." Baxter faced me, his lips curved in pious forgiveness. "I wanted to talk to you before church. You know the Bible says we're not to worship God if someone has something against us. We're to go make things right with that person first. I know there's this … problem sitting between us, and I hoped we could resolve it."

I'll just bet he did. In front of his pastor, of course, so he'd have a witness as to his gracious character.

I looked from him to Steve. "Whose idea was this?"

"Baxter's." My pastor's tone was firm, as if the answer alone supported Baxter's claim.

My arms folded. "I see. Baxter, why couldn't you do this alone? Why bring Steve? As I remember, the passage you're talking about also says to go to the person quietly, by yourself. And if that doesn't resolve the problem, *then* take a witness along."

Steve hesitated. What could he say? He knew I was right.

"You've been so against me, Joanne." Baxter raised a hand in supplication. "Frankly, I didn't know if you *would* talk to me alone."

He had that right. I'd have never opened the door.

Baxter saw my hardening expression and flicked a glance at Steve—*see what I mean?*

My cheeks grew hotter. Here stood this detestable man in my house—this wife beater, this *murderer*, and all the while his voice dripped with feigned hurt at my shortcomings. I couldn't imagine how Linda survived living with such a hypocrite.

Oh, wait. She hadn't.

"Joanne." Steve shifted on his feet. "Can we resolve this?"

"What's to resolve?"

He tilted his head. "You've made some pretty strong allegations against Baxter publicly—"

"I did *not* make them publicly. They were overheard, and a reporter printed them. That was never my intent."

"Okay. But now that's happened, the allegations are out there."

"So talk to the reporter."

Surprise flicked across my pastor's face. He'd never seen me act like this—toward him or anyone else.

"We came here to talk to *you*, Joanne." Baxter's voice remained ever so calm, his eyes gleaming with sincerity. "I just want to reassure you that I never did anything to hurt Linda or Cherisse. I mourn the death of both my wives more than you can know."

"Jackson will kill you if he finds out."

My arms shook. I wanted to punch out Baxter's lights. This man was the reason I'd been driven from my own home last night, why I was now afraid to sleep here at all. How dare he come here? Even for Baxter Jackson, this was over the top.

"This involves more than just you and Baxter," Steve prodded. "Many in the church are upset about it. I just hoped we could talk it out."

A horrifying thought spun through my head. What if Baxter was doing more than playing righteous in front of his pastor? Inside, he had to be livid. If something bad did happen to me after that newspaper article, surely someone would raise Baxter's name as my only known enemy. Now he had a witness that he'd never want to do me harm. That he'd been so forgiving, despite my transgressions.

Fear intertwined with my anger. That combination—and the caffeine and no sleep—prickled my whole body with heat. I glared at Baxter, my eyes telegraphing that I knew the truth. He'd sent someone here last night. He would do anything to silence me.

His disgusting charade was over.

My finger raised, pointing at Baxter. I turned narrowed eyes on Steve. "*This* man beat his first wife." My voice trembled, but I didn't care. "I don't know about Cherisse, but I know about Linda. She showed me the bruises, Steve. Big, purple. On her back, where no one else could see. She sat right here on my deck, raised her shirt, and showed me."

Baxter's head pulled back as if he'd been struck. "That's a *lie*."

"No, Baxter, *you're* the liar. You walk around Mr. Perfect Christian, Generous King of Vonita. I know who you really are. And so, don't forget, does God."

"Joanne," Steve's voice rose, "that's just preposterous. I've known Baxter for years. And I knew Linda. Never once did she come to me—"

"Of course not. She was the newcomer. It would be her word against the whole town's. And she was scared to death of what Baxter would do to her if she told."

"You have no proof of that!" Baxter's face crimsoned. He leaned toward me, a vein pulsing in his neck. "And I'm telling you, you'd better stop. I'll sue you for slander—"

"Wait." Steve pressed a hand against Baxter's arm. "Let's just calm down."

Baxter straightened, breathing hard. A saw blade wouldn't have cut through his jaw.

"Joanne." Steve swallowed. "I don't know what was on Linda's mind. But I just can't believe what she told you was the truth."

My eyes burned. I loved Steve. He was a good man, a caring pastor. He was just so deceived. "And *that* is exactly why she never came to you."

Baxter made a growling sound in his throat. Steve flicked a look at him, and he flexed his shoulders, clearly working to get hold of himself. How hard it must have been for him. How he must have wanted to strangle me right then.

Is that how he killed Linda?

"Clearly, coming here has been a mistake." Baxter's voice hardened to ice. "Sorry I wasted your time, Steve."

My pastor cast me a pleading look. My heart squeezed. He didn't deserve to be in the middle of this. How devastated he and my whole church would be when they learned the truth.

At that thought, a little vial within me broke, spilling over the rage. Did I really want to hurt my church like this? People would be torn up for months. It's not easy learning you've been deceived by someone you deeply trusted. Some may blame it on God, especially the younger folks who hadn't before experienced betrayal. If one of the church's strongest Christians turned out to be a sham, how could God be trusted? How could any other Christian be trusted? Their faith could be shaken to the core.

I could stop the search for Melissa right now, somehow manage to apologize to Baxter. Let the church just go on as it always had.

But how could I ever live with my conscience before God?

"I'm sorry too, Steve," I said. "I never wanted this. Don't worry about church today—I won't be there."

"No, Joa—"

I held up a palm, shook my head. "It's okay. Really. I don't want to make anyone uncomfortable. Just . . . go now. Please? I have work to do here."

My eyes locked with Baxter's.

Steve hung back, as if still trying to find a way to fix it. I opened the door. My pastor sent a sad smile my way, then stepped out on the porch.

In the moment Steve's back turned, Baxter cast a burning look of pure hatred upon me. His lips curled into a snarl. Only Steve's presence kept him from going for my throat.

Fear shriveled down my spine.

Baxter's murderous expression melted as he stepped outside. He turned back, puffed with righteous indignation. Amazing, how he could do that. "God will judge what you have done to me."

I slammed the door behind the men and bolted the lock. Leaned against the wood, listening to their footsteps fade down the sidewalk. Two car doors opened and closed.

My legs went weak. I'd done it now. Crossed a Rubicon with Baxter Jackson. Until Melissa led authorities to Linda's body, I'd have to watch my back every minute. Even in daylight.

TWENTY-ONE

It took me some time to settle down after Steve and Baxter left. I wandered around the house, drinking water to dilute the caffeine in my system, and praying. And worrying. What my pastor must think of me right now. I could only imagine the words Baxter filled his head with on their drive away from my place.

Once I passed Billy Bass and forgot to duck. He flipped into song—and I jumped so hard I hit the opposite wall.

After about twenty minutes my jitters subsided enough to return to what must be done. I found my way back to the computer, perched in my chair. Refocused my thoughts.

Time to call Tony Whistman. Find out if Melissa Harkoff still lived at his address, and if so, was she the right one. The one who could put Baxter Jackson behind bars.

I brought up Tony's website and honed in on his phone number. Most likely a cell. Realtors needed to be available to potential clients at all times. I jotted the phone number down on the yellow pad on my desk. My mouse clicked to the page on Tony's site that I'd registered after some delay last night. It was a recently updated page of his current listings. Today he was conducting an open house for the home at 3007 Tradden Lane. The picture showed an off-white stucco with dark blue shutters and a well-kept front yard. The description labeled it as a four bedroom, two-and-a-half bath on a quiet cul-de-sac.

Just the kind of home I found myself in the market to buy.

I picked up the phone and dialed Tony's number.

Please, God. Let this lead me to her.

"Tony Whistman." The voice was deeper than I'd expected. A little gruff around the edges.

"Hi, my name is Sarah Blair. I'm interested in looking at the house on 3007 Tradden Lane. Your website lists it as an open house today. Is that still on?"

"Yes, I'm opening it from noon to five. Be happy to have you come down."

"Great. So you'll actually be at the house? Not an associate?"

Tony chuckled. "It's just me around here, trying to hang on and make a living."

I laughed with him. "I hear you're a good realtor. I can't remember where I first heard your name. I think it was some friend of Melissa Harkoff's."

Silence. I felt a shift over the line.

Tony grunted. "Well. At least she did something for me."

Ah, so his relationship with her *was* personal. Which meant this Melissa was likely somewhere around the right age.

"Sorry. I didn't mean ..."

"Hey, if it gets you to my open house, I'm happy. You buy the place, I'll forgive her everything."

My hope snagged. Sounded like this relationship was over. So where was Melissa now? My mind raced for a way to push Tony further on the phone. But his antennae would surely go up.

"Okay." I gave another laugh. "Sounds like a deal for everyone. Anyway, I'll see you at the open house."

"Good. About what time will you be coming by, Sarah?"

Realtors—ever the salesmen.

"I'm hoping pretty soon after you open up."

"All right. See you then."

I clicked off the line and said a silent prayer of thanks to God.

Under "My Pictures" I clicked on the file for 2004 and found the photo of Melissa and Linda. I printed it on three-by-five photo paper, then trimmed it with a sharply bladed cutter to fit in my wallet.

MapQuest gave me directions to 3007 Tradden Lane.

My phone rang. Dineen's ID. I picked up.

"You sure left early," she said.

"I had things to do. Sorry to visit and run."

She laughed. "Did you have to wait long for your electricity?"

"It was on when I got back. A little while later my whole house lit up."

"Huh?"

"Baxter came to my door."

"Baxter?"

"And Steve." I told Dineen the sordid details.

"You think Baxter knows you're looking for Melissa?" Anxiety tinged her voice.

"I'm not sure it matters. He does know what the article said, and that's enough."

"What're you going to do?"

"I'm going to put the man *away*."

Just speaking the words coursed fresh determination through my veins. Linda should have stood up for herself when she had the chance. Baxter Jackson was not going to take me down too.

"Joanne, I don't like this."

"I'm not liking the fact that you're my sister right now. I don't want *you* in danger."

Silence. I could feel the repercussions sinking into Dineen's brain.

I stared at Melissa's picture. Her smile now looked taunting, as if she dared me to believe I'd ever find her.

"How's Jimmy?" I asked.

"A little better but still feverish. He's down for the day."

"Give him a kiss for me. I need to go now. I'll check in with you later."

"Joanne. Be careful."

"You too."

I clicked off the line and stared again at Melissa, standing next to Linda and smiling. *Why* hadn't one of them told the world about Baxter's abuse? What went so wrong in that house that Linda ended up dead?

My eyes flicked to the clock on my office wall. Time to get moving.

I headed for the bathroom to put on some makeup, thoughts turning to my next bluff with Tony. Apparently he was no longer on good terms with Melissa. A point in my favor. He'd be less protective, more likely to complain to a listening ear. Still, I would be treading unstable ground. If Tony clammed up, I'd lose precious time.

As I crossed the threshold to my bedroom, sudden hard rain beat against the roof.

TWENTY-TWO

JUNE 2004

Four couples joined Baxter and Linda for their dinner party on Saturday. Melissa helped serve.

They'd invited her to eat with them, but she politely declined. She wasn't interested in being one of them. She wanted to glide in and out, as invisible and discreet as a server in an upscale restaurant. While she soaked up every word.

In the past few days Melissa had worked everything out in her head. Stay the course. Do what she needed to do to keep in the Jacksons' good graces. All week she'd been Linda's right-hand gal, writing down everything the woman rattled off in a long shopping list, going to various stores with her, unpacking all the bags of goods. After the grocery run for five courses, and the wine and flowers and centerpiece, Melissa added up the total in her mind. Over six hundred dollars. Baxter didn't bat an eye at the cost. In fact, he didn't even ask. Linda saved all the receipts as tax deductions, since the dinner was "for business purposes."

Maybe. But the Jacksons sure made it seem like those people were their best friends on earth.

They introduced Melissa to everyone, and she worked hard at remembering their names. Mr. and Mrs. Sanyon were probably in their sixties, both with gray hair and looking very refined. She wore a silk dress that had to be as expensive as the one Linda had on, with a diamond necklace and earrings. "Who are they, what do they do?" Melissa whispered to Linda when they retreated into the kitchen to make drinks. Linda looked absolutely stunning in a fitted red dress and matching heels, her hair up. Melissa had done her best to dress for the occasion too, in black slacks and a slinky black top Linda had bought her the day before.

"He's a real estate developer." Linda said no more, meaning Mrs. Sanyon did the same thing Linda did—took care of the house and her man.

Then there was Police Chief Eddington and his wife. Maybe in their late forties. The chief stood tall and porky, with a big nose and deep-set eyes. His wife looked a foot shorter. She was quite a talker. Oh, so chatty and charming. She gave Melissa a hug as if greeting her own granddaughter. "How wonderful to see you, dear. We know how happy you've made Baxter and Linda."

Baxter and Linda. It hit Melissa that everyone she'd met said their names in that order. Like Linda was an afterthought.

Chief Eddington looked Melissa over with a nod. "Nice to meet you." But an undertone edged his voice, as if Melissa's kind wasn't really good enough for this household.

Had she imagined that?

The chief flicked his eyes at Baxter. "This man treating you right?"

"Yes, sir. I'm very happy here."

A smile twitched one corner of the chief's mouth. "Can't imagine who wouldn't be, living in this mansion."

He held Melissa's gaze for a split-second too long. She turned away, uneasiness worming through her gut. She'd never liked policemen. Had no trust of them. What had they ever done for her? And she'd never forget being questioned by some cop after her mom's death.

Baxter caught Melissa's eye. Something in his expression told

Melissa he read her thoughts. Defensiveness rose within her. But then Baxter gave her a reassuring smile. Her insides settled.

As the Eddingtons joined the others in the formal living room, Baxter asked them what they wanted to drink. A gin and tonic for the chief, white wine for Mrs. Eddington. "Linda, honey, you stay." Baxter squeezed his wife's arm. "I'll help Melissa get these."

Surprise flicked across Linda's face. She covered it with a smile. "Okay."

With a glance at the chief, Melissa scurried after Baxter.

In the kitchen he reached for one of the glasses already set out on the counter. "I'll make Wayne's drink. You can pour the wine."

"Sure."

Wayne. Baxter said the name so easily. Melissa watched from the corner of her eye while he poured the gin with expertise. He looked good tonight in blue slacks and a dress shirt. But then Baxter always managed to appear in charge of every situation. As if the air itself in the house, at church, everywhere swirled around him.

Melissa pulled a white wine bottle out of its ice bucket. "So does Mrs. Eddington do anything? I mean, work?"

"She's the only wife here tonight who does." Baxter set down the bottle of gin and reached for tonic water. "Front desk for Dr. Bedrey, a dentist in town."

"Oh." Melissa poured wine into a glass until the bottle emptied. She pushed the bottle toward the back of the counter. She faced Baxter as he turned toward her.

One side of his mouth curved. "Wayne can come across sort of hard sometimes. It's just his way. Doesn't mean anything."

Melissa's lips firmed. Part of her wanted to deny. She never let anybody see her vulnerability. The other half warmed at the thought that Baxter had noticed.

She shrugged. Turned to pick up the wine glass.

Baxter lifted the gin and tonic. His eyes were still on her. "By the way, you look stunning tonight." He said the words as a proud father would speak to his daughter.

Stunning. The very word she'd thought about Linda.

Melissa cast a demure glance at the floor. "Thanks."

TWENTY-THREE

FEBRUARY 2010

I arrived at the Tradden Lane address without getting lost, courtesy of the GPS system in my car. It was shortly after noon. I saw one car in the driveway of the house—a blue Mercedes. It looked new.

Interesting. Tony's name had come up on a credit header just two months ago. From buying this car?

A RE/MAX "Open House" sign had led me to turn onto Tradden Lane. A matching red "For Sale" sign stood in the front yard, Tony Whistman's name and picture on top. His sign dripped water. The rain had stopped only in the last five minutes.

On the passenger seat of my car lay a manila folder containing a printout of my HM file. I set it on the floor. I'd also brought a yellow pad and pen for quick note-jotting. It lay on the passenger seat.

I took a drink from the water bottle I'd brought along and got out of the SUV. My gaze swept the wet yard and two-story house. Too bad I wasn't really in the market for real estate. This was a lovely home.

No other cars lined the curb. The rain couldn't be helping the attendance at Tony's open house. Good news for me. I hoped to talk to him alone.

My knees wobbled as I closed my car door. The lack of sleep had plagued me during the entire drive. A slow-moving brain I didn't need. I took a couple of deep breaths, leaning against the 4Runner. I could only hope Tony wasn't watching through a window.

A moment later I entered the house and closed the door behind me. Straight ahead lay a kitchen. I could see the edge of a black and silver granite counter top, a stack of flyers about the property upon it.

"Hello there," a voice called out. Tony's. A second later he appeared in the kitchen threshold. Tony stood under six feet, with a short torso and long legs. He smiled, but I could feel his gray eyes calculating my worth as a potential buyer. The vibes he gave off didn't sit right with me, the sense I'd gotten from his picture only flowing stronger from the real person. Tony impressed me as a man who'd be hard to live with. Someone who knew what he wanted and viewed compromise as a failure.

If that trait spilled over into his business, he wouldn't be selling many houses. Especially in this market.

"Hi. I'm Sarah Blair."

"Oh, yeah, you called. Glad you made it."

I smiled. "Nice car out there. New?"

"Got it two months ago. It's a fine specimen."

"That it is."

I cast my gaze up the staircase, pretending to survey the wall colors, the carpet.

"Go ahead and look around, Sarah. I'll be in the kitchen if you have questions."

"Thanks."

I started with the second level, taking my time, opening closet doors. Tony would expect to hear such sounds. Back downstairs I perused the living room, the den, a small office. By design I ended in the kitchen.

No one else had yet entered the house. I didn't want to push my luck. All the same, a woman in search of a house checks out the kitchen with a detailed eye. I went through the motions, looking in cabinets, noticing the appliances and size of the sink.

Tony and I talked about the home, its square footage, and "fair" price. I told him I was getting remarried soon, my fiancé living in San Mateo. I wanted to move down to the San Jose area, closer to his job. Of course he'd have to check out whatever place I was interested in.

"Sure." Tony leaned casually against the counter on one elbow, one foot crossed over the other. "I can show it to the two of you any time. Just give me a call."

I ran my hand over the smooth, swirled granite, my body language saying I was in no hurry to leave. Open houses could be lonely, boring events. A good realtor without other customers would always be up for a chat.

"So who was this friend of Melissa's who told you about me?" Tony asked.

Bingo.

I faced him, head tilted, frowning. "I'm trying to remember. It was some time ago. Maybe my friend Ellie, who used to work with her at Macy's?"

Tony screwed up his face. "When did Melissa work at Macy's?"

"I . . . are we talking about the same person? Brown hair, pretty. About twenty-two?"

"Sounds like the one."

My heart turned over. *Please let it be.* "Guess that was before you knew her."

"Guess so."

"Know what, I think I may even have an old picture of her with my friend." I set my purse on the counter and pulled out my wallet. "Let's see . . ." I flipped through a few pictures. "Yes. Here."

I held the wallet out to Tony, my thumb half covering Linda's face. He leaned over and checked out the photo. "Yup, that's her. Wow, she's young. Look how long her hair was."

He stared at the picture a moment longer, wistfulness flicking over his face. Then straightened, his jaw firming.

I gave him an empathetic look. "I haven't seen Melissa in a long time. You two have some kind of break-up?"

He snorted. " 'Some kind' is right. She got all weird on me and took off three days ago. Just—gone. All her clothes, everything. Have no idea where she went."

I'd missed Melissa by three days? My expression froze. I covered my reaction by putting my wallet back in my purse. "You must have some idea. People don't just ... disappear."

He scratched the base of his neck. "They do if they want to. Doesn't matter, though, I'm better off without her."

"Sounds like you're not quite sure you believe that."

He shrugged. "If I learned one thing from living with Melissa for four months, it's that she's hard-headed as can be. Nothing stands in her way."

"Have you tried calling her? I'm assuming she has a cell phone."

"Yeah, I called her." He sighed. "She told me she had somebody new in her life and I was not to call her again. Then she hung up."

"Wow. That's ... sudden. You had no idea?"

"None. I phoned the few friends of hers I'd met. They don't know anything either."

"What about going to her work?"

Tony snorted. "She didn't show up after she took off. They don't know any more than I do."

This didn't sound good. "You don't think something's happened to her."

"Nah. She just ..." Tony's gaze roamed across the room. "That's her other trait. Well, two traits. Independence and privacy." His mouth twisted. "Except when she wants something."

"I don't ..." I shook my head. "When I knew her she seemed unsure of herself, trying so hard to fit in."

Tony spewed a mirthless laugh. "Like you said, that was a long time ago."

"I guess."

I desperately wanted to keep Tony talking. If only I could pry the name of Melissa's "few friends" from him. If she'd moved in with some new man, one of them was bound to know, despite the denials to Tony.

"What kind of work was she in?"

"She answered phones at Whidbye Realty. That's how we met. I had to call a realtor over there, and we got to talking ..."

Real estate, how interesting. It fit.

Tony stood up straight and drew a deep breath, as if cleansing himself from the subject. "Enough talk about Melissa."

"I'm sorry it didn't work out for you."

He nodded. "Yeah. Me too."

My brain spun for something more to say, but the conversation had played itself out. At least I'd confirmed this Melissa was my gal. And she was still using the same cell phone number I'd uncovered.

But I didn't expect to persuade her over the phone to end six years of silence. I would have to find a way to talk with her in person.

"Well." I pulled myself up straighter, picked a flyer for the house off the counter. "I should be going." I looked over the sheet in my hand. "Nice job here. Good photos to show my fiancé."

I took my leave of Tony, promising to call him back if my fiancé was interested in seeing the place. I stepped outside to a sky bulging low and ominous, as if the clouds might crack any minute.

My watch read 1:10. In five hours it would be dark.

TWENTY-FOUR

As I drove away from Tradden Lane, I considered possible pretexts for my call to Melissa. My head was dulling by the minute, as if some drug had just hit my system. My body craved sleep. I sat up straighter, took a deep breath.

Didn't help.

After about a mile I spotted a church parking lot and pulled into it. Cut the engine.

Maybe if I ate something. But I couldn't be bothered with real food now.

I popped open the console and fished out a bag of emergency Jelly Bellies. It was a mixed bag, flavors for all situations, but I was beyond picking through them. I grabbed a handful, shoved them in my mouth, and chewed. Bursts of French Vanilla and Cotton Candy, Crushed Pineapple, and Jalapeño hit my tongue. I ate a second handful, and a third, reveling in the tastes, the sugar. An hour from now I'd probably crash. But I couldn't think of that now.

When I'd had enough I stuffed the half-eaten Jelly Belly bag into the console and took a long drink from my water bottle.

There. I felt a little better. Emphasis on *little.*

From my purse I pulled out my regular cell phone. I dialed 411 and got the address for Whidbye Realty. Jotted it down.

I put that phone away and withdrew another from my purse—a prepaid cell with a blocked ID.

This was it. I'd better make it good.

I had one chance to contact Melissa and coax an address from her. Melissa could well be suspicious of anyone who called, knowing Tony was trying to find her. If this didn't work, I'd be relegated to checking for new leads on my computer. But it could take days for her to apply for new credit or change her address on some bill.

Baxter's hate-filled expression bloomed in my head. As long as that man walked the streets, I would not feel safe.

The prepaid cell phone felt heavy in my hand. I still felt so tired.

I got out of the car, paced around. Swung my arms and stretched. If anyone saw me they'd surely wonder. Mine was the behavior of a tired driver at a long-awaited rest stop, not someone in a church parking lot.

As I walked I mentally practiced my spiel. Finally feeling a little more alert, I got back in the car—and punched in Melissa's number.

While waiting for the connection I asked God's help on this one.

"Please enjoy the music while your party is reached," said a woman's canned voice. Some horrible rap begin to play as a ringback tone. I held my cell away from my ear. *Come on, come on.* The tune—if you could call it that—seemed to go on forever.

This was the downside of a blocked ID. Melissa would most likely ignore the call and let it go to voicemail.

The rapper sang a few real notes—then cut off.

"Hi, I'm not here. Leave a message." *Beep.*

Even though I hadn't heard her speak in six years, I knew it was Melissa. Skip tracers tend to become quite astute at recognizing voices.

"This is Janet White with UPS." My tone sounded clipped, professional. "I have a package for special Sunday delivery from Whidbye Realty for a Melissa Harkoff at 820 Willmott, San Jose.

The owner there refused the package and could give me no forwarding address. If you call with that information, I'll reroute the package. Otherwise it'll need to return to sender."

I rattled off my number and hung up.

Now—the waiting game.

I leaned back against the headrest and closed my eyes.

TWENTY-FIVE

The ringing of his special cell phone shot prickly heat through his veins. He snatched it up and pushed *talk.* "I'm here."

"Just checking in like we agreed."

"Where is she?"

"In her car, sitting in a church parking lot in San Jose."

"Why? What's she doing?"

"Sleeping."

His head drew back. "Sleeping."

"Looks like it."

His jaw pulled to one side. He took a long, slow breath. Exhaled. "Tell me, is *that* what we want her to be doing? With time running out?"

"No."

"Think maybe you should do something about it?"

"Yeah. Sure."

His teeth clenched. "That would be most helpful."

He punched off the line before the idiot could reply.

TWENTY-SIX

JUNE 2004

"You look stunning tonight."

The compliment rolled through Melissa's head as she followed Baxter to the living room, carrying the white wine for the police chief's wife.

More guests were still to come. Now it didn't matter what any of them said. Melissa would cling to Baxter's words.

"Here you go." She handed the wine to Mrs. Eddington with a charming smile.

The third couple soon arrived at the dinner party—the Brewers. Mrs. Brewer looked twenty years younger than her husband. Around Linda's age. She was dressed in black, with shiny black hair and big brown eyes. Her eye shadow and liner were in shades of purple and looked like a professional had applied them. Melissa watched her eyes as she blinked, trying to figure how to duplicate that look. Mr. Brewer's thick, gray hair, tanned face, and piercing blue eyes made him appear like some big-shot criminal lawyer on TV. He even had the voice. He *was* a lawyer, Linda informed Melissa in the kitchen. But not on the criminal side.

"I thought all lawyers were criminals." Melissa deadpanned.

Linda smiled. Either she was really enjoying herself or she deserved an Oscar. Melissa had heard that hearty laugh of hers more than once tonight.

Maybe Baxter had made it up to her, promised never to hit her again. Who wouldn't want to believe Baxter? Despite the argument Melissa had heard, despite the new bitter suspicion of his hypocrisy, she couldn't dislike him. Every day since that argument he'd warmed to her even more. He'd been nothing but nice and encouraging, and she'd seen him and Linda hugging more than once. Some moments Melissa told herself she'd imagined the slap. Every couple argued now and then. That's all she'd heard. Now, after Baxter's kindness to her in the middle of a dinner party of important people, she found herself even more convinced of that.

"You look really great tonight," Melissa told Linda. They stood side by side, Melissa watching as Linda poured two glasses of white wine. Linda herself never drank. Only fancy bottled water for her.

"Thanks, hon. So do you."

Melissa looked down at her new clothes. "Yeah, well, thanks to *you*."

Linda set down the wine glass and turned to face Melissa, her expression turning serious. "No, thanks to *you*. You're beautiful no matter what clothes you're wearing. True beauty comes from the inside. And you are beautiful on the inside, Melissa Harkoff."

Melissa stared. No one had ever said anything like that to her before. For a crazy second she wanted to throw her arms around Linda. But the feeling blitzed away like fairy dust. Was this for real? Maybe Linda was aware she knew Baxter smacked his wife around in their bedroom. Maybe this was some silent plea for Melissa to keep her mouth shut.

"You're beautiful inside too," Melissa said. A calculated answer, meaning anything Linda needed it to mean.

Linda's smile etched itself in pain. She gave Melissa a tight hug, as if the words meant more to her than Melissa could ever know. They stood there for a moment, Melissa trying not to feel too stiff. With an audible breath, Linda let her go. "Well. Better get back to those guests." Her voice held that overbright ring Melissa had heard before. Linda picked up the wine glasses. "Bring in some cocktail napkins, okay?"

Melissa followed like the good foster daughter she was.

The fourth and final couple arrived a few minutes later. "So sorry," Mrs. Drake breathed, raising both hands and spreading long fingers. Her hair was brown and curly. Her eyes looked tired, even though she couldn't be much older than Linda. "Harry got a business call while we were walking out the door—on a Saturday. But you know how that goes."

"I sure do." Baxter grinned. "Come in, come in."

Mr. Drake shook hands with Baxter, a smile stretched across his narrow face. Melissa tried to guess what he did for a living. Doctor? Another attorney?

Owner of a concrete company, Linda whispered.

Melissa had gone through the drill with Linda. Present plates from the left, remove from the right. Serve women first. Keep the wine flowing. Apparently Melissa did so well Linda had more time to sit and enjoy her guests than she usually did. Which left Melissa alone in the kitchen, ear cocked toward the dining room conversation as she rinsed dishes from each course.

"How's the Enclave development going?" Sounded like Mr. Brewer's voice.

"Fine, fine." Mr. Sanyon. "No slowing down for us. So many people are wanting to move farther and farther out of San Jose. Vonita's looking great to them, and so are the prices. Half the houses are sold already—most of 'em by Baxter. And phase one won't even be done for another three months."

Melissa felt a swell of pride for Baxter. Probably no realtor in fifty miles came close to his sales.

"You developers, messin' up my town," Chief Eddington said. "More people will just mean more crime."

"Ah, you love it, and you know it." Baxter laughed. "Gives you something to do."

"I'd rather retire."

"Retire! You're not even fifty yet."

"All the more years to play golf."

Mrs. Eddington chimed in. "As long as you finish playing by five and make me dinner."

"Make dinner? That's your job."

"Not when I'm working and you're not."

Good for you. Melissa smirked.

Mr. Eddington huffed. "Guess the town's stuck with me as police chief, then."

Mr. Brewer talked about some lawsuit he was leading against a San Jose real estate developer. People had bought homes that were never finished or built badly. Floors sagging. Front sidewalks cracking.

"Should've used Harry for those sidewalks." Mrs. Drake's voice.

"And if Ken were the developer, you wouldn't be suing in the first place." Another woman—Mrs. Sanyon. Ken must be her husband.

"Well, if the likes of present company ran this world, I'd be out of clients." Mr. Brewer chuckled.

"Here, here," Linda said.

Glasses and silverware clinked.

Interesting, the way all these people interconnected, Melissa thought as she set plates in the dishwasher. She'd pulled on a pair of rubber gloves. Never figured she'd wear such ugly things, but as long as she was playing slave she didn't want to ruin her manicure. Mr. Sanyon built the homes that Baxter sold. Mr. Drake probably did the concrete. Mr. Brewer was suing some competitor of Sanyon. And Sanyon's development was drawing people to Vonita—which made Eddington chief over more people.

Was this the way the business world worked? The way adults

with money worked? People helping others to help themselves. Do for me, and I'll do for you.

Melissa wanted to be part of that world. Somebody with a good career who made lots of money. Somebody everyone would want to invite to a fancy dinner party. She'd show up in her silk dresses and diamonds. She'd throw around important names and projects between bites of honey-shrimp salad and prime rib au jus.

At that moment, her yellow-gloved hands holding a dirty plate, Melissa felt something crack within her. A feeling, a *knowledge* trickled out.

She was better than this.

Melissa stilled, caught by the sensation within herself. Yes. She *was* better. She really could forget her past. Forget her abuse and the ratty trailer and her mom's live-in men with roving hands. Staying in this house as a lowly foster child wasn't enough, even if the house belonged to Baxter Jackson. Melissa could *be* somebody. She'd be *better* than Linda. Not just some wife of a rich man who claimed she saw beauty on the inside. Melissa would make her own money. Live in her own place.

Maybe Baxter would help her go to college. She got good grades in high school. Why shouldn't she pursue a higher education?

Melissa put down the plate and turned off the water. Voices chirped and chuckled from the dining room, but now she barely noticed. She focused out the window into the gorgeous backyard full of flowers and trees and green, green grass. A backyard tended twice a week by gardeners.

"You look stunning tonight."

Baxter had seen something in her. She was born to live in a place like this. To live this kind of life.

Hope flamed within Melissa, so blazing and sudden she clutched the counter tile, barely able to breathe. For the first time she saw her childhood as a mere blip on the screen. It hadn't ruined her. None of it, not even the death of her mother. It had strengthened and prepared her for the big world out there. She really could do anything she wanted. She could make things happen. All she had to do was go after it.

Tears biting her eyes, Melissa made a promise to herself. From this day forward no one, no circumstance, no setback would ever stand in her way.

TWENTY-SEVEN

FEBRUARY 2010

A cacophony of hammers startled me from sleep.

My body jerked. My bleary eyes flew open to behold my car windshield sheeted with rain. Some distance across the parking lot, my view of the Baptist Memorial Church warped and wavered. Drops pounded the roof of the SUV.

"Unh." I blinked hard and checked my watch. Almost 3:00. What in the world? How could I have fallen asleep?

Sinking back against the headrest, I vaguely remembered doing that same thing after leaving the message for Melissa. I'd laid the prepaid cell phone on the passenger seat ...

My head swiveled. The phone was still there. Along with the yellow pad and pen.

My body felt like a truck had hit it. I *had* to eat something. Real food.

My phone rang.

I bounced up straight, heart quivering. Only then did I realize it was my regular cell, not the prepaid. I dug it out of my purse and checked the incoming ID.

Private caller.

I stared at it. Should I answer?

The second ring stabbed my nerves. On the third one I hit *talk*. "Hello?"

"Joanne." The unmistakable roughened voice of Hooded Man filled my ear.

My eyes fixated on the windshield, words sticking in my throat.

"I know you're there."

I swallowed. He was calling me now? Why hadn't he called the first time, instead of stopping me on a deluged road?

"Are you doing what I told you?" he pressed.

"Were you at my house last night?"

"Why would I be at your house?"

"Someone slammed the garage back door. Just after the electricity went out."

"Oh. *No.* I told you he would kill you if he found out."

"But I didn't tell *anyone.* I hadn't even been home that long."

Air seeped from his throat. "Then he doesn't know, but he wants you dead anyway, after that newspaper article."

Fear gripped my throat. No words would come.

"Don't stay in your house tonight, Joanne."

"Why won't you tell me who you are?" My voice rose. "Why the mask? You're a *coward*. Why should I listen to you?"

Silence throbbed in my ear. For a moment I thought he'd hung up.

"You're right." His voice hung low, grating. "I *am* a coward."

My eyes closed. "Please tell me who you are."

"You're clearly in danger. Your only hope is to persuade Melissa to tell what she knows. *Are* you looking for her?"

"Yes, okay? Yes!" Perry's words flashed in my mind— *"Do what you have to do."* "Are you the only one who knows about this? Are there others with you?"

"You have to find her *now*."

"I'm trying!" My fist pounded the steering wheel.

"You can't spend another night in your house until you do."

"What do you expect me to do, go on the run? You're the one who got me into this. I should go to the police."

"You can't." Hooded Man's voice flattened.

"And just why not?"

I could hear him breathing.

"Tell me!"

"Because the chief's in with Baxter."

All air sucked from my lungs. I slumped back against the headrest, refusing to believe, knowing it was true. Chief Eddington had barely looked into Cherisse's death.

But not everyone on the force was "in with Baxter." The two policemen who'd come to my house last night had been helpful.

Or had they? What if they *had* seen evidence of a break-in and hadn't told me? By the time I returned to the house the next day, footprints would have been long gone, erased by the rain.

"And don't go to your sister's," Hooded Man warned.

"You leave Dineen out of this!"

"No, *you* leave her out. By not staying at her house."

Did he know I'd stayed there last night?

My fingers curled around the cell phone. This was too much. I wanted to strangle this man. Because of some personal vendetta against Baxter, he'd used me as his perfect pawn. He'd played my sense of injustice, hung me out on a limb. Now there was no turning back. "*Why* did you do this to me?"

"Just. Find. Melissa."

The line clicked.

"Wait! Are you there?" I thrust a hand in my scalp. "Don't go!"

No response.

"Please!"

The emptiness echoed. I threw my cell phone on the floor and leaned over the steering wheel. Tears bit my eyes. What was I doing? How had I gotten here? This was *crazy*.

My cell rang, a different tone.

The prepaid.

My head jerked up. No, no, not *now.*

I picked up the phone as if it were a ticking bomb. Peered with blurry eyes at the ID.

Melissa Harkoff's phone number filled the screen.

TWENTY-EIGHT

The prepaid cell phone rang a second time. I clutched it, breathless. For a horrific second I couldn't remember the false name I'd given Melissa.

Rain pummeled my car. The air around me thickened with humid heat.

The phone rang a third time. I punched on the line.

"Janet White, UPS." My heart banged. I fought to keep my voice steady.

"Hi, this is Melissa Harkoff. You called about some package?"

"Uh, yes. Let me just retrieve that paperwork."

"You said it's from Whidbye Realty."

I sat up straighter. Picked up my yellow pad with the addresses I needed written upon it.

"Here it is. Yes, Whidbye Realty, 2415 W. Sharon Street. Addressed to Melissa Harkoff at 820 Willmott. You have an updated address?"

"How'd you get my phone number?" Suspicion nicked her tone.

"We always ask for the addressee's number, just in case something like this happens."

I rubbed a hand across my forehead. It came away wet.

"Oh." Melissa was silent a moment. "What is it?"

"What's in the package? I have no idea. I just work for the delivery service."

"I don't know why they'd be sending me anything."

"Miss Harkoff, do you want the package or not?"

"I don't ... *What* is that noise?"

I threw a look out the windshield and winced. "It's raining hard. This building's roof sounds like tin."

Melissa paused. "I used to work at Whidbye." She spoke the words as if thinking out loud.

"Maybe they're sending you some personal items you left. Who knows? What's your address, please?"

Silence.

"Miss Harkoff, I don't have all day."

"When will I get it?"

"Today, if you'll just tell me where to deliver it."

She breathed a sigh, indecision wafting over the line. I wanted to reach across cyberspace and pull the information from her tongue. *Come on, Melissa.*

"Okay. It's 264 South Anniston. In San Jose."

I grabbed my pen. "Two-sixty-four South Anniston." I jotted it down on the yellow pad. "Will you be home?"

"Why would you ask that?"

Not good. "If you're not home, is there a porch to leave the package on, where it'll be safe from the rain?"

"Oh. Yeah. And I'll be there to get it in a couple hours."

A couple hours. It would be nearing sunset by then.

"Fine. I'll try to get it on the right truck for you today. If I can't, then look for it on Monday."

"Okay. Thanks."

I hung up and closed my eyes. My heart galloped like some runaway colt. For a few minutes all I could do was breathe. The car felt so hot. I cracked the passenger window open, ignoring the fat splashes that punched onto the seat.

Thank God. I'd found Melissa.

I felt no elation, only sick relief.

The hardest part lay before me.

No wonder Melissa had kept quiet for six years. If Baxter wanted to silence *me* just because of that newspaper article, imagine how he'd threatened her. How in the world could I ever convince her to go public now? She'd take one look at me and run.

A couple hours, she'd said.

My insides trembled. No way could I confront Melissa in this weakened state. I needed food. And a lot more than that. I needed a plan that would save my life.

TWENTY-NINE

JUNE 2004

Melissa's epiphany the night of the dinner party grabbed onto her and wouldn't let go. The next day in church, while the pastor's sermon droned on—something about real love versus false—Melissa's mind fixed upon her new goal to make something of her life, starting *now*. And thanks to information from Baxter she'd overheard at the party, she had the perfect idea of how to go about it.

After church Nicole asked if Melissa wanted to hang out on Wednesday. "A bunch of us are going to go to a movie or something. Want to come?"

Melissa gave her a wide smile. "Oh, thanks. Maybe I can. But I need to check with Linda first. I'll call you later, okay?"

Truth was, she needed to check with Baxter.

She hit the subject head-on in the kitchen as the three of them sat down to eat chicken salad and fruit for lunch. No use looking hesitant. That wouldn't get her anywhere.

"Baxter, I want to come work in your office."

Linda's eyebrows raised. She slid a look at her husband. Baxter stopped chewing for a moment, then swallowed. "Oh, yeah? You want to learn about real estate?"

"Yes. I'll help you do anything you need. You don't have to pay me. You do enough for me already. I want to pay you back somehow. And in the meantime I'll learn."

Baxter shook his head. "You don't have to pay me back for anything, Melissa. You don't have to pay either of us back."

His final sentence zinged through her nerves. Melissa forced herself not to look away. Had she singled him out too much over Linda?

"That's right, you don't." Linda patted her arm.

Melissa put down her fork. "Okay, I don't, but I want to. I'll still help you all I can in the house, Linda. But during the day I don't want to just hang out with friends. I want to *do* something, *learn* something. I have to find a way to make my own living some day." Her gaze dropped, and she traced a finger on the edge of her plate. "I mean, until I came here I had to fight just to survive, you know?"

Silence. She sensed Baxter and Linda exchanging glances, but she didn't look up.

"Well." Baxter cleared his throat. "I think we can work something out."

Melissa's head jerked up. "Really?" Excitement filled her voice.

He nodded. "Just so happens I lost my office assistant on Friday. I asked our guests last night if anyone knew someone to take her place, but then we got off on some other subject."

"You're kidding. That's perfect! I mean, I'm sorry you lost her, but . . ."

Baxter smiled. "You don't look sorry."

"Okay, I'm not." Melissa smiled back. "But I'll make you glad she's gone. I'll work twice as hard. And for free!"

"Melissa. I'm not going to have you work for free."

She shook her head. "I don't need to be paid, really. You buy me so many clothes already—"

"*Who* buys you the clothes?" Linda's mouth curved.

Was that a tease or a dig at being overlooked? "Oh, *you* do, of course. I meant *you* as in both of you."

"Actually"—Baxter's eyes cut to Linda as he slid his fork into his chicken salad—"*I* buy the clothes."

Linda shifted in her chair, her shoulders pulling in. Her whole body seemed to tighten, even as she aimed a forced smile at her husband. Carefully she cut a slice of pineapple on her plate and put it in her mouth.

A memory struck Melissa of herself at three and her mother, for once sober. Playing the "hidey" game. Melissa thought if she covered her eyes in the middle of the room, no one could see her. "No, stupid," her mother said. "If you're not hiding your whole body anyone can see you."

But people hid all the time in plain sight, didn't they?

"So can I start tomorrow?" Melissa leaned forward. "What will I do?"

Linda took another bite of pineapple.

"Yes, you can start tomorrow." Baxter sipped his water. "This is an unlicensed assistant position, which means there are certain things you can't do. You can't relate real estate information to clients. But you can run off flyers, maybe even learn to compose them. You can answer my phone and set up some of my appointments. You can call selling clients and set up open houses for their listings."

Anticipation welled within Melissa. "That sounds great! How many hours do I get to work?"

Linda concentrated on her plate, vibrations rolling off her like cold waves. Melissa hadn't counted on this idea driving a wedge between her and Linda. What might this cost her?

In the end, did it matter? Baxter was the one in power.

"Let's wait and see," Baxter said. If he noticed Linda's reaction at all he didn't show it. "Don't want to wear you out too quickly. It means you'll have to get up in the morning. Linda can bring you in around nine."

"When do you go? I can just ride with you."

"Early for you. Around eight."

"I'll be ready."

Baxter nodded at Melissa. "Well, Linda. Looks like we've got a working girl here."

"That's wonderful," Linda chirped around her glass of ice water. "Good for you, Melissa."

Melissa beamed at her. "And don't worry, I'll still help with dinner and everything."

"I'm sure you will."

"And we'll still have time to do things together. Right, Baxter? I mean, I'll still have time to hang out with Linda."

"Absolutely. Wouldn't want to stand in the way of that."

"Okay, then." Melissa leaned back in her chair, her gaze roaming from Baxter to Linda. Excitement jumped around inside her like a little kid. "This is *so cool*."

When they finished eating Melissa waved them both out of the kitchen. "Go on, I've got the dishes." She couldn't keep the anticipation from her voice. She was going to work with Baxter!

The dishes only took a few minutes. Melissa headed up to her bedroom. Soon after she closed the door she heard the telltale sound through the ceiling heater vent. Another argument in the master bedroom. Melissa dragged her desk chair over and stood on it to listen, but she couldn't make out the words. She did, however, hear the smacks. One, two this time. Then crying. The muffled slam of a door.

Slowly Melissa replaced her chair near the desk.

Had she caused this?

Maybe Baxter didn't like Linda being upset at the table. Maybe Linda didn't want some foster kid working with her husband and told him so. Would she be brave enough to say that?

Melissa hugged herself. She knew what it felt like to be the victim. It was awful and horrible and helpless. But that was behind her now. She would not look at it anymore. And neither did she need any reminders. This was a time to cling to new hope. The shining promise that she would make something of her life despite her past.

Linda didn't face half what Melissa had overcome, yet the woman couldn't seem to stand up for herself. If she played Perfect Pretend Marriage in her house and church and life—whose fault was that?

All the same Melissa's heart beat too fast. The very thought of abuse made her throat close.

Melissa cracked her bedroom door and stuck her ear against the opening. She heard the vague swish of clothes, feet on hardwood floor. Baxter was going down the stairs.

She pulled her head back, closed her eyes. A wild thought trailed through her head: whatever she did next was going to set the course for the rest of her life.

The caring thing would be to comfort Linda. Knock on the master bedroom door, open it anyway when Linda said she wanted to be left alone. Go in there and say hey, I'm with you. I know what it's like.

Melissa's pulse beat in her ears. She willed it to slow.

She thought of her stepdad. Butch was his name. Appropriate. Melissa had been eleven. Butch had caught her in her tiny bedroom one evening while her mother was at the store. What he did to her in that never-ending half an hour had butchered her soul. She hadn't spoken a word for weeks after. When Melissa finally told her mother, the old witch didn't believe her. Until she caught him in the act one day. Only then did she kick him out.

That's when her mother started drinking more than ever. From guilt? Ironic, if that was the reason, since the woman ended up beating on her. As if everything was Melissa's fault. The victim always deserved it.

The few slaps Linda endured were nothing compared to Melissa's life.

Melissa's mind flashed to the sight of her dead mother on the kitchen floor. The scene filled her head like a movie on pause.

Her jaw tightened. She'd handled that, hadn't she? She could do the same now.

Melissa drew herself up straight, smoothed her hair, and stepped out of her room.

Pasting on a blithe expression, she headed toward the stairs. One hand grasped the top of the banister and swung her around to face her descent.

Halfway down the staircase Melissa could hear the TV in the den, switching from channel to channel. Something men always did. Men, the kings of their castles. The ones with the power.

Baxter sat on one end of the leather couch.

"Whatcha watchin'?" Melissa crossed into the room and sat on the other end of the sofa.

"Can't find anything decent." He clicked the button again.

"Where's Linda?"

He shrugged. "I think she's taking a nap." *Click, click.*

Melissa drew her legs up onto the couch. "I found some cool channel the other day, like way high in numbers. Five hundred thirty, I think. They show movies there with no commercials."

"Really?"

Baxter punched in the numbers. The TV screen switched to the opening scene of *Back to the Future*. "Hey, this is a great movie."

"Yeah, I love it."

Melissa settled into a comfortable position. It occurred to her she would need to call Nicole, tell the girl she couldn't hang out this week. She would be at work. Melissa could imagine Nicole's jealousy over working in Baxter Jackson's office.

When thoughts of Linda nudged into Melissa's mind, she pushed them away. She didn't care that Linda was up in the master bedroom by herself. If she wanted to join the family, she could.

Part of Melissa was almost glad. For once she had Baxter to herself.

For the next two hours they enjoyed the movie. Melissa made popcorn.

Linda did not venture from her room.

THIRTY

FEBRUARY 2010

Five-fifteen. The sun would soon be setting.

I perched behind the wheel of my 4Runner, some distance down from 264 South Anniston and directly beside a little park. The neighborhood looked well kept, upper middle class. Melissa appeared to have no lack of well-housed friends.

I'd been at my post for the past hour, just in case Melissa returned early. Before that I'd driven through Burger King and eaten my fill of a Whopper Junior and fries. Food I don't typically eat. But this was no typical day.

I finished off my nutritious meal with the last half of my bag of Jelly Bellies.

Forty minutes ago the rain had stopped. The overcast sky at dusk looked frayed and weary. Like I felt.

My eyes constantly flicked up the street and in the rearview mirror. I saw no one following me. I was afraid a cop would drive up, ask what I was doing. But the street remained clear.

Worry about Dineen plagued me. I wanted to check on her but didn't know how much to say. She'd be sure to ask questions. When I could stand it no longer I pulled out my cell phone and called her. "How's everything there?"

"Fine. Jimmy's sleeping. How are *you*?"

I bit my cheek. "I found her."

"You're kidding! What did she say?"

"Haven't gotten that far yet."

"Oh. Will she talk to you?"

"She's been quiet for six years, Dineen; no doubt she'll be thrilled to see me."

Thick silence.

My mouth twisted. "I'm sorry. That wasn't fair. No need to take this out on you."

"It's okay. Just . . . Will you call me after you see her?"

A woman came out of the house next to Melissa's, dressed in an exercise outfit. She turned down the sidewalk and started jogging toward me. I listed far over to my right, pretending to pick something off the passenger floor. A small grunt escaped me.

"Are you there, Joanne? What are you doing?"

Footsteps pounded past. I hung there a second longer before raising my head. The woman jogged on.

I straightened. Such a little thing, but it had shaken me. If someone noticed me sitting in my car so long, they might become suspicious, call the police. *Please, Melissa, come soon.*

"Better go, Dineen. I'll call you when I can. *Don't* call me, okay? I may be in the middle of talking to her."

"Okay." My sister sounded reluctant. "Just don't forget me."

"Never."

I punched off and checked the time on my phone. Almost 5:30.

"Don't go home until you've found her." Hooded Man's words.

Worst case scenarios ran through my head. What if Melissa didn't show? I couldn't stay here all night. And I couldn't go home, and I couldn't go to Dineen's. A lot of choices that left me. Some hotel. How long could I keep that up?

What if Melissa *did* appear, and I blew the surprise confrontation?

What if, amazingly, she agreed to break her silence? Who would I take her to? Surely not Chief Eddington.

Reporters, that's who. Get the media involved. Then the public would be watching. The Vonita police wouldn't be able to sustain a cover-up.

Baxter would still try to lie his way out of it. He couldn't be allowed to pin blame on Melissa. She would need an attorney's advice before leading authorities to Linda's grave. Maybe she'd need some kind of immunity in exchange for her information? I didn't know.

But that whole process could take days. Meanwhile Melissa and I could still be in danger.

Fresh anger at Hooded Man rose within me. If I only knew his identity. *Had* he acted alone—or did a circle of justice-seekers silently urge me on? Would they come out of the woodwork if Melissa went to reporters? Would *anyone* come forward with corroborating evidence? Would they help keep us safe?

Six o'clock arrived. The sky was darkening.

Six-twenty. The streetlights had come on. Fortunately, I'd parked some distance from the closest one.

My muscles were tight, every nerve on edge. Helplessness filtered through me, untamed and fiery. I had to do *something* other than just sit there.

On impulse I pulled my regular cell phone from my purse and dialed 411 for the number to Perry's convenience store. He answered on the second ring.

"Hi, it's Joanne Weeks." My eyes remained on my target house.

"Hey, Joanne." He sounded pleased. I never called his store.

"Anybody else around at the moment?"

"Just yours truly."

Now that I had him on the line, how to pose my question? I wanted to trust him. I wanted ... I wasn't sure what. But I didn't know whose side he was on.

If he was on any side.

"I need to ask you something, Perry. This morning as I left your store you said, 'Do what you have to do.' What did you mean by that?"

Hesitation prickled the distance between us. I pictured Perry's kind eyes, his detective novel on the counter. I pictured him in his house, alone. "Just that I admire you for speaking out about what you believe."

"That's it?"

"Yeah." He paused again, as if awaiting an explanation. "Should there be more?"

"I don't know; you tell me."

A red car passed, headed up toward Melissa's house. My eyes flicked to the driver. A man. My muscles relaxed.

"Joanne, I'm not sure what you're trying to say."

I gripped the phone, Hooded Man's white and bloodied cheek flashing in my brain. I could see those shadowed eyes, hear the roughened voice.

"Do you know what I'm doing right now?" I asked.

"Is this a trick question?"

"No."

"You're talking to me on the phone."

My chin sank.

He made a sound in his throat. "Are you okay, Joanne? Can I help you with something?"

Fear and frustration welled up my throat. Yes, I needed help. But I still hadn't the slightest notion whom I could trust. I just wanted to go home and wake up on a new day. Discover this was all a horrible nightmare.

"No, Perry. I'm ... fine."

"You don't sound fine."

Headlights appeared up the street. I sat up straight, watching with hawk eyes. Was it slowing down?

"Joanne, you there?"

The car *was* slowing. And it was approaching Melissa's house.

The garage door at house number 264 began rolling up. The car turned into the driveway.

"Gotta go, Perry." I threw the cell into my purse.

The car drove into the garage. The door rolled down.

God help me; this was it. I'd promised myself I wouldn't hesitate, lest fear paralyze me.

Purse in hand, I hefted out of the SUV and locked it. On trembling legs I walked swiftly up the street to confront Melissa.

THIRTY-ONE

As I hit the porch of 264 South Anniston, an overhead light flicked on. Footsteps muffled through the door.

Melissa—coming out to check on the package.

I froze. *No, no, not yet!* I wasn't ready. I'd needed to gather myself before ringing the doorbell.

Everything in me wanted to turn and run.

A lock clicked, then a bolt. The door pulled back.

Melissa stuck her head outside, gaze aimed downward. She caught sight of my feet, and her head jerked up.

We ogled each other.

Her cheeks had grown a little rounder, her brown hair now cut to her shoulders. But I'd have known her in a crowd. Her eyes latched onto mine as emotions rippled across her face. Surprise ... recognition ... indignation ... fear. My tongue couldn't utter a word.

A small gasp escaped her. "What are you doing here?"

"I need to talk to you, Melissa."

"Why?" She threw wild looks up and down the street, as if searching for ghosts. "How'd you find me?"

"No one's with me. Please let me come in."

"*How* did you find me?"

"I—"

Anger cinched her face. "The UPS lady. That was *you*."

"Please, I—"

"Get out of here! Now!"

She pulled back into the house, started to shove the door closed. I thrust my foot across the threshold. The door hit it hard. I winced.

"Get out of here right now, Joanne." Melissa's words spit through clenched teeth. "Or I'm calling the police."

"You *can't* call the police. You want me to tell them why I'm here?"

"I have no *idea* why you're here." She pushed harder against my foot. I couldn't have pulled it out if I wanted to.

"Melissa, please. Let me in." My voice shook.

"What do you want?"

"I *have* to talk to you."

"Who knows you're here?"

"Nobody. I promise. Please. Give me five minutes."

"You *lied* to me."

"Do you know Baxter's second wife is dead?"

Melissa's shoulders arched back. "What does that have to do with me?"

"Everything."

She glared at me, her hand still on the doorknob, her cheeks blanched. My foot throbbed. I clutched my purse, a trembling supplicant.

Air whooshed from Melissa, deflating her chest. She dropped her chin, anguish and ire etching her forehead. She stepped back. Opened the door.

I pushed inside before she could change her mind. We stood in a tiled entryway, illumed by an overhead light. To the right lay a darkened living room, leading to a dining area. A large den with a staircase at the far side was on the left. Straight ahead up a hall I could see a little of the kitchen, the only other room in the house that was lit.

Melissa banged the door closed, folded her arms, and assailed me with her eyes. "Five minutes."

My throat constricted. None of this was going right. I struggled to find a starting point. "Can we sit down?"

"No."

I nodded.

"This is about Baxter." Melissa spoke his name with contempt.

"Cherisse, his second wife, died two weeks ago. From a fall down the stairs, so he said. I don't believe it."

"Why should I care?"

"Because you saw him kill Linda."

Melissa's jaw moved to one side. She singed me with a look on slow burn. "Says who?"

"Linda told me he was beating her. She showed me the bruises. I never believed Baxter's story of what happened that night. And now Cherisse is dead, and he's going to get away with that too."

"Not my problem."

"You want him to kill a third wife someday?"

"I don't know anything about Cherisse."

"Doesn't matter. They'll have to reopen that case once they see Baxter lied about Linda."

She shook her head.

"Melissa, *please.* I'm begging you to tell what you saw. Don't let Baxter get away with this."

"He already has. The Vonita chief of police is one of his best friends."

"He doesn't have to get away with it forever. You can change that."

"No, I can't."

"Yes, you *can.*"

"Joanne." Her eyes closed, her voice dulling. "You don't know what you're asking. He'll kill me."

He'll kill me *if you don't.*

I touched her forearm. "I'll be with you every step of the way. We'll go to a reporter first, not the police. A reporter will be all over the story—"

"Baxter will deny everything."

"But you can prove it. You know where Linda's body is."

Her eyes widened, and abject fright seized her face. "Who told you that?"

"It doesn't matter."

"Oh, yes it does! *Who* told you?"

A *clack* sounded from the rear of the house. Like metal on metal. Melissa stilled, and her eyes locked with mine. She hunched forward, mouthed *Did you hear that?*

I nodded.

The unmistakable whir of a sliding glass door opening filtered to our ears.

Melissa focused past me, ancient horror in her eyes, as if she'd known for years this day would come. For an endless second neither of us moved.

The light in the kitchen blacked out.

Melissa twisted and smacked off the entryway light switch. Grabbed my arm and pulled me toward the unlit living room. Instinctively, we crouched low, moving on panther feet across the tile.

Our feet hit carpet. I couldn't see a thing in the sudden darkness. A streetlamp two doors up gave no light to the room. I stumbled after Melissa, clutching my purse to my chest—and praying.

Somewhere in the distance footsteps skulked.

THIRTY-TWO

JUNE 2004

By the second week of working in Baxter's real estate office, Melissa's dreams of her mother's death came less often. But they were no less vivid when they did invade her sleep. The blood on the trailer's kitchen floor, the gash in her mother's forehead, the wild and furious reality that the woman whom she hated, loved, hated was gone. *Gone.* Such relief from that stunning knowledge. Such abject fear.

But Melissa's past life was fading. Almost like she was two people—the Melissa before coming to the Jacksons' house, and the Melissa after.

"Baxter Jackson's office." Melissa answered the ringing phone at her small desk in the corner of Baxter's large office. As the top-selling realtor in the firm, he claimed the most square feet. His desk faced away from hers so he could look out over the surrounding hills. In June, with no rain since early May, the hills had turned brown.

Although Melissa's desk faced a plain wall, she didn't mind a bit. She was a real estate assistant! Unlicensed, sure, but she'd change that as soon as she could. Melissa saw herself working with Baxter well into the future—until he taught her everything he could. Then she'd strike out on her own.

"Is the man himself around?" asked a male voice on the line. Melissa recognized it at once. Chief Eddington. Melissa's chin raised.

"He's here, Mr. Eddington, but he stepped out of the office for a minute. May I have him call you right back?" Her voice sounded the utmost in professional.

"Ah, you knew me. Who's this?"

"Melissa."

"Melissa! Baxter's got you working there now?"

"Yes, sir." *And I'm good at it too.*

"Well, that oughtta keep you out of trouble." The chief's voice held a hint of tease. All the same Melissa's eyes narrowed.

"Oh, you can be assured of that."

Movement on Melissa's right caught her attention. Baxter was entering the office. He wore a gray suit and coral tie today. As always he held himself upright and confident. Every day Melissa worked for the man she became more convinced he could move mountains. Everybody in this whole building thought he walked on water.

"Hold on a moment, sir," she said into the receiver, then pulled it from her ear and placed her hand over the mouthpiece. "Chief Eddington."

"Put him through on line one."

Melissa did as she was told and hung up.

Baxter picked up the phone at his massive desk and settled into his black leather chair. "Wayne, my man." He listened a moment. "They *what*?" Irritation clipped his voice. Baxter swiveled his chair toward Melissa and held up his index finger—Melissa's signal to leave him alone in the office for the call. He did not look happy.

Melissa rose and picked up the flyer she needed to run off in the copy room down the hall. Leaving the office, she shut the door behind her.

She knew better than to ask about the calls Baxter took alone.

They didn't happen often. When they did it was always some businessman on the line—or Chief Eddington. Never a woman. Baxter had never done anything to make Melissa think he was running around on Linda. Melissa *had* wondered. If he shoved his wife around at home, what else might he do in private? But she'd seen nothing.

Disappointing in a way, Melissa thought as she positioned the flyer she'd created on the copy machine glass. Because she never would have told a soul. It would have given her one more opportunity to prove to Baxter how loyal she was.

The machine chugged, spitting out its copies. Melissa stood back, arms crossed, and waited.

Truth was, part of her would have been crushed to discover Baxter was running around.

Five minutes later, copying done, she gathered the papers and returned to Baxter's office. She could see through the large window that he was no longer on the phone.

Melissa entered and crossed to his desk. She laid the stack of flyers neatly upon it. This close she could smell his aftershave.

He frowned up at her, as if still upset by the phone call. Then smiled. "Chief Eddington says I'd better watch out for you. Or next thing I know, you'll be outselling me in real estate."

The chief said *that?*

Melissa made a sound through her teeth. "I'm not even licensed."

"You will be someday."

"And I'm going to work with you, right? You'll teach me everything."

"Sure. Long as you cut me in on your deals."

She spread her hands. "What I have is yours."

Immediately Melissa's body flushed with heat. She wanted to melt through the floor. She hadn't meant her answer to sound like that. But she would not show her embarrassment. Forcing herself to hold Baxter's gaze, she gave him a shrug and an innocent smile.

His eyes locked with hers. An expression of surprise flitted across his face. Followed by one of hunger.

Melissa knew that look.

Her heart did a little stutter step. Part of her couldn't believe it. The other part, deep inside, had known all along.

Her left fingers curled into her palm. What did she want to happen next?

The moment ballooned, then stretched ... stretched ... Still Baxter surveyed Melissa—until her heart sizzled ... splayed open under the heat of his stare. Until she could take ... no ... more ...

Baxter blinked.

The balloon popped.

Abruptly he turned back to his listings.

THIRTY-THREE

FEBRUARY 2010

In the darkness Melissa and I crouched at the end of a sofa. Somewhere close by, the living room gave way to the dining room through an arched entryway. That much I had seen when the light was on. I couldn't see it now.

Melissa balanced beside me, one hand on my arm. She knew the house. I had to follow her lead. We didn't dare talk. We hardly dared breathe.

Questions flailed in my mind. *Who* was here? What kind of trouble had Melissa gotten herself into?

A cautious step hit the tiled entryway.

Melissa edged forward, making no sound. I stayed right behind, scared that I would knock into furniture, create a disturbance that would give us away.

In the dining room we crept by the wall. My adjusting eyesight could dimly make out a long table and chairs to our right. If I could see them, surely someone entering the room could see our movement.

The entryway light burst on.

Melissa surged through the rest of the dining room, through an opening into the kitchen. Light spilled from the front door area, past the den and up the hall, diffusing at the kitchen's entrance.

Cool air filtered from the back of the room. I could barely see the opened sliding door.

The house's layout formed a circle. Any minute now the intruder could appear from the dining room.

Unless he thought we'd fled to the den and upstairs.

Maybe it was just a burglar. Maybe he didn't want to hurt us at all.

But Melissa's horrified expression, her immediate reaction had screamed that he did.

Melissa pushed me around a central cooking island and down behind it. She scurried without noise toward the kitchen table, yanked up a purse. She plunged her hand inside.

It came up with a handgun.

Melissa swiveled toward the open sliding glass door, motioning me to follow. I rose from a crouch—and movement from the dining room caught my eye. I gasped, turned. Melissa spun around.

A man appeared in the kitchen doorway. Dressed in black right down to gloves, his face in a ski mask. He raised a gun. I hit the floor.

Somebody fired.

THIRTY-FOUR

I cringed behind the cooking island. In my mind's eye I saw Melissa fall, the gunman come for me next.

A grunt of pain burst from the dining room doorway. Followed by Melissa's footsteps at the sliding glass door. I twisted my head to see her escaping into the night.

I sprang up and raced after her.

Something whizzed by my ear as I flung myself outside.

Bullet.

I ran harder.

I found myself swerving left across a patio, Melissa before me. We careened around the corner of the house and down the side. Across the front yard toward the sidewalk. A street lamp two houses up sprayed far too much light—our pursuer could easily see us.

Gritting my teeth, I sprinted to catch up to Melissa, thumped her on the shoulder blade. "To my car." I spun left.

We sprinted down the sidewalk, my right hand scrambling within my purse, seeking my car keys. My legs ran of their own accord, my mind spinning new fatal images. How far was the man behind us? How badly was he hit?

We reached my SUV. I angled off the curb, toward the driver's side. My hand closed on metal, the plastic of my key ring. I yanked it out, frantically pushing the "open" button.

With a blessed *click,* the locks released.

Melissa and I threw ourselves into the car. I thrust the key into the ignition, casting desperate glances up the street. No one.

The car started. I gunned the motor, surged through a U-turn, and sped down the street. Melissa perched forward in her seat, hands gripping the dashboard. At the next block I veered right. Two more blocks, then left. I zigzagged through residential streets until I knew we hadn't been followed.

"Where can we go?" My words pushed through clenched teeth.

"I don't know."

"You have to know someone."

"You did this to me!"

What?

We hit a stoplight at a major intersection. A sign read "Left to 101." I turned onto the busy road and hit the freeway a half a mile up. Took an exit heading south.

Melissa pushed back in her seat, cursing under her breath.

"Did you kill him?" I asked.

"I think I hit him in the thigh."

The thigh. Enough to slow him down. He'd have to go to the hospital.

Would someone soon take his place?

"Melissa, where's your gun?"

"It's not mine; it's gun-crazy Tony's," she spat. "I just borrowed it."

"I don't care *whose* it is. Where is it right now?"

"In my purse!"

It's Tony's. "He know you have it?"

"Would you stop with the questions!"

"I just want to know, Melissa." Ice layered my voice.

"Shut *up*! He's not going to miss one little handgun!"

I drove on, both of us fuming.

Two exits down I got off the freeway and drove down a street until we passed a housing development on our right. I turned into it, zigzagged through streets again. Nice two-stories, well-kept lawns. A quiet neighborhood.

At an empty lot I pulled over to the curb and cut the engine. For the moment we were safe. No car had followed us. I *knew* that. "Who— "

"You almost got me killed." Melissa's voice spewed venom.

"Me?"

"Somebody obviously followed you to that house."

"Nobody followed me. I've been out looking for you all day. I've been all kinds of places. *No one* followed me."

"Yeah, right. It just so happens the minute you show up, so does a gunman." She blazed me with a look. "*Who* told you I know about Linda's death? That I know where she's buried?"

My eyes closed. "I don't know. A hooded man in a mask. On the road at night."

"What?"

"He told me to look for you. That you could bring Baxter to justice."

Melissa snorted. "And you just *believed* him? Just did what he told you, without even knowing who he was?"

"Well, it's true, isn't it! You know where Linda's buried!"

She cursed under her breath.

"I wanted Baxter to pay, Melissa. I've wanted that for six years. When the man told me you know how she died—that you *saw* it—I *had* to look for you."

Melissa thrust her hands in the air. "*Don't* you get it? *Baxter* sent that man!"

THIRTY-FIVE

JULY 2004

On the Fourth of July Melissa stood at the kitchen counter, making sandwiches and a salad for dinner. Neither she, Baxter, nor Linda needed much to eat after pigging out at the town-wide holiday lunch picnic. Linda was now in her bedroom, nursing a bad cold that had turned worse after being out all afternoon in the hot sun. She had obviously tried hard to be cheerful and social with their friends, even managing a couple of her deep-throated laughs. But Melissa knew she felt miserable. By the time they made it home Linda was coughing and looked flushed. The thermometer said she had a fever of 101.

It had been a week since that pulse-stopping moment between Melissa and Baxter at the office. The moment when nothing happened, and everything did. Since then Melissa had felt ... different. Shaky and excited and fearful all at once. Like amazing new things could appear just over the horizon, but she wasn't sure she dared look.

Things hadn't been the same at home since then.

Today at the picnic where he reigned as king, Baxter had been his typical Mr. Social. He'd hidden his sour mood that showed at home. Melissa attributed it to sudden problems at work. Just days before the papers were signed on the sale of a large office building, the deal had fallen through. Baxter lost a lot of money. He was not happy. No one at work would have known, and Baxter still acted fine toward Melissa. But at home with Linda he prowled around like an edgy tiger, practically daring her to set him off. She'd been extra careful around him all week.

This bomb couldn't tick forever. Something was going to blow. Melissa had sensed the countdown more strongly in the last two days. She walked around nerves tight, waiting for the explosion. Wondering what pieces she'd have to pick up.

Meanwhile Linda apparently believed she was hiding her eggshell walk from Melissa. How naive, as Baxter seemed to care less and less about keeping up a front for Melissa regarding how he treated his wife. As if their tie at work weighed enough to outbalance anything he did at home.

Baxter entered the kitchen as Melissa laid thin-sliced roast beef on the bottom halves of three large sourdough rolls. He headed for the refrigerator and pulled out a diet soft drink. Without turning to look at him Melissa was aware of his every move.

She laid Monterey jack cheese on top of the roast beef. "How's Linda?"

"Feeling lousy."

"Should I take her food up to her?"

"Nah, she'll come down." Baxter popped the top of the soda can and took a drink. He eased over to the sliding glass door and gazed at the flower-drenched backyard. A look of satisfaction and owncrship.

"It'll be too bad if she misses the fireworks," Melissa said. "She'll probably want to be in bed."

"She'll go."

"You sure?" Melissa wouldn't mind if Linda stayed home.

Baxter turned his head and surveyed Melissa. She met his eyes. "I'm sure. Because I *say* she's going."

Their gaze locked for a second too long. Melissa's spine tingled.

It was the first time Baxter had said anything overtly about the power he wielded over his wife. Melissa turned back to the sandwiches, mind whirling. What was he *really* saying? That he could make *her* do whatever he wanted too? Or that no matter what happened in this house, Baxter could control his wife's reaction?

Melissa spread mayonnaise on a roll top and placed it over its prepared other half. Lately, even with all her strength and determination, she wondered if she could keep pace with this man. There were depths to him she couldn't fathom. He had years of experience on her.

"Those about done?" Baxter posed the question casually, as if knew he'd driven home a point and now chose to back off.

If only Melissa knew *which* point.

"Yeah." She put the second and third sandwiches together.

Baxter took another drink of soda and sauntered to the intercom on the far wall. Melissa heard the faint click of the *talk* button. "Hey, babe, dinner's ready. Come down."

Once the *talk* button had been pushed, the intercom line remained open for ten seconds, allowing the other person to answer hands-free. Half that time passed before Linda's feeble voice responded. "I'm not hungry. You two go ahead." Sounded like she'd been sleeping.

Baxter compressed the button. "You need to eat. It'll give you strength for tonight."

"I really don't want anything."

"Linda. Get down here."

Linda came down.

They were quiet around the table. Linda's eyes drooped, barely able to stay open. She chewed woodenly, eyes fixed downward.

Melissa sneaked an accusing look at Baxter. Really, what was the point of this? Did it make him feel good just to boss his wife around? Baxter's glance happened to cross Melissa's face, then cut back and hung there, as if he read her thoughts. Melissa felt her expression flatten. She lifted one corner of her mouth, then concentrated on her sandwich.

Baxter sniffed. "We'll leave at nine for the fireworks. They'll wait until it's good and dark—around nine thirty—to set 'em off." He was looking at Melissa, but she knew his statement was aimed at Linda.

His wife stopped chewing and closed her eyes, as if mentally weighing her next move. Melissa could almost hear the laden wheels turning in her head.

Linda set down her sandwich and leaned back in her chair. As if bracing herself. "I don't want to go tonight, honey. I just need to go to bed." Her voice remained light, not at all in keeping with her body language.

Melissa couldn't help but feel sorry for her. Linda tried so hard to keep peace. Was a little rest too much to ask?

"You can't miss tonight." Baxter's tone sounded dismissive. "These are *my* fireworks, remember? *I* pay for them. What would it look like if you weren't there?"

Linda focused on her plate. Most of the sandwich remained upon it. "People know I'm sick. They'll understand."

"Well, *I* won't. You're going, and that's all there is to it."

Baxter's eyes remained on his wife, but somehow Melissa knew his attention still fixed upon *her*. Like he was testing her, daring her to interfere. The air around Melissa rumbled, as if a long-threatened earthquake approached. She sat very still.

Linda pushed back her chair and rose. Her face looked stretched, taut.

"Where are you going?" Baxter demanded.

"To bed."

"You're not done eating."

"I've had enough. If I'm going tonight, I need to rest now." Linda looked pointedly at me, then at her husband, as if reminding him their perfect little facade was looking ragged at the edges. She turned away.

Baxter's expression blackened. He jumped up and grabbed her arm. "Sit down! I didn't say you could leave."

She tried to yank away. He gripped her harder. "I *said* sit down!" With both hands he shoved her back into the chair. Her body hit with a heavy thump. The chair legs bounced against the wood floor.

Linda's face crumpled. She bent over, her shoulders jerking in a silent sob. Sick as she was, she clearly lacked the energy to pretend. Baxter stood over her, glaring, hands low on his hips. His mouth formed a tight line, one strand of his thick hair out of place. The fire in his eyes dared his wife to make one more stupid move.

"Stop crying." His words forced through clenched teeth.

Linda ducked lower, stuttering in a long breath. But a wail escaped her throat.

"Shut *up*!" Baxter punched her behind her right ear.

"Unh!" Linda's head ricocheted left, and she almost fell out of the chair. She shot out a foot, regained her balance. Her body sank lower, arms thrown up to protect her head. Her whole torso shook.

Melissa's lungs curled inward. She perched in tight-throated silence, her limbs like stone. Now he'd done it. He'd upended the game board. It was one thing for her to ignore abuse behind a closed door. Now he'd thrown it in her face.

Baxter cursed and threw himself into heavy-legged pacing, his shoulders rounded, head down and shaking. Three steps away, he heaved himself up and whirled around. "See what you've done, Linda? *Why* do you make me have to do this? Why can't you just do what I say?"

"I'm ... s-sorry." The words rose from Linda, soggy and bloated.

"You're sorry, all right! What's Melissa going to think of you now?"

His barbed accusation cut deep into Linda—Melissa could tell by the way the woman shrank, the twitch of her body. Pain and humiliation rolled off her in waves. Melissa sensed the shame far outweighed her physical pain. Shame that the life Linda had modeled for a foster daughter had suddenly been exposed as a lie.

Melissa turned her gaze on Baxter, fear trickling through her veins. She'd been crazy, thinking she could match wits with this man. Now that the charade had disintegrated, nothing would keep him from hitting her next. Could be today. Could be tomorrow. But it would come.

Unless she found a way to stop it.

Baxter raised challenging eyes to Melissa—and the world stopped. What she saw in that burning stare made her head reel. A mad defiance borne of guilt.

Guilt.

In that moment she understood his recent mood. It had nothing to do with a lost sale and everything to do with *her*. The perfect church-going man who somehow justified beating his wife now faced a new temptation—one he was scared to death he couldn't conquer.

Melissa's eyes drifted to Linda, who was still crying. So alone in her chair. For a moment Melissa wanted to lay a comforting hand on her arm.

The crazy thought quickly passed.

She looked again to Baxter, meeting his glare head-on and steady, as if gazing straight into his soul. This was her defining moment. Sides were aligning here, and one wrong step could cost her everything.

Melissa raised her shoulders. And her chin. But she turned her head and tilted it, just a little. Lifted one side of her mouth in a whisper of a knowing smile.

I know what you really want, she told Baxter Jackson, saying nothing. *And I'll never tell.*

THIRTY-SIX

FEBRUARY 2010

"Baxter sent that man!"

Shock spritzed my veins. I shifted in my seat to look Melissa in the face. "Why would Baxter do that? Why would he want me to find the person who can tell the truth about him?"

The moment I asked the question, I knew the answer.

Melissa leaned forward, as if talking to an idiot child. "Because he wants to *kill* me."

I stared at Melissa, open-mouthed, still not wanting to believe Baxter had sent Hooded Man. Because if that was true, I had been *so duped.*

But Hooded Man *had* called this afternoon, just to be sure I was looking. As if there was no time to waste. He'd played on my fear of Baxter. Even told me Chief Eddington was in on Baxter's schemes . . .

Then who had broken into my house? If Baxter wanted me to find Melissa, he wouldn't have sent someone to hurt me last night.

I could barely find my tongue. "Does Chief Eddington know Baxter killed Linda?"

"No way, no one knows. Baxter and me, that's it. He would never tell, and neither would I. That's how I know he's behind this."

No. I just didn't . . . I peered out the windshield, searching the darkness for answers. They swirled beyond my reach.

My chin dropped. "The hooded man who told me—he said the police were in on it."

"Let me guess—he told you that *after* you said you'd go to them."

The words stabbed a knife in me and twisted. I couldn't raise my head to look at her.

"So you wouldn't go." Melissa just had to press her point. "So you'd look for me all by yourself, with *no one knowing*. And lead Baxter straight to me."

"But *how* did I lead him to you? I waited for you on your street for hours. I saw no one."

"Well, you didn't look hard enough."

I rubbed my forehead, picturing Hooded Man in the rain. Was he our pursuer? I'd seen the gunman only in a flash. No way could I tell.

"And in case you're too stupid to get this too, Joanne—he also wanted to kill you. Perfect, huh. He gets rid of me, his one witness, *and* the person who led him here."

I stared at the steering wheel, unseeing. Melissa had to be right. Hooded Man ... the break-in at my house last night ... the one at hers today—they had to be connected. Although I still couldn't understand the break-in at my place. Who had done that, and why? My lagging brain sensed I was overlooking an obvious piece of the puzzle, but try as I might, I couldn't think through it.

"That man in the mask you saw," Melissa said. "Did he look like the gunman?"

"I don't know. Same build I guess, but ... Do you know who he is?"

"Probably some hired lowlife. Obviously not a professional or we'd we dead."

Exhaustion crawled through my system. My brain was turning to mush. "We need to go somewhere safe for the night, figure out what to do."

Melissa glared at me. "Aren't you even going to apologize?"

"I'm sorry."

"Wow. What an apology. You sure sound sorry."

"I *am*. More than you know. It's just that . . . I have to get some sleep. So I can figure this out."

"Another wild guess — you were up late last night looking for *me*?"

I dropped my gaze.

Melissa thrust her arms into a fold and focused out her window. "Great. We'll go to some hotel. And *sleep*." She emphasized the word as if that's the last thing she wanted to do. "You're paying."

My mind was shutting down fast, my thoughts hazy. "What hotel should we go to?"

"*I* don't know! Somewhere far away from here."

I shook my head and blinked hard. Started the car engine. "We'll go . . . north."

We got back on the freeway. At a Mountain View exit we pulled off and found a hotel. After checking into a second floor room with two double beds, I moved the car around back, where it couldn't be spotted from the street. I put the car keys in my pocket instead of in my purse, just in case Melissa decided she wanted to take a little ride while I was asleep.

In the room Melissa hustled over to close the curtains. I visited the bathroom, then sat down hard on a bed. Melissa punched the pillows up against the headboard on the other bed and heaved herself into a sitting position, staring at the far wall. She pulled her purse next to her, took out the gun, and laid it beside her.

"You're not going to take off as soon as I'm conked out, are you?" I barely felt my own mouth ask the question. I collapsed on my back, hands folded on my stomach. My body ran like melting wax.

Melissa made a disgusted sound. "And just where would I go — thanks to *you*?"

I sighed. My eyes closed. "Whose house were you staying at?"

"A friend. He's gone for a week on a business trip. Said I could housesit."

"Why did you leave Tony?"

"None of your business."

Yes, it is, I wanted to retort. But my mind couldn't push the words to my tongue.

A quicksand of sleep bubbled up around me. My body gave in, began to sink. The muck rose … rose … until it closed over my head, swallowing me whole …

A ringing cell phone shrilled the air.

THIRTY-SEVEN

A second ring resounded in the hotel room. My entire body jumped. Slowly my weighted brain drifted up from the quicksand, so . . . very . . . heavy.

Ring three.

"Whaa . . . ?" my mouth said, the word thick and rumbling. My eyes opened, unfocused.

Melissa was rooting around in my purse, which lay on the floor by my bed. She pulled out my cell and peered at the screen. "You know a Perry Bracowski?"

"Uh-huh."

She held the phone out of my reach. "Is he safe?"

"Yeah."

"You sure?"

"Give me the phone, Melissa."

She handed it over. I took it with fumbling fingers. "Hi. Perry." I stayed on my back, staring at the cream-colored motel ceiling.

"Joanne, you okay?"

"I was just . . . falling asleep."

"Oh." His voice held surprise that I would go to bed so early. What time was it, anyway? "Sorry to wake you. I just wanted to know if everything's all right. Last time we talked you didn't sound like yourself."

No kidding. Enervation warped his comment into downright

funny. My laugh bordered on a hysterical giggle. "Never had a better day. Even got shot at."

A stunned silence played over the phone. "You got *shot* at?"

Melissa flapped a hand at me, warning me to shut up. I ignored her.

"Joanne. *Who* shot at you?"

"Somebody who apparently wants me dead."

"Who? Someone you're skip tracing?"

"No. It's complicated."

"Stop talking *right now*." Melissa stepped toward me, her expression menacing.

"I'll talk to him if I want to."

"Who?" Perry cut in. "Are you talking to me?"

"No. To Miss Priss here."

Melissa's face twisted. She swept a hand toward the phone. I jerked away from her.

A portion of my mind cleared. With the clearing, all humor died away, replaced with one cogent thought.

I sat up, swung my legs to the floor, my back to Melissa. "Perry, hold on a minute." I swiveled toward Melissa and thrust a finger at her. "*Don't* do that again."

She stood her ground, folded her arms, and glared at me.

I returned the phone to my ear. "Perry. You read detective novels all the time, right? I need to run a scenario by you."

"Okay."

"Say someone's out in their car all day. Going here, going there. Sees no one following them. But then something happens that proves somebody *was* following. How could they do that without being spotted?"

"If the person's good at tailing, he should be able to keep out of sight easily enough."

"But . . ."

Frustration bounced around within me. My question sounded

so naive. But it wouldn't have been that easy for someone to keep out of sight when I was parked on Melissa's street. I'd constantly checked for cars and hadn't seen anyone lurking around. And when I was in the church parking lot Hooded Man had phoned me, demanding to know if I was looking for Melissa. If he'd been following me, wouldn't he have known where I was?

"Of course he could also have put a GPS on the person's car," Perry added. "Then he could track without being close by."

I stilled. A GPS system. Not the kind of equipment a law-abiding skip tracer would use. But that intruder last night, in my garage. Drops of rain leading to my car . . .

The missing puzzle piece my tired brain couldn't find earlier.

How *stupid* of me. I should have guessed this. I should have *known.*

My body stiffened. Wait a minute. If a GPS was on my car, whoever Baxter had hired would know where we were *right now.* They could be at the motel any minute.

"Where would he put it, Perry?"

"Different places. Inside, maybe, like in the glove compartment. Or underneath the car, using a magnetized case. Why— "

"How big is it?"

"Pretty small."

If it was underneath the car I'd never find it in the dark. I had no flashlight. And no way would I even go out to the parking lot.

Melissa came around the foot of the bed to watch my face.

"We have to get out of here." I blurted the words into the phone, my eyes locked with Melissa's.

Her eyes rounded. "What?"

"He thinks they put a GPS tracking system on my car."

She shoved both hands into her hair, her face whitening. "Where do we go with no car?" Melissa's voice pinched like a scared child's. "And how do we leave the room if they're out there?"

"I don't know."

"Well, you'd better *think* of something!"

My eyes squeezed shut. How had this happened? I was a skip tracer; now *I* was on the run.

"Joanne!" Perry's voice drilled into my ear. I punched on the speakerphone so Melissa could hear. "*Who* is with you? Tell me what's happening."

Briefly I did. Melissa paced at the end of the beds, palms together and pressed against her mouth. When I told Perry about the break-in at my house, she came to a stop and glared at me. "Why didn't you tell me that?"

"You need to call the police," Perry said.

"I— "

"No!" Melissa shook her head furiously. "She calls the police, and I'm out of here right now. The first thing they'll do is take us down to the station and try to force me to tell what I know. And I'll never do it. I'd be dead before they even tried to do a thing to Baxter."

I knew she meant it. Melissa could run again at any time. How would I ever convince her to change her mind? "You hear her?" I spoke into the phone.

"I heard. No police." He paused. "I'll come get you."

"But your store— "

"I'll close early."

Melissa thrust herself toward me. "He's not coming with cops!"

"No, he's— "

"Melissa!" Frustration coated Perry's voice. I held the speakerphone toward her.

"You're *not* bringing cops." Fire blazed in her eyes.

"I hear you, already."

"I swear if you show up with them, I'll deny I ever said anything about Baxter."

"Melissa, *chill out*. I'm coming by myself."

Her eyes narrowed.

"And you're welcome."

She puffed out a martyr's sigh.

"Nice companion you've got there, Joanne," Perry said.

Melissa rolled her eyes and turned away.

"So tell me where you are."

I told him.

"Okay, I'll leave right now. *Stay in your room.*"

I calculated how long it would take Perry to make the drive.

"Thanks, Perry. Thank you so much."

"Just one more day in my exciting life." He hung up.

I threw the cell phone back into my purse and faced Melissa. "He's trying to help, you know. He doesn't have to do this."

Her expression flattened. She licked her lips. "I know. It's just ... We almost got killed. And it's all because of Baxter. I don't want anything to *do* with his problems. For six years I've tried to forget what happened, but it never goes away. I just *want to live my life.*"

A new wave of tiredness hit. I just wanted to live my life too. Imagine what it must be like for someone as young as Melissa to carry such a burden.

"You will, Melissa. You will."

She brushed aside my platitudes and headed for her purse. Pulled out her cell phone. "I have to call a friend. I was supposed to meet her tomorrow for breakfast." Melissa's hardened tone had returned—a reminder to me that I'd thoroughly messed up her life. "I'll think of some excuse." She walked into the bathroom and shut the door. I heard the dull *whir* of the fan come on.

I sank upon my bed and scooted up to lean against the headboard. Checked the clock. Five after eight. We had over an hour to wait for Perry.

THIRTY-EIGHT

JULY 2004

When to dive off a sinking ship? And where to go, except back to the shark-infested waters of Social Services? Did Melissa really think another foster home would be better than living with the Jacksons?

Maybe the ship wouldn't totally sink after all, she told herself in the volatile days following July Fourth. Maybe only one end would, while her end tipped higher and safer than ever.

Besides, where would Melissa be without Baxter Jackson? Sure, the man had his faults. But he was her ticket to a career, a better, solid life. A magnificent life. And there was more. He'd gotten under her skin, piercing like a long, fine sliver. There was no pulling him out, not now. They worked together well; they understood each other. Melissa recognized the need for power and control in him and knew he saw the same in her. She had one thing Linda lacked—backbone. Baxter admired Melissa for that. She was sure of it. Instead of trying to dominate her, he now seemed to revel in displaying his domination of Linda in her presence.

The more their bond grew, the harsher Baxter treated his wife.

Melissa did nothing to stop him. How could she? When he lashed out at Linda, Melissa somehow managed to fade from the scene. But she walked a balance beam. It was not in her best interest to lose Linda's trust, even as Melissa built her loyalty to Baxter. When she and Linda were alone, Melissa oozed sympathy for the woman. As a result Linda began to lean on Melissa as the one person she could talk to, while she kept up appearances with everyone else.

Clever Baxter made his wife's charade easy. Melissa soon saw his strategy: never punch where someone would see a bruise. It was always in the head, or Linda's side or back. If he slapped her face it was a controlled hit, leaving red fingerprints that didn't last long.

July roiled on.

The temperature was hot—high nineties. Sunny day after sunny day, beating down on Vonita. Melissa thrived in it. The days energized her, the sizzling outside matching her sizzling inside. She lay out in a bikini in the backyard on weekends, her skin turning a deep brown. Feeling Baxter's eyes on her body.

Linda stayed out of the heat.

She didn't see her friends much anymore, as far as Melissa knew. Linda had even drawn away from Joanne Weeks. Instead she read a lot. Found projects to do in the house. She remodeled the guestroom and bought expensive new drapes and a Persian rug for the dining area. She potted plants and set them around the kitchen and den, throwing out the old ones. Linda took Melissa shopping for clothes, both of them buying lavishly. Spending was the one way Linda could get back at her husband.

Not that Melissa could complain about that. By now she had a designer wardrobe to die for. Shoes and handbags to match. Her skin looked perfect, thanks to the expensive moisturizers and toners. Her makeup was all MAC, with just about every eye shadow color the company made. Linda had even bought her professional lessons on how to apply makeup. Melissa had never looked better in her life.

Baxter didn't miss that fact either. He didn't say it but Melissa knew.

"You know why he'll never complain about my spending?"

Linda told Melissa as they drove home from the mall one Saturday. Melissa was behind the wheel. She loved driving the BMW. "His own ego. How could Baxter Jackson ever admit he didn't make enough to keep his family happy?"

Melissa nodded. "Yeah, you're right." She focused on the road, picturing Baxter, how he looked at her. The man was being eaten alive inside. What a dupe Linda was. Baxter paid the bills out of sheer guilt.

At the real estate office Melissa's job remained busy. She arranged open houses, answered phone calls, learned all she could. But Baxter's sales were way down for the month, even as the other realtors did well in the booming housing market. No reason the streak of bad luck should last. Baxter kept telling her this was the way business went. You had your good months and your bad months. He'd been through the cycle plenty of times. Sales would start going up; he was convinced of that.

Better start going up fast, Melissa thought. Bills rising and income falling. Not a good combination.

Besides, Melissa knew better than to think rising sales would calm Baxter down.

And so the three of them played their game. Baxter walked his unsteady line between wife and foster daughter. Melissa trod her own between husband and wife. And Linda pretended to the outside world more than ever.

Melissa tried hard to keep her mind focused—and succeeded most of the time. But in her moments of doubt she told herself this house of cards couldn't last.

One day it was bound to come tumbling down.

THIRTY-NINE

FEBRUARY 2010

By 8:40 Melissa and I had been waiting for Perry for over half an hour. We'd said little, ears attuned to any sound in the hallway. Melissa had resumed pacing. Her nervous movements were about to drive me crazy. I slumped on my bed, nerves humming.

Melissa turned to me abruptly. "I thought you called yourself a Christian."

I blinked. "I *am* a Christian."

"Then why do you lie?"

"I don't."

"You lied to *me*."

"Well, I . . . Sometimes in my work I have to."

"Uh-huh." She shifted her weight, hands on her hips. "Is that what the Bible says—don't lie except when you 'have to'?"

I surveyed her, my tongue stuck out against my top lip. "I had to find you, Melissa."

"Don't rationalize. I *hate* that. People rationalized to me my entire life. My mother had a reason to drink. She beat me for good reason—I was in her way. My stepfather raped me with good reason—I was *there*. Baxter hit Linda with good reason—she took it."

"But you're talking about *lifestyles*. I don't make a habit of lying. It's only once in a while. To locate someone. For a good cause."

"So the end justifies the means."

Her sarcastic words dug into me. "How dare you put me in the same category as Baxter! Don't forget he wants us dead. Do you know he came to my house today, with Pastor Steve as a witness, to try to make amends, like a good Christian man? He played his part to the hilt. He's nothing but a total hypocrite."

"Not total. He *does* help people in the church. He *does* help the town. And I worked with him, so I know how honest he is with his clients."

What was *this*? What happened to Baxter ruining her life? "You're forgetting the part about beating his wife. Hard enough one night that he killed her. At least I'm assuming that's what happened."

"He did hit Linda. I saw him. You can bet he hit his second wife too."

"Then—"

"That's his weakness. Control. And yes, he lies about it to the world. And Linda lied by covering up for him. So in the end she was no better. And *you* lie too."

My spine wrenched straight. "And what exactly have *you* done for six years? Lied by your silence. You've let a cold-blooded killer get away with Linda's death!"

Melissa's eyes grew hard. "There's one difference, Joanne. Between you and Baxter and Linda—and me. *I* don't call myself a Christian."

Her accusation stung me to the core. I stared at her, open-mouthed, wanting to defend myself. No words would come.

Melissa watched the emotions play across my face, her mouth twisting in grim satisfaction. With a shake of her head she turned away and resumed pacing. "Little wonder I rejected everything I heard in that church."

That was a rationalization itself, and she knew it. "Christians aren't perfect, Melissa. God is. Don't judge him by our shortcomings."

She threw me a look—*yeah, right.*

I dropped my head into one hand. Rubbed my temple. Her words still burned.

Long minutes ticked by. Melissa and I did not speak. Eventually she sank onto the edge of her bed. She stared at the wall, the blank TV. Who knew where her thoughts now took her?

Mine remained on my seared conscience until I wrenched them away.

They eventually cycled back to the gunman. Was he at the hospital? If his shot was a flesh wound he could be here by now, just waiting for us to show ourselves. Or did Baxter have other people working for him?

Why was he pursuing Melissa now, after six years?

"Where is she, Melissa? Where's Linda?"

Melissa shook her head, stubbornness thinning her mouth.

"You need to tell me! Don't you care what happened to Linda? Don't you want him to *pay*?"

She whirled on me. "No, I *don't* care! Like I told you, I just want to live my life!"

"You have to care. You can't be that hard."

"Don't you judge me." Her voice steeled. "You have *no idea* how that night has haunted me. If I'm hard, it's because life's made me that way."

"It's haunted you because you've run from it. Deal with it. Tell what you know. Your conscience will be clear."

"If I live that long!" She turned away from me, furious. Seconds later, the anger seemed to seep right out of her, air from a pricked balloon. Her shoulders slumped, and she dropped her head.

"Going to live with Baxter and Linda was the one break in my life." Melissa spoke to the floor. "When I started working in his office, I thought I could take on the world. I'd be an agent too someday. I'd make millions. *Be* somebody. Then it all fell apart. Linda was killed, and Social Services took me away. They sent me to a horrible foster home. I lasted there one week before running. I've been on my own ever since, just trying to make it. Couldn't even graduate from high school. Living with this man and that one just so I could have a roof over my head." Melissa shifted on her bed and looked me in the eye. "I thought the world of Baxter."

My voice softened. "But how could you, when you knew he was hitting Linda?"

She shrugged. "I got beat all my life. It's what men do."

I thought of Tom. His smile, his quiet strength. The comfort of his arms. *Not all men, Melissa.*

"Baxter turned on me after Linda's death," Melissa said. "Like everything was all *my* fault."

"Probably because he knew you were a witness. Deceivers don't like anyone who knows the truth about them."

"I guess." Another lift of her shoulder. "He made me hate him. For six years I've hated him. And now he's trying to kill me. I won't give him that satisfaction." She pushed from the bed and went back to pacing. "*Where* is Perry?"

The clock read 8:55. "He'll be here soon."

I hoped.

Exhaustion washed over me. I wanted to curl up on the bed and sleep. Forget everything. What was I even doing here? Melissa was not going to change her mind about talking. Now with her life on the line she was more adamant than ever. Bottom line, she didn't trust anyone to keep her safe until Baxter was behind bars. I could hardly blame her. Tonight, the minute Perry and I got her to safety, she'd run. And she'd go far, maybe even out of state. I wouldn't be able to find her so easily next time.

Why should I even try?

Because if Baxter managed to find her first, he'd kill her.

My head lowered into my hands. So it had come to this. I'd started out with dreams of bringing Baxter to justice. Now I had to worry about keeping Melissa alive.

I stared at my lap, frustration and fear zinging my nerves. Then, out of nowhere, a new thought landed like an errant ball in my dull brain. I picked it up, turned it over. Examined its every side. It was a dirty ball, scuffed. One that would make you want to wash your hands after touching it.

I closed my fingers around it.

Voices sounded in the hall. My head jerked up, and Melissa stilled. We cast feverish looks at each other. The voices grew close, passed the door, then faded.

My muscles refused to relax.

I checked the clock. 9:05.

What if Perry never showed? My plan would fall apart.

I watched the clock turn 9:10. Then 9:15.

A soft knock rapped at the door.

Melissa gasped. Heat shot through my veins. I pushed off the bed and scurried on silent feet to the door. "Who is it?"

FORTY

"It's Perry."

I unlatched the bolt and eased open the door. Perry pushed inside and bolted all the locks behind him. He looked out of breath and tense, wary. A strand of his gray-black hair stuck out from the side of his head. "Hi."

"Hi."

"You okay?"

"Looks like it's going to be 'One of These Nights.' Like the Eagles' album."

His dark brown eyes searched mine.

"Track five," I said.

Knowledge flicked across his face. He gave me a slight nod.

"*What* are you *talking* about?" Impatience rolled off Melissa.

Perry looked past me to her. "This would be a good time to thank me for putting my life on the line for you."

"Thank you. Unless you've got the police waiting outside the door."

His jaw tightened. "I don't."

She nodded, her forehead creasing until once again she looked like a frightened child. "How do we do this?"

"I cruised the parking lot before coming in. I didn't see anyone lurking around. Granted, I may have missed someone. But my car's unlocked and parked right near a side door. We hop in and take off."

"And what if it doesn't work?"

"You got a better idea?"

"I had my own ideas. Then *she* came along." Melissa gestured toward me with her chin. "Now look at me. Running for my life."

Perry flexed his forehead, and his entire scalp moved. He and his wife had raised two daughters. That experience now played across his face. "You listen to me. Joanne's trying to help you, and so am I. But I've had about enough of your attitude. So tell you what—she and I are leaving. You want to stay and fight this thing on your own, have at it." He focused on me. "Let's go."

No way was I leaving Melissa. Either Perry's frustration was getting the best of him, or he was bluffing. I hurried over to get my purse, then planted myself in front of her. "I have a plan."

"Really. Better than your last one?"

"Let us get you out of here. Once we're safe, you and I will have a long talk. I'm going to teach you how to disappear—for good."

Melissa blinked.

"I know how to find people. Which means I also know what they can do to *not* be found."

Perry stood behind me. I prayed he kept silent.

Melissa's eyes narrowed. "Why would you do that?"

"I don't want to. I want you to tell authorities what you know. Once Baxter's put away, you'll be safe. You won't have to hide."

"That'll never happen, and you know it, Joanne. Somehow he'll go free. And he'll come after *me.* I wouldn't even live to see the trial."

I nodded, defeat in my expression. "Then you're going to need my help."

Melissa's gaze roamed from me to Perry and back. "You'll really do that?"

"Yes."

She surveyed me a moment longer, then walked over to pick up her handgun from the bed and placed it in her purse. "Okay."

Perry eyed her handbag. "That thing legal?"

Melissa shrugged.

"No wonder you don't want to face the police."

She threw him a withering look. "So where are you taking us?"

"Let's just get out of here." I waved a hand. "We'll talk about it in the car."

We gathered at the door, animosity and grudging kinship vibrating between the three of us.

"I checked around before coming to the room." Perry kept his voice low. "There's a stairway to our left. It leads to a side fire exit. My car's parked right by it."

My heart fluttered. We were really going to do this. "What if he's out there, watching for us?"

"It's a chance we have to take. If anything, he's probably watching the front door. Once you're in the car, duck down in the seat. But remember, he's wounded. He may not be here at all. Yet. So the sooner we get going, the better." Perry raised his eyebrows. "Ready?"

I nodded. He looked at Melissa, patted his waistband. "I have a gun too."

He *did*? Maybe I should have known. Perry and his detective novels. I managed a smile.

"But we can't go walking through the hotel with weapons drawn." Perry pulled back the bolt latch. "Keep yours in your purse."

He opened the door, stuck out his head, and checked both directions. Stepped out, waving us to follow. We scurried in a tight group down the hall and came to a stop at a corner. Perry peered around it, then urged us on. On our right was the stairwell. He went through the door first, peering down toward the first level. Melissa and I followed close behind.

My legs trembled. Quiet as we tried to be, our breathing seemed to echo up every level. My palms were sweating. I glanced at Melissa, saw my fear in her face.

We reached the bottom. The door sat straight ahead.

My throat dried up. An image of the gunman dressed in black flashed through my mind. He was out there, wasn't he? The hunter waiting for his inevitable prey.

Perry pulled car keys from his pocket and put them in his left hand. Leaned in close to Melissa and me. "Once we go through the door, move *fast.*"

We nodded.

He lifted his shirt and withdrew his gun from its waistband holster. Inched the door open and peered outside. He glanced over his shoulder. "Now."

Perry pushed out into the night, Melissa and I right behind. Perry's car faced us. I scurried to the passenger front, Melissa to the rear. In peripheral vision I saw a few parked cars, a tall parking lot light. No one lurking. No gunman.

We threw ourselves inside the car. Melissa and I slid down in our seats. Perry put his gun in the console. He backed out, braked hard, and lurched forward toward the street. I sat half on the floor, the edge of my seat digging into my back, watching the streetlights slide by the window. The night sky hung starless and gray-curdled, threatening more rain.

We stopped again, then turned right. I squirmed to look over my shoulder. The hotel faded in the distance.

Perry's eyes flicked from road to rearview mirror. He drove straight-backed, headlights from oncoming cars washing over his face. "Don't see anyone following. But stay down."

He went right. Then left. Right. Left. My mind flashed back to my own white-knuckled drive away from 264 Anniston. "See anybody?"

"No."

Clothes rustled from the back seat.

"Stay down, Melissa," Perry barked. "Don't get up till I tell you."

He made more turns until I lost all sense of direction. Out the window, commercial buildings gave way to houses. I could no longer hear sounds of traffic.

My legs were getting cramped.

Perry slowed. Veered right.

He exhaled a long breath, flexed his fingers against the steering wheel. "We did it."

I wriggled up into my seat. Melissa did the same. We were on a quiet residential street, no cars around. We'd made it. I could barely believe it. We'd *made* it.

A prayer of gratitude breathed through my lips.

But this night wasn't over. Far from it.

"Now what?" Melissa's voice mixed relief and anxiety. "Where do we go?"

Perry shot me a sideways questioning look.

"Now I make a phone call." I reached in my purse for my cell phone.

FORTY-ONE

JULY 2004

Melissa was synching Baxter's schedule on his computer with his Blackberry when a call came in from Rex Shalling in Texas. Mr. Shalling and his wife were moving to the Vonita area and were buying a multimillion-dollar home in an upscale area. The sale would go through in a few days. It was a sale Baxter badly needed.

"Just a moment, Mr. Shalling." Melissa put him through to Baxter.

"Hello, Rex." Baxter leaned back in his chair. "How are things with your job transfer?"

A long pause. "I see. How wonderful for you." Baxter's voice held a different tone. Jovial but forced. A client wouldn't have heard the deep disappointment. Melissa did.

She turned to watch Baxter. His shoulders slumped.

He hung up the phone and stared at it.

"Bad news?"

A moment passed before Baxter answered. "He's ending up getting a promotion in Texas. Won't need to move after all." He spoke without turning around.

Melissa closed her eyes. Baxter had lucked out by being both listing and selling agent on the deal. Even after cutting his fee from 6 percent to 5, he stood to make around $140,000.

All that money—gone with one phone call.

Baxter slammed his fist against his desk. He shook his head, rubbed his temple. "I can't *believe* this. *What* is happening with my sales?"

Melissa rose and walked over to him. Laid a hand on his shoulder. Her palm prickled. Never had she touched him like that. "I'm really sorry."

He shrank away from her touch, his voice sharpening. "Not now, Melissa."

She pulled her arm away, stricken.

Baxter straightened and threw a glance out the office window. No one was in the hallway. He raked his gaze up to her face. "Sorry, didn't mean that. I just ... someone might see you."

Understanding flooded Melissa. She backed up one step and gave a tight nod. *Not now*, he'd said. *Not now.*

Baxter turned away. Melissa went back to her desk.

She blinked at her computer. What had she been doing?

The atmosphere in the office tremored. Two minutes passed without a sound. Melissa sneaked a peek at Baxter. He sat with one leg stretched out, his left arm on the desk. Staring out the window. His fingers rose and fell in a slow, silent tap.

"Melissa?"

"Yeah."

"That was nice of you."

She gazed at his back. How she wanted to throw her arms around him and comfort him. Hang on and not let go. He worked hard all day, and what did Linda do? Spend money. Well, let the woman shop till she dropped. Melissa wasn't going to spend another dime. She had enough clothes for a lifetime anyway.

"No problem," she said.

On their drive home an hour later Melissa clutched her purse in her lap, toying with its handle. There was so much she wanted to say. Not one word of it would come.

"Not now, Melissa."

They stopped at a red light. "Don't tell Linda about the sale falling through," Baxter said.

"You know I never tell her what happens at work."

Baxter turned his head and surveyed her. Melissa met his gaze with meaning-filled eyes.

The light turned green. Baxter focused on the road. "She's out tonight after dinner." His tone was so casual. "Got some church volunteer meeting."

Melissa's heart flipped. "Oh. That's right." She pushed the purse around on her legs. "I'll do the dishes for her."

"You always do the dishes."

"Well, then, all the more reason to do them tonight."

Baxter smiled.

As they drove into the garage his mood darkened. Melissa could almost see the weight descend upon him. He slammed the Mercedes' door. His jaw hardened, eyes turning cool as the moment when he faced his wife approached. Melissa trailed Baxter into the kitchen, giving him plenty of room. Not for herself, but to send a message to Linda.

They found her standing at the stove, fluffing rice in a pan with a fork. The smell of baking salmon filled the air. "Hi, honey." Linda smiled at her husband, her eyes gauging. Melissa gave a slight shake of her head. Linda's body tensed. "How was your day?"

"Fine." He walked past her and left the kitchen, on his way upstairs to change.

Melissa and Linda exchanged glances. Melissa lay her purse on the counter and walked to a cabinet for plates. "Let me help. I hear you have a meeting tonight."

"Yes, at seven-thirty." Linda stilled and cocked her head. No sound from Baxter. "Did something bad happen today?" she whispered.

Work questions were one of the hardest parts of trying to keep balance in the household. Melissa couldn't betray Baxter by telling Linda the truth. At the same time she needed to play Linda's ally.

"I don't know. I had a lot of copying to do. If he took some bad calls it was while I was out of the office."

Linda set down the fork. "I just don't understand why he's gotten so bad the last few weeks."

Melissa moved closer to the stove, one ear tilted toward the stairs. "I don't either, but I'm so sorry. I mean, when I first came here I never would have guessed . . ."

"I know." Linda's voice tainted in bitterness. "You and the rest of the world." She replaced the lid on the rice and turned down the heat. Such simple movements, but to Melissa they symbolized Linda's life. Keep a lid on it. Try to keep Baxter from boiling over.

Why did adults have to be so confusing?

"When did he first hit you?" Melissa kept her voice low.

Linda stared across the room as if watching her own private screen. "Three months after we got married."

"Nothing before that? Not a clue?"

"Not one. He had me fooled like everybody else." She cradled her hands at her waist, watching one thumb rub over another. "The first time he did it I was so stunned. Just . . . shocked. He apologized later. Promised he'd never do it again. But of course he did." Linda's mouth twisted. "After awhile he stopped promising."

Indignation rolled up Melissa's spine. Linda was beautiful and smart. She could live her own life. "Why don't you *leave*?"

Linda turned world-weary, resigned eyes upon her. "I love him."

"How *can* you, when he treats you like that?"

A long moment passed as Linda's gaze fastened upon Melissa, as if staring into the depths of her. "Why don't *you* leave?"

Melissa's jaw flexed. Just what was *that* supposed to mean? Anger bubbled within, her mind flashing through a series of pictures. The trashy trailer she grew up in . . . her drunken mother's slit-eyed, hateful looks ... bruises on Melissa's body ... her bedroom at the Jacksons' house ... Baxter's face. Melissa stared back at Linda, her mouth hardening. "Because my life right now is a hundred times better than where I came from."

A hint of a pained, knowing smile flickered across Linda's lips. Her expression read so many things at once. That at sixteen, what did Melissa understand, and who was she to judge? That she could not begin to know Linda's heartache, because she'd never been betrayed by the man she loved. (Stepfathers and a lousy mother didn't count?) That Melissa would change her tune in a hurry if Baxter started mistreating *her*. (*That* would never happen.) Linda opened her mouth — maybe to say one of these things, maybe to say them all. Then she closed it. She turned away.

Baxter's footsteps sounded on the stairs.

Melissa swiveled to a drawer and started pulling out utensils. Linda opened the oven door and slid out a pan of baked salmon.

Dinner went pretty well, although all three of them were quiet. Melissa figured the church meeting was a point for Linda's side. It wouldn't do for Baxter to hit her too close to her seeing her church friends. She might get all teary, and how to explain that?

Or maybe he just had other things on his mind.

Melissa could hardly eat. Her veins burned. She hated Baxter's abuse of his wife, but neither did she like Linda's know-more-than-you attitude. Fact was, Linda got hit because she wouldn't stand up for herself. She was an *adult*, not the kid Melissa had been in her trailer days. If Linda really thought Baxter was so bad, she'd march into church and tell everyone the truth about her husband. Press charges against him. And if her friends and the police didn't believe her story — show them her bruises. But she wasn't about to do that, was she? Because Linda knew the truth. She was the only one in the world Baxter treated like that. Everyone else knew him as a great man. The problem lay with *her*, not *him*.

After dinner Melissa did the dishes while Linda prepared to

leave. At exactly 7:25 she pulled out of the garage on her way to church. The perfect volunteer, never late.

Baxter was watching TV in the den, sitting on his end of the couch. Flipping through channels, as usual. Melissa went upstairs to brush her teeth, then joined him on the opposite end of the sofa. For five minutes they were silent, staring at the TV, seeing nothing. The air between them shimmied. Then it rippled. Melissa found herself breathing fast and shallow, trying hard not to show it. Baxter crossed his legs male-style, one ankle against the other knee. Feigning relaxation. A man in his castle at the end of a work day, chilling out.

His muscles itched. Melissa felt it.

The channels kept switching, as if all of Baxter's energy released through his thumb. Local news to an old movie to a commercial to another commercial to a cop show. Baxter returned to the movie. Some oldie that didn't look a bit interesting. They watched it for a couple minutes.

Abruptly Baxter leaned forward, as if yanked by a noose. Melissa watched from the corner of her eye. He focused on the remote, eyes searching for some button. His finger moved, and he pressed. The sound muted.

Melissa turned her head and looked at him.

Baxter dropped the remote. He gazed back at Melissa, lips pressing.

He rose and crossed the four steps to her end of the couch. Sat down beside her. His eyes darkened with guilt-ridden hunger.

The next thing she knew they were in each other's arms.

FORTY-TWO

FEBRUARY 2010

"Who are you calling?" Suspicion sharpened Melissa's voice. I'd already punched in the number, my stomach trembling. If this didn't work, I had no back-up plan.

"My brother."

Rain began to fall. A few drops, then steady. Perry switched on the wipers. We were on El Camino, a major street in San Jose.

"He doesn't live in Vonita, does he?" Melissa pressed. "I'm not setting foot in Vonita!"

"If I'd wanted to take you to Vonita, we'd go to Perry's." The line began to ring in my ear. "He lives in Hollister."

Perry gave me another sideways glance but said nothing. Hollister was the San Benito County seat. We'd need to head south, then veer east.

Second ring. I checked the car's digital clock. Nine-forty. On a Sunday night. Dan would certainly wonder when he saw my caller ID.

The third ring cut off in the middle. "Hello, Joanne?"

Dan's reedy voice vibrated in my ear. I clicked down the volume. "Yeah, Dan, it's me. Sorry to call you so late, but I need to come over."

"Right now?"

Dan stood six-two, a wiry man in his mid-fifties. Divorced, kids grown. A no-nonsense kind of guy. His unlikely combination of dark hair and intense blue eyes commanded attention. That piercing gaze could bore right through a person when he wanted to make a point. Which was often.

"I have to see you now. I've ... run into some trouble. Got shot at. It's not safe for me to go home."

"*Shot* at! By some skip?"

"Look, could I just come and talk? I'll tell you about it."

"Want police here?"

"*No*. No police."

Melissa made a gasping sound. "*No!*"

"All right," Dan said. "You coming from Vonita?"

"Mountain View, so it'll be a little while. And, Dan, when we get there—"

"We?"

I winced. Hadn't meant to let that slip just yet. "I've got two people with me. I'll call you when we're on your street. Can you watch for us and let us in quickly?"

"Joanne, if you think you're still in danger, I'll call the police. They'll intercept you wherever you are and escort you here."

"No. Please. Just trust me on this one. Okay?"

He hesitated. "All right. But once you get here, I call the shots."

That was Dan—always gaining control. A fighter by birth. If Melissa thought Perry had been short-tempered with her, wait till she got in Dan's face. "Fine by me."

The rain became a downpour as I hung up.

Perry turned on 87 South toward Gilroy, where we'd catch 101 and then Highway 25 into Hollister. The drive was close to fifty miles. In the rain—over an hour.

"Tell me, Joanne." Melissa tapped me on the shoulder. "Tell me how to disappear."

"Let's wait till we get to Dan's house."

"Just tell me about getting a new ID. You know people who can get me one?"

A faint smile crossed Perry's lips.

"Buying a fake ID is what you *don't* want to do," I told her. "How do you know whose life you're buying? She could have warrants out on her, unpaid parking tickets, creditors after her. Something, anything that would cause authorities to come looking for you. That's exactly what you don't need."

"So what do I do?"

My eyes closed. I leaned back against the headrest. "You keep your own ID. And learn how not to leave a trail."

One thing I remembered about Melissa—when she needed to learn something for her own advantage, she learned it. Linda had bragged how quickly she picked up the necessary skills for working in Baxter's office.

"Is it complicated?" Melissa's tone had returned to one of reined-in excitement, as if she relished the challenge.

"Yes. You'll have to keep at it. One slip—and someone like me can catch you."

"I want to know!"

"We'll talk when we get to Dan's."

"Tell me *now.*"

"When we get to Dan's."

She argued. I wouldn't budge. After a time she muttered a curse and fell silent. Wonderful Perry said nothing. I wished I could talk to him, tell him how grateful I was. Later. When this was all over.

My eyes remained closed. I drifted, the drum of raindrops fading. A blanket settled over my brain, warm and smothering ...

The next thing I knew Perry was pushing my shoulder. "Joanne."

"Hmm?" My mouth moved before my mind engaged. I opened my eyes, blinked a few times. The rain had stopped. "Did I fall asleep?"

"Yeah. We're just outside Hollister. Where do I go?"

"Oh. Okay." I sat up straight and stretched my neck one way, then the other. Tried to shake loose the fog in my head. Not a sound from the backseat. I twisted around. Melissa sat with arms folded. Her eyes met mine, then cut away. The meaning was clear. I'd told her she had to wait for what she wanted, made her subservient. To Melissa, an unpardonable sin.

I pictured the upcoming scene at Dan's house, and a chill trickled down my spine.

My focus turned to the road. "Turn right at the next stoplight, Perry." I fished my phone from my purse and called Dan. "We're here. See you in about three minutes."

"I'll be watching."

Melissa's clothes rustled. "I don't see why we had to come all the way down here."

"You see anybody following us?" Perry shot her a look in the rearview mirror.

"No."

"Worked, didn't it?"

"There's the street—Maxley Lane." I pointed. "Turn left. It's the third house down on the right."

We pulled up to Dan's place, a white stucco rancher with black shutters. Stark-colored and neat, like its owner. I'd last been here on a weekend to pick up some last-minute papers on a skip.

"Okay, Melissa." I grabbed my purse. "Let's go."

"About time."

I breathed a prayer.

The door of the house opened as we piled out of the car. Dan stood silhouetted in his entryway, one hand low on his hip. We scurried up the short sidewalk, tense to be out in the open, even though no one could have followed us. Our host stepped back, ushering us in with a wave of his arm, as if hurrying along errant children. We stopped in the hallway. Dan closed and locked the door.

"Joanne." He nodded at me. He was wearing jeans and loafers, a tucked-in long-sleeve shirt. His gaze moved to my companions.

"This is Melissa." I touched her arm, feeling her stiffness. She muttered a hello, both hands clasping her purse in front of her. "And Perry." The two men shook hands.

Melissa's eyes darted from Dan to me, making comparisons. Clearly, we didn't look a thing alike.

"Let's go sit down." Dan gestured toward his living room.

We followed him in. Dan and Perry settled in matching armchairs, Melissa and I on opposite ends of a couch, facing them. I made sure she took the side further into the room. We placed our purses on the floor. She cast me a look that read *this better not take long*. Her own agenda to glean from me all she could played out in the impatient shake of her right leg, her fidgeting fingers. Perry sat with back straight, large hands spread on his thighs. Alertness and keen curiosity shone in his eyes. He surveyed Melissa and her handbag, directly across from him, then focused on me.

A trickle of sweat itched the nape of my neck. *Here we go.* I didn't know enough about the law to grasp exactly how my scheme would play out. But one thing I did know. Melissa was packing a gun that wasn't registered in her name, not to mention that she didn't even have a permit to carry it.

My dry throat swallowed. I desperately wanted Jelly Bellies. Wild Blackberry and Piña Colada.

"Dan." I licked my lips and plunged in. "Melissa's last name is Harkoff. She was a foster child in the home of Baxter and Linda Jackson when Linda disappeared. You remember that case."

"Of course. Unsolved murder."

Melissa swiveled toward me. "What're you—"

"Melissa can solve it. She saw Baxter kill Linda. She knows where the body is buried." I turned to Melissa. Her jaw was set and hard, her eyes boring into mine. "Melissa, this is Dan Marlahn. District attorney of San Benito County."

Before Melissa could move, Perry shoved from his chair and snatched the gun-toting purse away from her feet.

FORTY-THREE

AUGUST 2004

The Jackson house of cards wasn't going to fall. It was about to explode.

By the third week of August Melissa could barely sleep. Nightmares of her dead mother had returned with fury. And every minute of the day felt electrified. She and Baxter had so little time to be alone. Linda had attended two more church volunteer meetings at night—that was it. The rest of the time Baxter and Melissa were near each other, yet so far. Their presence in the same room became a live wire, her nerves thrumming with his every move. She knew he felt it too, maybe even more. In the office there was no privacy because of the large window looking out to the hall. When Melissa and Baxter were at home with Linda the sparks between the two of them popped wildly. One wrong move, one lustful look intercepted by Linda would be gasoline on embers.

Melissa quickly learned how to handle Baxter—the poster man for duplicity. She knew he admired her stubborn determination and strength, even as he needed to control the women in his life. Each day in the office she asserted herself a little more. Hadn't she earned that right? It was all a balance. The more self-assured and poised she acted, the more he wanted her. The more he wanted her, the stronger she became.

Slow business didn't help the situation any. Sales were down for the second month in a row. Some big house would nearly sell, then the deal would fall through. After losing five sales in a row Baxter accused God of cursing him.

"Oh, come on, Baxter, things will pick up again." Melissa's fingers poised over her computer keyboard. "That's what *you* always say."

He snorted. "They'd better pick up fast. Linda's going to break me."

"We're not shopping anymore. I told her I have enough clothes."

He swung around in his chair and surveyed Melissa under lowered brows. "Newsflash—she's not waiting for you. What do you think she does all day?"

Melissa's jaw loosened. "Why don't you tell her to stop?"

"Because it keeps her busy and her mouth shut." He shrugged. "Besides, she ... needs it. Makes her feel better."

Ah, the guilt again.

"Yeah, well, you need less bills."

"The money will come, Melissa. Sales will pick up, like you said."

How fast he changed his tune.

"But you're right." His expression twisted into a half tease. "I'd be better off financially without her." His voice dropped into a mumble. "Not to mention her life insurance."

"What?" Melissa eyed him with indignant surprise. "What'd you say?"

He waved a hand in the air. "Nothing. Just a bad joke." He rotated toward his desk, ending the conversation. Melissa surveyed his back for a long moment before returning to her work.

Every day—the tension and desire. The tightrope walk. Baxter's inner demons.

In church on Sundays Melissa sat next to Linda (she didn't dare sit next to Baxter) and listened to the sermons about living a Christian life in the twenty-first century. Linda would nod and Baxter mutter his *amens*. Talk about a disconnect. Those hours in church formed Melissa's most confusing moments. Pastor Steve's words pierced her soul more than once. He spoke of Jesus' love, his forgiveness, his burning desire to set each person free of the past, no matter how bad it might be. There were times when Melissa yearned for that cleansing with aching intensity. The pastor's promises of wholeness, of a new and stunning *purpose* that no circumstances could take away shone upon the wreckage of Melissa's life like a beacon in roiling dark waters. But every time, the Jacksons' secrets would roll over her and drown the ache inside. They amened and nodded at the pastor's every point. They projected everything the pastor talked about.

All lies.

How could Melissa stake her life on any of the pastor's claims, no matter how bright they seemed, when she knew the truth about Baxter and Linda?

Sometimes Melissa wondered which one was the bigger hypocrite — the wife-beater or the one who covered it up? And how strange that Baxter should suddenly develop a conscience when it came to sleeping with Melissa. Why the remorse over cheating on his wife when he felt none about mistreating her in other ways?

Melissa knew one thing — it never feels good to face your own guilt. Much better to channel the energy into something else. Baxter practiced what he did best and took it out on Linda — worse than ever. He hit her almost every day now, the slightest *anything* from her setting him off. She spoke too loud, she spoke too soft. The meat was overcooked, the vegetables undercooked. She smiled too much, she smiled too little. Linda withdrew into a dazed and brittle shell. Alone with Melissa she cried, *"Why?"* Melissa gritted her teeth and comforted Linda, cursing the woman and her husband both. Linda was a wimp, Baxter too hot-headed. One of these days either one of them was bound to do something really, really stupid. And Melissa would find herself out on the street.

"You've got to lay off Linda," Melissa accosted Baxter as they drove home one day. He hunched over the wheel, hard-eyed and tight-jawed. Melissa didn't care that he was in a foul mood. The man needed to get hold of himself.

"Don't tell me how to treat my wife."

"Baxter, one day you're going to hit her too hard, and she'll really be hurt. Have some bruise she can't hide. Then what?"

"I said lay off."

Melissa pressed back in her seat, air pushing from her mouth. She made a face at the road. Sometimes this man could be so knuckle-headed. "Look, I'm not trying to tell you what to do, but—"

"Sure sounds like it to me."

"Well, what do you *want*, Baxter? You want her telling her friends at church?"

"She'll never do that."

"Don't be so sure. Linda's a volcano waiting to erupt. The right moment with the right friend asking what's wrong with her lately, and she'll blow."

"Melissa. *Shut up*."

"*Don't* tell me to shut up! That's the way you talk to Linda, not me."

They hit a red light. Baxter braked hard, jerking Melissa's body against her seatbelt. He turned on her, his expression black as coal. "You listen to me. Nobody tells me what to do in my own house." His finger pointed at her, stiff and thrusting at air. "You're just a sixteen-year-old kid without a home. I let you in mine, and I can kick you out tomorrow. Got that?"

Shock and pain spun through Melissa. She stared at Baxter, open-mouthed. Speechless.

He swiveled back to glare at the stoplight, fingers drumming a mad beat on the steering wheel.

Fine, then. Act like a two-year-old.

The silence in the car pricked.

A minute later they turned a corner. Far ahead the Jackson mansion came into view. The moment she'd first seen it flashed in Melissa's mind. Had that really been just two months ago? Seemed like a lifetime.

She would not lose this house. This life. Baxter.

Just a sixteen-year-old kid. Oh, really. In some ways she knew more than Baxter Jackson. At least she wasn't lying to herself.

The driveway approached. They had little time left. Like a wind goddess Melissa swept around inside her body and gathered her whirling emotions. Shoved them down into a hole.

"You won't kick me out, Baxter." Her voice shifted low and soothing. She stretched her hand across the seat and grazed his thigh. "I'm on your side, remember?"

He threw her a look, not quite so dark. Melissa's hand pressed against his leg. He shook his head as if in defeat, air seeping from his throat. Slowly his right hand found hers and squeezed.

"It's been too long." He turned into the graceful driveway.

Melissa flicked a look at the windows and pulled her hand into her lap. "I think Linda's done having church meetings for a while."

"We have to find another way."

Melissa gazed at the front porch. The beautiful carved wood door that symbolized entrance into the splendid and shining Jackson world. "You have any ideas?"

"I'll think of something."

"When?"

His expression turned smug. "Tonight."

FORTY-FOUR

FEBRUARY 2010

"Hey!" Melissa launched off the couch and lunged for her purse. Perry clutched it to his chest and twisted away from her. She screamed a curse and swerved around him, hands scrabbling for it. He jerked away again and bent over it. Melissa pummeled his back with her fist.

"Melissa, stop!" I jumped up.

Dan was on his feet, head swiveling from me to Melissa. "What's going on?"

"She has a gun in there."

Dan strode to Melissa, grabbed her arms, and pulled her away from Perry. She turned on him like a banshee, arms and legs flying. Dan fought to hold her off. Perry turned to help, still holding the purse. I ran to take it from him. He pivoted toward Melissa, captured her from behind in a bear hug. She screamed and squirmed, but he held tight. He pushed her forward until her legs hit the couch, spun her around and forced her down.

Dan stood to one side of Melissa, Perry on the other. Their faces were flushed. "*Don't* you move." Perry pointed a finger at her.

Melissa glared up at them, teeth clenched and trembling. She was outweighed, outnumbered, and betrayed. Her glare cut to me, glistening with hatred. And a telltale glint of something else she would never admit.

Fear.

"All right." Dan held up a palm. "Let's just all calm down. I need to hear this from the beginning."

"There's nothing to hear." Defiance pinched Melissa's face.

"Joanne says there is."

"Joanne's a *liar.*"

Dan looked to me and spread his hands. Baxter Jackson was no stranger to him. They may not be close friends themselves, but Chief Eddington provided a strong link. Baxter was a prominent citizen in Dan's county—and no DA would pounce on such a person without good reason.

My legs felt suddenly weak. The last twenty-four hours had been the longest in my life. Now that my ploy had worked—so far—what energy I had left seemed to drain right out of me.

I still held Melissa's purse. I didn't trust her anywhere near it. I backed up and sank into the armchair Dan had left. He and Perry continued to guard Melissa. I set her handbag in my lap.

"It started last night on a road near my house ..." Quickly I related the story of Hooded Man, the break-in at my home, finding Melissa, the gunman in *her* house, Perry's rescue. Perry listened as intently as Dan, equally amazed at the parts he didn't know. Melissa pressed back against the couch, head down, arms folded. Even in her silence I could almost smell the burning gears of her mind. She would not give in easily.

"So I brought her to you, Dan. I told her I was bringing her to my brother's house." I dared a glance at Melissa. She shot me a look of pure venom. "She can tell you everything about Linda's murder. Baxter has to be caught quickly. Now he's after both of us."

"I'm *not* telling you anything." Melissa leaned toward Dan. "'Cause guess what? I lied to her. I don't know *anything* about Linda's death."

"Then why is Baxter after you?" Perry retorted.

"Maybe he's not. Maybe it's someone else, who knows? She has no proof it's Baxter."

Dan raised his eyebrows at me. "Do you?"

"I ... no. You'll have to find the gunman. Make him talk. Baxter will never admit to anything."

Dan ran a hand through his hair. "Let's put that aside for a minute." He regarded Melissa, two fingers at his lips. The stance of a prosecutor pondering argument. "So you don't know about Linda's death."

"No."

"But someone told Joanne you do know. And now that someone may be trying to kill you. Mere coincidence?"

"You can't make me stay here."

"You want to call the police?"

Melissa seared him with a look.

Dan walked two steps toward me, turned back, and pointed at Melissa. "Stay there." He approached me. I held up the purse. He peered inside until his expression indicated he saw the handgun. "You got a permit to carry this?"

"It's a friend's. I just borrowed it a few days ago."

"I take it that means no."

No response.

Dan focused again inside the purse. "Unlawful carrying and possession of weapons. That could get you a year in state prison."

Melissa shoved upright, her eyes wide. "You can't do that to me! It's not my gun!"

"That's the point."

"But it's just borrowed. I can give it back."

"You're carrying it. You shot someone with it."

"He was trying to shoot *me*!"

"Tell that to the DA."

Melissa's shoulders arched. Her eyes sought Dan's, silently begging him to take back his words. Dan stared back at her with his hard prosecutorial gaze. With a loud expelling of air, Melissa fell against the couch. Her chin dropped. "I can't believe this."

Dan handed the purse back to me. Shrugged. "We *could* forget about the gun."

From beneath her lashes, Melissa eyed him warily.

"Unlawful carrying and possession of a concealed weapon is a small thing compared to homicide. That's a crime that should never go unpunished. Tell me what you know about Linda Jackson's murder, and we'll let the gun thing go."

"I *told* you. I don't know *anything*!"

He headed for the couch and sat down beside her. Too close. Melissa leaned away.

"I think you do." Dan's voice ran smooth. "I've known Joanne for years now. She's done some skip tracing for me, did you know that? Whenever I've had to find a witness that we'd lost track of. Joanne's reliable. I believe what she says. And *she* tells me you've admitted to her that you witnessed Linda Jackson's murder."

"I didn't. Really." Melissa's voice sounded dull. "I lied."

Dan eyed her, waiting. Silence throbbed the air. Melissa focused blankly on the floor, her face a mask of stubbornness.

Perry eased away from her, back to his armchair.

Dan shifted his position. "Ever hear of a material witness?"

Melissa made no response.

"That's what you are. You witnessed a crime, and your knowledge of that crime is material to prosecuting the case. Under California law you can't just walk away with that knowledge. If you refuse to tell what you know, I can put you in jail. Right now."

"No!" Melissa's head swung toward him, her cheeks blanched.

"I can keep you in jail up to forty-eight hours. Which means Monday morning I'll take you before the judge. He will order you to face the grand jury and tell them what you know. If you fail to appear before the grand jury, a warrant will be issued for your arrest."

The district attorney's words fell like hammers upon Melissa. I watched her body shrink with each blow. When he finished, her gaze roved the floor as if seeking an answer to this nightmare.

"Why are you so against testifying?" Perry asked. "You lived with Linda. I saw the two of you come into my store plenty of times, and you seemed to be great friends."

"We were." Melissa's words were barely audible.

She said no more. Dan and I exchanged glances. I hadn't known he could jail Melissa for refusing to cooperate. The illegal weapon charge, I'd thought, would be threat enough. Now she was indeed trapped. The knowledge should have soothed me. I'd hunted her and found her. Mission accomplished.

But a niggling voice inside taunted this wasn't over.

"Have it your way." Dan pushed to his feet. "I'm going to make the call."

Melissa jerked her head up. "What call?"

"The police. They'll take you down to jail. The gun charge is going with you too."

"No!" Melissa sprang to her feet. "No, I ... Baxter will *kill* me, don't you see? He's already tried. Why haven't you asked more about *that*? He tries to kill two people tonight, and you want to take *me* to jail?"

"At this point I have absolutely no proof of who was chasing you and Joanne."

"I *know* it was Baxter! Somebody he hired."

"Maybe we can prove that. We have a better chance if we tie it to Linda's murder. Baxter killed his wife, and you witnessed it. Then he tried to silence you for your knowledge. Without that tie, what have we got?"

"And what about me until you arrest Baxter?" Melissa demanded. "Who's going to keep *me* alive?"

"California has a witness-protection program. We'll take care of you."

"I'd rather take care of myself."

"Doesn't look like that's worked too well."

Melissa glared at the DA, shallow-breathing. He raised his eyebrows, waiting. Emotions flitted across her face—anger ... blame ... indignation.

The silence spun out.

From somewhere in the house a clock ticked. Outside a dog barked in the distance. Perry looked at me, gave me the slightest smile of reassurance.

Melissa closed her eyes. Resignation dragged at the sides of her mouth. She pulled her top lip between her teeth. Crossed her arms in a self-hug. Another minute passed before she spoke the words I never thought I'd hear. "If I tell you, how long until Baxter is arrested?"

"We'll protect you until he is."

"How long?"

Dan tilted his head. "You can lead us to the body?"

She nodded.

"Were you with Baxter when he buried Linda?"

Another slight nod. "He made me go."

Perry and I exchanged a look. The mere thought sent chills through my veins. How could Baxter have done that to a teenager? I couldn't *wait* to see the man behind bars.

Dan surveyed Melissa, then gazed across the room, his expression blending disgust and empathy. It was the mixture that made an effective DA. He possessed passion for bringing criminals to justice without becoming calloused to the plights of witnesses who helped him do so.

"Is Linda's body in this area?" he asked.

"Yes."

Dan dipped his chin. "Okay. When we find the remains, which will corroborate your story, he'll be picked up."

Which didn't mean he'd stay in jail. If some expensive attorney managed to get him bail, he'd be back out on the streets until trial. That could take months. Maybe a year, even longer. The thought punched holes in my lungs. I peered down the long days ahead, envisioned the uproar in Vonita, two camps taking sides—including the people of my own church. Saw myself trying to live within the vortex, go to the store, pass people on the street. At least half of them would hate me. How could I even stay in Vonita?

Guilt stabbed me. How could I be thinking of myself while Linda's body lay out there somewhere, crying to be found?

"How long will that take?" Melissa asked.

"I'll get a forensics team together first thing in the morning. You lead us to the site, we'll dig. It'll take some time to assemble all the bones. Once the dig is done we'll have to positively identify the body as Linda's. If we can match dental records, it will take only a day or two. But because of the apparent danger you're in, I'll want to get Baxter off the streets as quickly as possible. I'll push for picking him up before identification."

Melissa dropped her chin and stared at the floor. Calculations played across her face.

Come on, Melissa.

"Could he be arrested as early as tomorrow night?"

"Yes. If you can lead us to the exact site quickly. After six years, maybe you've forgotten the spot, and we'll have to dig here and there to see if we can turn up anything. That could turn into days."

Melissa shook her head. "I know the exact spot. I haven't forgotten." Her voice lowered. "I'll never forget."

Dan cast me a look that read he still couldn't believe this was happening. *Baxter Jackson.* With all the cases Dan had prosecuted, all the dregs of humanity he had seen, this one still seemed to surprise him.

"I've worked with a lot of witnesses over the years." Dan's tone gentled. "I know the toll that seeing a crime takes on people. We're the good guys here. We'll keep you safe and see that justice is done for Linda. You just need to fulfill your part, and I'll do the rest. Will you do that?"

Melissa rubbed her forehead as if to buff away the unwanted

knowledge in her brain. She would not raise her head. A blush grazed her cheeks, her lips thinned in futility. One hand palmed the other, squeezing and relaxing, squeezing, relaxing. In that moment she looked like the girl of sixteen who came to live with Linda and Baxter. The young, damaged girl who so wanted to fit in.

Melissa swallowed. Determination dawned in her expression. She raised her chin and looked the district attorney in the eye. "Okay, I'll tell you. And I'll take you to the grave."

FORTY-FIVE

Melissa's words echoed in my head. *"I'll take you to the grave."* Her defeat, my victory. I wanted to jump up and cheer. I wanted to fall on my knees and thank God. But all energy had left my limbs. I could only stare at her numbly, her purse like an anvil on my lap.

My murdered best friend would have her justice. Linda, who'd lit up a room, even as she lied to the world. To *me*.

"Thank you, Melissa." Dan stood up. "You're doing the right thing."

She lifted a shoulder.

"What happened, Melissa?" My mouth moved of its own accord. "Why did he do it?"

Her gaze dropped to the floor. She pressed her lips together, spots of color appearing on her cheeks. "It's my fault." Melissa's voice caught. "If I hadn't been there, in that house."

"Melissa." Dan shook his head. "It's not your fault."

Her mouth turned down. She made no reply.

Perry looked at me, sympathy shining in his eyes. It struck me—he knew how much I'd loved Linda. He *understood*.

A sudden violent longing seized my limbs. I wanted Perry's arms around me. I wanted a man's comfort, and my husband was gone.

Dan touched Melissa on the shoulder. "I'm going to make a call to the Vonita police, alert them we're bringing you down for a statement."

"No!" Melissa's chin jerked up. "Don't take me to Vonita! Why can't I just tell you everything right here?"

"We need to tape and video your statement. I don't have the equipment here— "

"*Don't* take me to Vonita! They won't listen to me. The chief's too good a friend of Baxter's."

"What about your office, Dan?" I could understand Melissa's fear of returning to Baxter's stomping grounds.

Dan thought a minute. "I'll see what I can do."

Melissa pushed off the couch. "Can I use your bathroom?"

"Sure." Dan gestured with his chin. "I'll show you where it is."

She hesitated. "I'll need my purse."

"I'll need to take the gun out."

Melissa shrugged.

"Hang on a minute." Dan left the room and returned with a dish towel and sealable plastic bag. Using the towel he extracted the handgun from Melissa's purse and slid it into the bag. Sealed it shut.

Melissa watched his every move. "I thought you said you weren't going to use that against me."

He faced her. "I won't. As long as you keep your end of the bargain."

She cast him a sullen look, as if ticked off that he still didn't fully trust her. Dan picked up the purse from my lap and handed it to Melissa. "Follow me."

They left the room, half the air sucking away with them. My lungs felt like bricks. I slumped in the chair, elbow on the armrest, and leaned my head against a fist.

"You did it, Joanne." Perry spoke in low tones. In the distance I could hear Dan talking to someone on the phone.

I managed a weak smile. "*We* did it. I'd still be stuck in that hotel room if you hadn't rescued us. Plus you were smart enough to figure out my message."

"Ah, that was easy. Eagles' *One of These Nights* album, song five." He chuckled. "'Lyin' Eyes.'"

"You did great. Just went along with everything."

"I know you don't have a brother."

I lifted my head off my fist. We smiled at each other.

Dan returned. "One of my investigators is going to meet us at my office. We have recording equipment there." He scratched the side of his face. "Man. Baxter Jackson. If we find that body, this case is gonna be a doozy."

"And Cherisse's death," I reminded him. "If Baxter's charged with Linda's murder, they'll reopen that case, won't they?"

"Yeah. We'll have to. I'll get a second pair of eyes to look at the autopsy findings. And a court order to disinter the body, if necessary."

I leaned my head back against the armchair. A minute passed in silence, each of us busy with our own musings. I imagined Dan peering down the road, envisioning Baxter's trial for Linda's murder, the prosecutorial arguments. Baxter would be sure to hire an expensive attorney. It would be a hard fight.

The thought made me dizzy. I couldn't go there now.

I needed sleep.

Dan looked toward the entryway. "She's taking a long time."

My head came up. He was right. "I'll go check on her."

"It's down that hall to the left." Dan pointed.

I stood up on rubber legs, crossed the room into the hall. At the bathroom door I knocked. Called Melissa's name.

No answer.

"Melissa? Melissa." I knocked harder. "You okay?"

Silence.

My heart stumbled. I slapped both hands on the knob and shook the door. "Melissa!"

Dan and Perry appeared at my side, concern on their faces. "Melissa!" Dan pounded on the door. "Open up!"

No, I thought. *No*. What had she done to herself?

Perry pushed in. "Melissa." He rattled the door knob. "Open up right now, or I'm coming in."

We waited, hardly daring to breathe. Listening for the slightest sound.

Nothing.

Perry raised his eyebrows at Dan. The district attorney nodded.

"Stand back." Perry positioned himself and kicked the door viciously. It splintered but did not fully give. Chilly air seeped past my shoulders. Perry aimed a second kick. The door shot open. A cold breeze tumbled out.

Perry jumped into the bathroom. Dan and I crowded behind. I saw the toilet and sink—empty.

And an open window, curtains fluttering.

FORTY-SIX

He paced the kitchen, fingers dug into the sides of his scalp. His special cell phone, clipped to his belt, sat maddeningly silent. The last call he'd received on it had sent him on a rampage through the house, alternately cursing and begging God for a break. The sound of his own voice cussing dropped lead into his veins. He never did that. It was beneath a man of his morality.

"I lost them," the caller had said. "And I got shot."

"You *what*?"

"I got shot in the leg, man. I got to go to the hospital."

"Don't you *dare* leave a trail by going to the hospital. You do that, I'll find you. I'll put you away myself."

"I got a *bullet* in my leg!"

"Better than one in your heart."

The exchange still buzzed in his head. He'd wanted to reach through the invisible connection and strangle the caller. And if that wasn't bad enough, his house phone had rung less than an hour later, a taunting voice on the line. A voice that wrenched such hatred through his gut he nearly threw up.

Right now he wanted to hit somebody. He wanted to bellow and scream.

Another curse spit from his lips.

He strode to the sink, filled a glass of water, and guzzled it down. *Pull yourself together, man.* This would all still work. He'd figure it out—didn't he always? Didn't he *always* come out on top?

The house phone rang.

He swung around and glared at it.

A second ring.

He took a deep breath and walked to the end of the counter. Picked up the receiver to check the ID.

Melissa Harkoff.

He raised his hand to throw the phone across the room, then caught himself. Maybe he could pull out some inkling of usable information.

With a growl in his throat he hit *talk*. "What makes you think I'm not recording these calls?"

"I'm sure you are, Baxter. Every word." Melissa sounded out of breath.

"Blackmail's a crime, in case you didn't know it. I could take the tapes to the police."

"Sure you will. Including all the parts in which I talk about you killing Linda."

"I—"

"Would you like to record where you buried the body? Let me start with instructions on how to get there."

"Shut up, Melissa."

"You listen to me." Melissa's voice turned acid raw. "Because you've got very little time left—"

"I'm not paying you one dime!"

"You don't have a choice anymore. Your sloppy mess of a killer *missed*, remember? I got him instead, remember that?"

Back to the taunts of her last call, some three and a half hours ago. When she claimed she'd been on the run with Joanne Weeks and had holed up in a hotel bathroom just long enough to "give her favorite hypocrite an update."

There are plenty more hired killers I can find to hunt you down, girl.

"Where are you now? Still with Joanne?"

"Oh, Baxter. Are you sitting down? You won't *believe* where I've just been."

He wouldn't dignify her ridicule with a response.

"Joanne took me to the district attorney's house."

Yeah, right.

"In Joanne's car?" Baxter knew that couldn't be true. For the last two hours his hired man had been watching the SUV, traced through the GPS to a hotel in Mountain View.

"Oh, right, like we'd leave in *that* wired car. You think we're stupid? Joanne had a friend come get her. We escaped out a back door."

Slow heat trickled down Baxter's spine. They'd gotten away *again*? What kind of incompetent fool had he hooked up with?

". . . took me to the district attorney's house." That's just the kind of stunt Joanne Weeks would pull.

On the other hand, any word that came out of Melissa Harkoff's mouth was most likely a lie.

"Just how would a visit to the DA fit in with your plans to blackmail me?" Baxter spat. "You tell them your story about how I killed Linda—and your money goes up in smoke." Not that he ever intended to pay it in the first place.

"She tricked me. Told me she was taking me to her brother's house to hide out."

Joanne didn't have a brother.

"Once we got there the DA—his name is Dan Marlahn. You know him? He lives in Hollister, on Maxley Lane."

The heat in Baxter's spine flickered into a burn and spread down his limbs.

"Anyway, Dan the DA told me I'm a 'material witness.' And I can't refuse to say what I know or he'll put me in jail."

Baxter's knees weakened. He dropped into a kitchen chair. Material witness? That sounded too knowledgeable of the law. Not something that would come solely from Melissa's devious mind.

"I kept refusing to talk. You know I don't want to tell them how you killed your wife. But Dan the DA wouldn't budge. Said it was jail time for me—right on the spot. I told them 'Okay, I'll do it' because—what choice did I have? Then I went to the bathroom and escaped out the window."

Baxter breathed into the phone, his heart grinding into an erratic beat.

"So, dear Baxter, your deadline has just moved up. Tuesday won't do. I'm not sure I can stay on the run that long. Now I have both you *and* the law after me. Any cop who finds me will haul me in, make me talk. Do you understand, Baxter? I have *no choice*."

He stared across the kitchen floor to the place where Linda had fallen six long years ago. The exact spot where he'd been forced to make the horrific decision that had led to this moment. "There's always a choice, Melissa." The words dripped with meaning.

"Not this time. I'm *not* going to jail."

"So run. You're good at that."

"I'll have the law on me wherever I go. You want that hanging over your head, Baxter? The day I'm found is the day you go down."

He fixated upon the infamous spot, hatred churning in his gut.

"Go ahead, Melissa, tell them your story. I'll tell them *you* must have killed Linda and buried her all by yourself, while I slept. I didn't know a thing about it. It'll be my word against yours. Who do you suppose the jury's going to believe?"

"Interesting story. Not quite sure it fits with your original one. You know—Linda went to the store for aspirin and never returned?"

Baxter seethed but could think of no reply.

Melissa laughed. The sound drove Baxter's heels into the floor. "There are things you still don't know, Baxter. Besides, you want to take the chance on who they believe? You want to go through an arrest, a trial? Your name dragged through the mud? And let's not forget the strange death of wife number two. What if they reopen *that* case?"

Rage coursed through Baxter. He hunched forward and gripped the phone, his throat tightening at the too-recent memories. It wasn't his fault; he hadn't meant for any of that to happen. If Cherisse hadn't mouthed off in their bedroom at the end of a long day as he was inserting a wooden stretcher into his shoe. If she hadn't run out the door when he ordered her to stay, and if he hadn't followed, that stretcher still in his hand, and if she hadn't reached the top of the stairs as his arm pulled back and whammed that solid block of wood into the side of her head, and if she'd fallen sideways instead of forward—

"*Don't* you talk to me about Cherisse. Don't you *dare*."

"I don't care about Cherisse," Melissa shot back. "What I care about is the money. The price has just gone up, due to my circumstances. Which *you* caused. I want $300,000. *And* your deadline's been pushed up. Now it's Monday, ten a.m. That gives you time to get to the bank."

"I'm not giving you a *cent*."

"Fine. Then count on being arrested Tuesday. That's about how long it'll take them to dig up Linda's body. I know, because I asked. *Don't* think I won't talk, Baxter. Between you trying to kill me and the police looking for me, I'll have *no choice*. If your deadline passes and you haven't paid the money, I'm going straight back to the DA."

Baxter's eyes closed. He knew she meant it. She'd called him out of the blue last week after six years. Said she'd heard about Cherisse's death through happening to read the *Vonita Times* online—the issue with Joanne Weeks and her big mouth as the cover story. Melissa wanted money by Monday or she'd tell the police he'd killed Linda. Now pushed to the brink, if she didn't get her way, vindictive Melissa would pile it on. The tears, the manipulation, the wide-eyed innocence. The lies. Their affair would turn into his seduction. Or worse, statutory rape would become *forced* rape. And Linda's death . . .

Baxter straightened in his chair. His gaze roved through the glass doors to his beautiful backyard. The yard he'd enjoyed with two equally beautiful wives. How he'd missed Linda. How he now missed Cherisse.

He'd lost enough. He would never lose his freedom. His reputation, his life. *Never.*

"All right." The words lay bitter on his tongue. "Monday at ten. Three-hundred thousand."

He could hear the smirk over the phone line. "I knew you'd come around, Baxter."

They discussed drop-off details. He was to put the money in a box, taped up. Write the name "Ann" on top. Melissa gave him specific instructions to a place in the woods on the west side of 101.

"Leave it there, then get in your car and drive away," Melissa commanded. "And don't think I haven't thought through how it'll be picked up safely. I won't be such an easy target this time."

This was the scenario Baxter had so wanted to avoid. Better to trick Joanne Weeks into leading him to an unsuspecting Melissa than to try killing Melissa when she was on the alert. And that's exactly how she'd be when picking up his package. All the more now, thanks to his scheme being uncovered.

What a backfire. He never should have done it this way. He should have gone through with a fake drop-off, stayed around, and killed Melissa himself. But that would have involved buying a gun. Getting rid of another body. Too many trails.

"I don't ever want to hear from you again." Baxter's tone would freeze steel.

"Have a good life, Baxter. Just get me the money."

Melissa hung up.

Slowly, Baxter rose and replaced the phone. Anger surged through him. He couldn't even tell who he was more mad at—Melissa or his hired man. If they walked into his kitchen right now he'd strangle them both—with a smile on his face.

Wait.

What if Melissa's call was a ruse? Maybe she and Joanne were still trapped in the hotel and cooked up this story so he'd pull his man away from Joanne's car . . .

But if he did pull off his man, how would they know it? They couldn't be sure it was safe to leave.

Baxter paced to the refrigerator and back, shoving down his emotions, forcing himself to think logically. He pulled up short in front of the sliding glass door.

No. That kind of ruse would be too open-ended. Joanne was smarter than that.

For once Melissa had to be telling the truth. They'd escaped the hotel. As for the DA part, Joanne could have fed Melissa that information . . .

But she wouldn't be calling Baxter to blackmail him in front of Joanne. They must have parted ways.

Baxter unclipped his private cell from his waist and punched in a number. Mr. Idiot answered on the first ring.

"They got away, you moron. *Again.*"

"*What?* The car— "

"Strip the car of the GPS and go home. You can't be anywhere around that hotel."

"But— " His man huffed over the line. "So then what?"

Baxter related the exact spot in the woods to watch on Monday. "There will be a box there, with 'Ann' written on top. You got all this?"

"Written down. When's she coming?"

"I don't know. Anytime after ten. Just hide and watch."

"Okay."

"Don't miss. And I don't *ever* want her body found."

"When do I do the other lady?"

"We'll talk about her later."

"What about my leg, man? It's still got a bullet in it. I got it wrapped up, but it hurts like—"

"Dig it out yourself."

Baxter smacked off the call.

FORTY-SEVEN

After our initial shock over Melissa's disappearance, Dan jumped on the phone to the local police. Perry headed out to search for Melissa himself. "She couldn't have gotten far." He threw open Dan's front door and ran outside.

I stayed behind, too tired and sick at heart to hurry after him. Perry wouldn't find her anyway. She'd skulk in the dark until she was blocks from Dan's house. The police with their spotlights were more likely to locate her.

Back in Dan's kitchen I listened to him request that Hollister police put out a BOLO—Be On the LookOut—for Melissa. If found, she would be arrested. They'd bring her in on the gun charge *and* the material witness thing. A little time in jail should change her mind about testifying against Baxter. But the fact that Melissa was on foot made the BOLO more difficult to be effective. Police wouldn't have a certain car to be searching for. Who knew what friend Melissa might call to pick her up?

"She's likely to call Tony Whistman," I told Dan as soon as he got off the phone. "The guy she just broke up with."

Dan stood in his kitchen, one hand on his hip, the other drumming his granite countertop. He looked none too happy. "You know how to contact him?"

"I have his cell number. I don't know his address, but I can find that quickly enough if you get me on a computer."

Dan reached for the phone. "I can have his name run for his address and driver's license. For now I can put some fear in him, in case Melissa's already called. What's his number?"

If Melissa had phoned Tony, he could already be on his way to pick her up. Fortunately it would take him some time to reach Hollister.

"Just a sec." I hurried to the living room and pulled my notebook from my purse. Back in the kitchen, I rattled off the number. Dan punched in the digits, then hovered over the counter, head down.

I watched him listen to Tony's phone ring. Anxiety pinged through my system like wayward electrodes. My legs threatened to give out any minute. I so needed sleep, but I wasn't about to get it now. More than that, I needed a new life. No matter what happened here, Vonita would never be the same for me.

My body wobbled. I pulled out a kitchen chair and fell into it.

Dan's head came up. "Tony Whistman?" He paused. "This is Dan Marlahn, district attorney for San Benito County. I need to talk to you about Melissa Harkoff..."

My nerves jittered and bounced—and just like that, some internal fuse blew. My mind dulled. I listened to Dan's conversation with Tony as if he spoke from the opposite end of a long tunnel. Dan warned Tony that any help he gave Melissa in fleeing would be against the law, and Dan would personally come down hard on him. "Again, Tony, understand that if she cooperates with us as a witness in this case, we will protect her and keep her safe. And free. If she doesn't, she'll face jail time herself. If you care for her, you'll do the right thing by contacting us the minute she calls you."

My eyes closed. Dan's voice faded. My head lowered...

I jerked up. My eyes blinked open, struggling to focus.

Dan was eyeing me, his phone on the counter. "He claimed she hasn't called."

I pulled in a deep breath, straightened in the chair. "Think he's lying?"

"Don't know." He sighed. "We need to get you down to the station so they can take your statement."

I nodded. "You got something to eat first? I need some energy."

"Yeah, sure." Distracted, his mind clearly running a mile a minute, Dan pulled out some lunch meat and cheese. I scarfed it down and drank two glasses of water. Then a craving for Jelly Bellies hit. When this night was over, I was going on a serious binge.

Perry stomped in as I was eating, thoroughly frustrated. "No go." He leaned against a counter and frowned at the floor. A ticker tape of emotions scrolled across his features.

Dan made another phone call to police with three more requests. First, to alert hospital emergency room personnel in the San Jose area to contact them if a man came in with a bullet wound in the leg. Second, to tow in my car so a forensics team could go through it for fingerprints and other evidence, as well as checking for any hidden devices such as a GPS unit.

Great. Now I'd lost my car to police. No telling how long it would take to get it back.

Third, Dan sent an officer to run down a judge for a court order for Melissa's cell phone records.

"On a Sunday night?" I asked when he hung up. "Aren't you pushing it with some judge?"

He lifted a shoulder. "I need to get the process started. Once I get that order, it'll still take me maybe twenty-four hours to get the records—and that's if I keep after the cell phone company. Those guys are overwhelmed with requests. They'd take days if I let 'em."

Perry looked up. "You'll track her via cell phone towers?"

"Yeah. She makes a call, we'll be able to locate her."

I left the kitchen to visit the bathroom. As I washed my hands I stared at myself in the mirror. Bags under my eyes, my mouth pulled down with tiredness. I looked like a truck hit me.

The night stretched out, long and unknowable.

Sadness bubbled up within me. I leaned over the sink, hands

supporting me on either side. Forget finding Melissa, forget bringing Baxter to justice. Forget even skip tracing. I just wanted to crawl into a cave and hide. And sleep.

Dear God, please help me. I don't turn to you enough. But I really need you right now.

Guilt surfaced as soon as the prayer wafted heavenward. Melissa's cutting words rang in my ears. *"The only difference between you and Linda and Baxter and me is* I *don't claim to be a Christian."*

In the living room I pulled my cell from my purse and called Dineen.

"*Where* have you *been*?" My sister's voice thickened with sleep and worry.

"I'm fine. Safe. I'm … working on things. I'll call you later."

Perry and Dan joined me. Perry handed me my notebook. I would have left it in Dan's kitchen. The DA held the plastic bag containing the gun he'd taken from Melissa. "I'll lead you to the San Jose station in my own car," he said. "I want to be there for your statement, Joanne."

"San Jose?"

"The break-in and shooting took place in their jurisdiction."

Oh. Right.

During the drive, I leaned back against the headrest in Perry's passenger seat and closed my eyes. The lyrics to "Don't Worry, Be Happy" sludged through my brain.

"I have a theory," Perry said. "About why Baxter's suddenly gunning for Melissa after all these years."

"Mm. Why's that?"

"I think she's blackmailing him."

My eyes pried open. "Now? After six years?"

"After his second wife died in an 'accident.' "

I stared at the darkened road, the scenario sifting down inside me.

"But she didn't even know Cherisse had died."

"You sure about that?"

I thought back to when Melissa and I had first come face-to-face. "She acted like she didn't know."

"If she's blackmailing him, she surely wouldn't want *you* to know."

But then she'd lied to me. Or at least kept important information from me. And she wasn't just a victim …

Deep inside I sensed Perry was right. But I didn't want to believe it. If Melissa was blackmailing Baxter, what would that do to her testimony against him?

"Perry." I closed my eyes again. "You've just doubled my need for a Jelly Belly hit."

At the station, Dan and I gathered in a cramped interrogation room with Officer Harvey Slater, a blond-haired man in his midforties. The room held a single worn table and three chairs. Intimidating and overly hot, permeated with the smell of sweat. Perry cooled his heels in a waiting area. With tape and video running, I related my sordid tale—again—this time starting with my accusations toward Chief Eddington, which ended up in the Vonita weekly paper. Officer Slater and Dan questioned me like pros, dredging up details I'd forgotten to include.

As I spoke, my mind turned toward Melissa. Where was she right now? She couldn't have wandered far into the night. She would need help. Someone had to come pick her up.

Tony? A girlfriend?

"Obviously Melissa can't be trusted," I said at the end of the interview. "What if she doesn't even know where Linda is buried?"

Although if she didn't know, why was Baxter after her?

Unless it wasn't Baxter at all.

My head hurt.

Dan shrugged. "Once we pick her up we'll find out soon enough what she does and doesn't know. And we *will* pick her up. Once we get her cell records, all she's got to do is use that phone."

I pictured Melissa in Perry's car, urging me to tell her how to disappear. How much did she know already? "She may be smart enough to know she has to stop using it."

Dan stood up. "No matter what she knows—we know more. We'll get her."

When? Next week? Next month? A year from now? In the meantime, how was I supposed to live? Someone had followed me. Tried to kill me.

My watch read 1:45 a.m.

At the entrance to the station Dan and I met up with Perry. Dan placed his hand on my arm. "Joanne, thank you for all you've done. I know you're exhausted. Go get some sleep. I'll keep you informed."

I stared at him. "Sleep where?" I'd done all this for justice, for the police, and now Dan was just turning me loose? "I can't feel safe in my house. It doesn't even have an alarm. And I'm not about to lead any trouble to my sister's home."

The district attorney inclined his head. "I can put an officer on you. Not sure how long we can keep it up, but hopefully it won't have to be for long."

I understood just how much Dan was offering. Personal protection cost money—dollars the county didn't have.

"No need." Perry held up a hand. "She can sleep in my guestroom. I'll watch her. I've got a gun."

Dan managed a wry smile. "Legal?"

"No worries."

I shook my head. "Perry, I—"

He put warm fingers against my lips. "Hush, Joanne."

"But—"

"Hey, Dan." Officer Slater appeared around the corner, phone in his hand. "I got a Mountain View officer on the line, calling from El Camino Hospital. He just brought some guy into the emergency room with a bullet in his thigh."

I gasped, all thoughts of sleeping at Perry's house falling away.

"All right." Dan took the phone from Slater. "Hi, District Attorney Dan Marlahn here. How bad's the wound? I don't want him walking out of there."

He listened.

"What does he say happened?"

Perry and I looked at each other. *Self-inflicted*, he mouthed. *Accident.*

"Does it look self-inflicted?"

Perry smiled.

"Okay. Stay with him. *Do not* let him leave. I'll send somebody to get him. And make sure the doctor gives you the bullet." Dan hurried to the counter, mouthing to the officer behind it for pen and paper. "What's the guy's name?" He wrote, asked a few more questions, and wrote some more. "Great. Thanks."

Dan handed the paper to the officer. "Run this guy for me." He gave the phone back to Officer Slater. "We got lucky. This officer, Miles, makes a routine stop for speeding, runs the guy's name, and finds a slew of unpaid moving violations, plus priors. Guy's name is Edgar Trovky, from San Jose. Then Miles notices Trovky's leg bleeding through a bandage. Guy gives some cockamamie story about shooting himself accidentally and how he's scared of hospitals and doesn't want to go. Miles doesn't buy it. He takes Trovky into custody for the unpaids, first stop—emergency room. Then he hears a boatload from the emergency doc about being on the lookout for a guy with a bullet in his thigh." Dan shook his head. "Sometimes the stars just align right."

Slater smiled. "Trovky." He thought a minute. "I think there was a Trovky on some burglary awhile back."

Dan grunted. "Can you go get this guy? I want to be present for his questioning. The bullet missed anything major. They'll get it out pretty quickly."

"Yeah, I'll go." Slater gestured with his chin toward the other officer. "I'll just wait for the rap sheet."

Officer Slater turned out to be right. Edgar Trovky's priors included jail time for a burglary, plus a couple of assaults. Age forty-eight. Six feet in height and 180 pounds.

The right build for Hooded Man.

"Let me stay," I blurted to Dan. "I want to hear the interview."

"I can't let you in the room."

"Don't they have one of those rooms here where I can listen from somewhere else? Watch through a one-way window?" I knew I was pushing, but I didn't care. No way could I just pack it in for the night now. "Maybe I'll think of something for you to ask him, based on what he says. Some detail I forgot to tell you."

Maybe my mind would turn to total mush, and I wouldn't think of a thing. Maybe this wasn't even our man.

The district attorney surveyed me.

"Come on, Dan."

He sighed. "Okay."

FORTY-EIGHT

AUGUST 2004

The hours after dinner dragged on like they would never end. Melissa's nerves sizzled as she waited for Baxter to get Linda out of the house. But as 7:00 turned into 8:00, and 8:00 to 9:00, with Baxter watching a movie in the den, it became clear he wasn't going to do anything. Frustrated to the core, Melissa couldn't stand to look at either Linda or Baxter. She retreated into her bedroom to watch TV. The previous month on one of their shopping sprees, Linda had bought her a flat screen television and her own VCR. Came in handy when she wanted to be by herself.

At 9:30 Melissa went down to the kitchen, telling herself she wanted a soda. She slowed as she passed the den, eyeing the backs of Linda's and Baxter's heads. They sat on opposite ends of the couch. How romantic. Melissa wondered if there was an ounce of love left in their marriage.

She opened a cabinet in the kitchen and shut it hard, scooted a chair in closer to the table. Made just enough noise to announce her presence to the adjoining room. As she was pulling a can out of the refrigerator, Baxter wandered in. Melissa caught his eye and raised her shoulders in a silent, *"Well?"* He walked to a cabinet and took out a glass. Stuck it under the freezer's outer compartment and pushed a button. As ice clinked into the glass he whispered, "Go to bed. I'll come to you."

Melissa pulled her head back, eyes widening.

Baxter pushed the button for water and waited until the glass filled. Without another word, without even looking at Melissa, he left the kitchen.

What was he thinking? Coming to her room at night was crazy. What if Linda woke up? What if she found them together? If Baxter thought his wife would keep quiet about a thing like that, he was too full of himself. Linda was on the edge already. No telling what she'd do. Only sheer stupidity on her part kept her from seeing what was going on under her nose already. Or maybe Linda did sense it on some level but couldn't bear to *see*. She could only deny. What was one more coat of polish over her rusting life?

Melissa leaned against the counter, head down, her soda forgotten. This train she'd boarded was picking up too much speed. It just might jump the tracks. Then where would she be?

At the same time, the very thought of being with Baxter tonight—with Linda in the house—left her breathless. Just proved how much Baxter wanted her. How much stronger in this triangle she was becoming.

Linda deserved whatever she got.

Melissa picked up the can of soda and headed for her bedroom.

There she took a shower. Put on a pair of pink silk shorty pajamas. She slipped into bed, turned out the lights. Turned the TV on low . . . and waited.

Ten o'clock ticked to 10:30. Melissa's eyes focused on the television, seeing nothing. She thought of her future. Maybe she could take a bunch of correspondence courses and get out of high school a year early. Go straight into studying for her real estate license. She could be an agent by eighteen. Make her first million by twenty.

"You'll never be nuthin' but trailer trash." Her mother's voice sneered through Melissa's head.

Yeah, right. Just where was her mother now? And where was Melissa? She ran a hand over her satiny sheets. Living in more luxury than her ignorant mother could have ever dreamed of, that's where.

The clock read 11:00. About the time Baxter and Linda went to bed.

At midnight Melissa rose for a glass of water. By the light of the television screen, she made her way to the bathroom. She could not begin to think of sleep.

At 12:30 Melissa was sitting straight up in bed, limbs tense. If Baxter didn't show up she would really let him have it tomorrow. She traced circles on her bedcovers, flipped through TV channels just like Baxter would do. Throwing down the remote, she jumped from bed and paced. On one pass by her desk chair she stopped, toying with the idea of dragging it over to the heater vent in the ceiling to listen. But if Baxter showed up at the wrong moment ...

She flung herself back into pacing.

Twelve-forty-five.

Okay, this waiting was getting plain *maddening.* This was exactly why she wanted to make her own way in life. She wouldn't wait for or on anybody. She'd have a dozen men working for *her.* She'd say "jump" and they'd jump.

Melissa got back into bed. Wouldn't do for Baxter to catch her walking the floor. *If* the man came at all.

He was probably doing this on purpose. Just to keep her in her place. The thought made her nerves sizzle.

Guess again, Baxter, who keeps who in place? What do you suppose would happen to you if I told people how you treat your wife?

At 12:50 her door opened without a knock. Just like that. Baxter slipped inside. Beyond him the hall was dark. He closed her door and locked it.

He hurried over to her bed and sat down, eyeing her with supreme satisfaction. "Told you I'd come."

"Where's Linda?"

"Asleep."

"What's to keep her that way?"

His lips curved in a slow smile. "I insisted she take a sleeping pill because she's been tossing and turning lately. She's *out*."

Melissa gave him a seductive look. "Nice going, Mr. Jackson." She reached for the remote and turned off the TV.

FORTY-NINE

FEBRUARY 2010

Two-fifty a.m.

A half hour ago Dan had heard from the forensics team that had gone over my car. They found no GPS. They did lift two sets of fingerprints.

Great. Those would be mine and Melissa's.

Had we read this all wrong?

Edgar Trovky slumped in his chair at the interrogation table, his wounded leg sticking straight out and the other jiggling. His hands laced and unlaced on the worn wood. Dan sat on one side of him, a finger at his upper lip. On the other side Officer Slater leaned forward, arms on the table. From the corner of a room a small camera was running.

Two sealed evidence bags sat on the table.

Perry and I watched through a one-way window from an adjacent room, just as small. The metal chairs were hard. My back ached and my eyes were gritty. Perry perched in his seat, alert as ever. The tilt of his body belied his thoughts—he'd give anything to exchange places with the officer.

I prayed Edgar Trovky would lead us to Baxter.

He'd come into the room limping, his expression hard as sour candy. His eyes were deep-set and beady, his gaze bouncing around as if every corner menaced. He had a narrow face, thin lips. Buzz-cut hair. His voice sounded nothing like the gravel of Hooded Man. But maybe that voice had been put on just to frighten me. Hooded Man had done everything else he could to scare me, from meeting me on that dark road to wearing a bloody mask. All to push me into finding Melissa as fast as possible.

What a pawn I'd been.

But if my mistakes led us to Baxter in the end, it would be worth it.

For the first fifteen minutes of the interview, Slater asked Trovky about everything except the bullet wound in his leg. Where he worked, what family he had, his hobbies, how long he'd lived in San Jose. I half listened, vacillating between frustration and fascination. Trovky's initial answers were in monosyllable. But little by little Slater opened him up until he was speaking in full sentences, offering information.

"He's a good interrogator," Perry said in a low voice. "He's read the guy. Now he's making him comfortable."

"So." Slater bounced a finger against the table. "What happened to your leg?"

Trovky's face clouded. "It was an accident, like I told the doc. I was cleaning my gun and it went off."

Slater nodded. "How'd you manage that?"

"It just went off."

"You were holding it how?"

Trovky focused on the table. "Like this." He mimed holding a gun, pointing it downward.

"Odd angle to clean a weapon."

Trovky shrugged.

"You had it pointed straight down?"

"Yeah."

"Hm." Slater leaned to the side of his chair and fisted his hip. "The doctor said the bullet entered your leg at an angle, higher in front, headed lower. If you had the gun pointed straight down, the bullet would have gone straight inside your leg."

Trovky shrugged again. "Okay. It was angled."

"Pretty odd position for your hand."

No response.

"What kind of gun is it?"

Trovky's eyes jerked to the floor. "Don't remember."

"You don't *remember*?"

"Uh-uh."

"When did this … accident happen?"

"Just before I got in the car, and then the cop pulled me over."

"Just before."

"Yeah."

"You're sure."

"Yup."

Slater and Dan exchanged a look. The officer refocused on Trovky. "See, that's what I'm not getting. The doc said for sure that bullet had been in there at least a couple hours."

"You can't keep me here. I ain't done nothin'."

"He's lying," I said to Perry.

"Yeah. Question is, about what? Somebody other than Melissa could have shot him."

Slater tilted his head. "You've got eight unpaid moving violations. That we know for sure. We *can* do something about that."

Trovky's mouth tightened. He glared at the wall.

Slater reached for the evidence bags, moved them around. Trovky's eyes snapped to the bags.

"What's in there?"

"I want you to tell me about your 'cleaning accident' again."

"What's in the bags?"

"You first."

"I told you, man!" Trovky repeated his story.

"Where's the gun?"

"At home. You think I'm gonna bring it with me to the hospital?"

Slater sniffed and moved the bags around some more. "If you're lying, we'll know. In one of these bags is the gun I'm willing to bet shot you. And in the other is the bullet taken from your leg. I'm thinking they're going to match."

Trovky went very still. Then shrugged. "So do your testing."

The three men sat in silence.

Dan spoke up. "There was a home invasion this evening at 264 Anniston in San Jose. You know anything about that?"

"Nope."

"Where were you this evening from six o'clock on?"

In his house, alone, Trovky replied. He'd been sleeping. Then cleaned his gun.

Perry and I exchanged a glance. No alibi.

Out of the blue I began to shake.

Maybe it was my thorough exhaustion, maybe frustration. Throw in my roiling anger at the lies and hypocrisy of Baxter Jackson. He'd gotten away with Linda's murder for six years. Despite all I'd tried, he just might win. If this man didn't crack—*if* he was the right man at all—and we didn't find Melissa, Baxter would keep right on living as king of Vonita, head elder at my church. The thought made me want to throw up.

Perry reached for my shoulder and steadied me. Without that I may have fallen out of my chair. "You okay?"

I managed a wan smile. Patted his hand. "Yeah. Thanks."

"You need sleep."

"I need justice."

Dan and Slater went over Trovky's story as to his whereabouts three times. The man wouldn't budge.

Perry scooted his chair next to mine. I leaned against him. My head weighed a thousand pounds.

Slater leaned forward. "You know Melissa Harkoff?"

"No."

"How about Baxter Jackson?"

"Never heard of him."

"Think hard."

"I don't *know* them!"

"Where were you last night between eight thirty and nine o'clock?"

"At home. Alone." In his anger, Trovky's voice was lowering, turning rougher.

"You sure are home alone a lot."

Trovky lifted a shoulder.

"You know Joanne Weeks?"

"No."

Hooded Man.

An invisible hand pulled me out of my chair. I headed for the door.

"Joanne." Perry rose. "What are you doing?"

"That's him. That's his voice."

I strode out of the room, knocked on the interrogation door. Stood aside before it opened so Trovky couldn't see me. Dan came out, closed the door behind him.

"It's him. I know the voice."

I wanted to shout. I wanted to hit something.

"You sure?"

"Can you make him show you his left hip? That's where my car nicked him. It should be bruised." Trovky hadn't favored that hip when he walked in. He'd had too much of a limp on his right leg.

"Okay."

"Let me go back in with you."

"No, Joanne."

"*I'll* question him. I'll *make* him talk."

"Slater knows what he's doing. If this is your man, we'll get there."

"It's *him*!"

"Okay, Joanne! Now go sit down."

Perry appeared and started to pull me away. I tried to shake him off. He pulled harder. Dan slipped back into the room.

"Perry, leave me *alone*."

"Joanne, you want to ruin this now? Let them do their job."

"They're not doing it fast enough!" My voice rose.

"Be *quiet*."

"I just want—"

"Joanne." Perry yanked me away from the interrogation room.

"I just want—"

"Jo-*anne*."

He pulled me into our area and closed the door. I smacked his hand away from my arm. Rage boiled up within me. This wasn't working. Trovky would lie his way out of this. Baxter would walk.

Linda, why *didn't you talk to me?*

My eyes burned. I fell into my chair.

Just like that the anger blitzed away, replaced with utter exhaustion. My head lowered. "I'm sorry. I just want people to stop *lying*."

Perry sat down and pulled me into his arms. His chin rested on top of my head. "I know, Joanne. I know."

FIFTY

At 3:45 a.m. Edgar Trovky cracked.

The ironic part? Officer Slater lied in order to break him.

Slater had taken the two evidence bags out of the interrogation room, telling Trovky someone would be running a firing test on them right away. Later he left again and returned with "the results": the gun and bullet matched.

"You're looking at some heavy-duty time here." Slater tapped his fingers against the table in slow metronome. "But we know this wasn't your idea. We can make you a deal. You tell us what you know about Baxter Jackson, and we'll go easy on you."

Trovky stared at the floor. "I can't go back to jail for years, man. My girlfriend's pregnant."

"So talk to us."

Trovky's eyes bounced from Slater to Dan and back. "How do I know I can trust you?"

Slater gestured toward Dan. "The DA's sitting right here. He calls the shots."

Trovky thought it over. Then talked.

Melissa *was* blackmailing Baxter.

No. My mouth opened. I exchanged a long look with Perry.

In response to the blackmail, Trovky said, Baxter schemed to have Melissa killed before his payment deadline. That's where Trovky came in, as of last Thursday. He'd contacted Trovky through a common acquaintance — a construction worker out of a job and eager to make a fast $1,000 for the introduction.

Tony Whistman's words surfaced in my brain: *"She got all weird on me and took off three days ago."* After Melissa first contacted Baxter, she must have been paranoid he'd try to hunt her down — scared enough to leave the place she'd lived in for the last few months and lie low in someone else's house.

"Was that you in the mask and hooded jacket that stopped Joanne Weeks on the road?" Slater asked.

"She hit me with that 4Runner. You should arrest her."

"What about at her house later that evening? You again?"

"Baxter wanted a GPS on her car."

"You put one on her 4Runner?"

"So I could know where she was."

"Where's that GPS now?"

"After they got away from the hotel, Baxter told me to take it off and get out of there. I threw it in a dumpster. Soon after that the cop stopped me."

Just to hear the GPS *had* been on my car. And that this murderer was waiting outside that hotel for us. If Perry hadn't come . . . I turned and gave him a long look.

"Where's the dumpster?" Slater asked.

Trovky told him. I knew Slater would send someone out to pick up the GPS.

"Okay." Slater thought a moment. "Just curious — what was with the garage door at Ms. Weeks' house? You slam it on purpose?"

Trovky lifted a shoulder. "I was leaving. The wind blew it out of my hands."

Another vindication. I *hadn't* been crazy.

Slater nodded. "What about Joanne Weeks? Did Baxter Jackson want you to kill her too?"

Trovky glared at the wall. "I think I'm done now."

"You want to take the rap for this whole thing?"

Trovky's mouth worked. He stuck his fingers into his scalp and rubbed. "No."

"Then keep talking."

A long moment passed before Trovky spoke again. "Yeah, he wanted that Joanne lady dead too."

The words blazed through my head. I closed my eyes, picturing Baxter Jackson in my house, pretending to set things right between us so he could worship at church. The sincerity he'd feigned in front of our pastor. How did people *do* that? How could a so-called Christian, a man who *knew* the truth of Christ, lead such a double life?

Slater leaned forward, folded arms on the table. "Why did he want her dead?"

"I don't know. I suppose so she couldn't figure out what happened and talk to you guys."

My whole body tingled. I could be dead right now. I was supposed to be *dead*.

Perry put an arm around my shoulder and rubbed.

"How much was Baxter going to pay you for Melissa Harkoff's murder?" Slater asked.

Trovky swung his head toward the wall, clearly brooding over his loss. "Ten thousand."

"And for Joanne Weeks?"

"Yeah."

"Yeah what?"

"Another ten thousand."

"Twenty thousand dollars all together."

Trovky lowered his forehead into his palm. "Me and my girlfriend need that money, man."

Dan and Slater exchanged a look.

"You get paid any up front?" Slater wanted to know.

"Half of it."

"Ten thousand? Five for each hit?"

"Yeah."

"Cash?"

"Yeah."

"When was this?"

"Thursday."

Slater tapped his bottom lip. "So you said Baxter called you tonight with a change of plans."

Trovky winced and shifted his wounded leg. "These chairs are hard."

"We'll try to wrap up here quick as we can, but there are still a lot of things we need to go over. You need something to drink?"

"You got Coke?"

Dan left the room and returned with a can of Coke.

The DA kept a poker face as the questioning about Baxter's schemes against Melissa's blackmail continued. But I knew from the tilt of his body, his knuckles brushing the edge of the table, that his mind whirled. Blackmail was illegal. His star witness had just dulled considerably. Even if he did find Melissa, if she did lead him to Linda's body, this was going to be one huge mess to sort out.

I closed my eyes and rubbed my forehead. Had all I'd lived through in the past thirty hours been for nothing?

"So now when's this drop-off payment supposed to take place?" Slater asked Trovky.

"Ten o'clock Monday morning."

Six hours from now.

"And you're supposed to watch the site and take out Melissa when she comes to pick up the money?"

Trovky's eyes pinged from Slater to Dan. "Yeah."

"You know when she's coming?"

"Nope. I was just supposed to wait till she showed up."

"What about Joanne Weeks?"

The suspect shrugged. "He said we'd talk about that later."

Later. Baxter still planned to kill me.

By the time the whole tale had unraveled, it was 5:00 a.m. My second full night without sleep. *Zombie* didn't begin to describe me.

Dan and Slater stepped out of the interrogation room for a moment, leaving a sullen Trovky inside. I met them in the hall as they conferred in low tones, Perry at my side. "You're going to arrest Baxter now, right?"

Perry touched me on the shoulder. "Joanne— "

"We need more on him," Dan said. "We want to be absolutely sure the charge of solicitation of murder sticks."

"What about murdering his *wife*?"

Slater shrugged. "That comes next, once we've discovered the body. Hopefully one thing will lead to another. But we have to catch Melissa."

"You will now. You can just watch the drop-off point for her, right?"

"That's the plan."

"So then you'll have Baxter in custody, and Melissa will have to talk." I looked from the officer to the DA, gripping my upper arms. I so wanted to believe everything was going to work out.

"Baxter won't talk," Slater said. "He'll lawyer up the minute we start asking questions."

"So you'll just let him *go*?"

Slater sizzled me with a look. The press of his mouth and hardness of his eyes betrayed his own tiredness. He'd been up all night questioning a witness, and he didn't need some uppity woman telling him what to do. Dan put both hands on his hips. The overhead light played up the circles beneath his eyes. "Joanne, why don't you go get some sleep? There's nothing more you can do here."

"*Why* can't you— "

"We'll handle this, okay?" Slater thrust his face at me. "Dan's right. You should go home."

My jaw tightened. "In case you hadn't noticed, I don't *have* a safe home to go to until Baxter's off the streets."

"Whoa, both of you." Dan held up his hands.

Perry squeezed my arm, nudging me away. I would not be moved.

"Okay, let's just ease off." The DA gestured toward the room where Perry and I had sat. "You want to stay here awhile longer, fine. Just ... you've done all you can now, Joanne. It's time to let us handle this thing."

That was a little too hard. And I was a lot too tired. *This thing* meant my life.

I would not rest until I saw Baxter Jackson in handcuffs.

FIFTY-ONE

AUGUST 2004

With Baxter in Melissa's room, time flipped into warp speed. The outside world didn't matter. When Melissa happened to glance at her clock again it read 1:35 a.m.

Baxter followed her gaze and sighed. "I need to go."

He slid from bed and started rooting around the floor for his clothes. Moonlight spilled through the window, illuminating the room in a pale haze. Baxter picked up Melissa's pajamas and tossed them to her. She slipped them on. He stood and ran a hand through his hair.

"We're going to be tired tomorrow."

She smiled. "You saying it wasn't worth it?"

"I— "

A knock hit the door.

They froze. Melissa stared at Baxter in horror.

"Quick," she whispered, "get in the closet."

He came to life. With long, quiet strides he scurried toward the walk-in, edged inside, and pulled the door closed.

Another knock. Louder this time. The handle turned back and forth.

Melissa cast a frantic look around the floor, searching for anything Baxter may have left behind. The rug was empty.

She clamped down inside, calming herself. "Yeah?" Her voice came out sleepy and thick.

"Unlock the door, Melissa."

Heart beating in her throat, Melissa padded across the room. She turned the lock and opened her door to a lit hallway, her eyes squinting against the light. Linda stood in her pajamas, hair mussed and circles beneath her eyes.

Melissa frowned. "What's going on?"

"Have you seen Baxter?"

"Baxter. No. What do you mean?"

"He's gone." Linda's voice edged. "I can't find him."

"Did you look downstairs? Maybe he can't sleep."

"I've looked everywhere." Linda leaned forward, peering past Melissa into the room. Suspicion etched her forehead.

"Is his car here?"

"Yes, I checked."

Melissa ran a hand across her eyes. "Well, I don't … do you want me to help you l—?"

"Is he in here, Melissa?" The question came hard, brittle.

"What?"

"You heard me."

"Why would he be in here?"

Linda shot her a twisted look of grief and fury. "When I came back up the stairs I thought I heard voices."

"In *here*? No way, I was sleeping."

Linda pulled herself up straight. Her bleary eyes looked deep into Melissa's. "Open the door all the way. I want to see inside the room."

"*What?* What's wrong with you?"

"Open the door!"

Melissa lifted her hand in an annoyed gesture and stood back. Linda swept past her into the bedroom. The woman strode to the middle of the carpet, turning her head right and left, shooting penetrating looks in the dim illumination from the hallway. She thrust a hand in her hair, then stumbled over to check on the other side of the desk, the dressers.

"Linda, *what* are you looking for?"

A moan escaped from Linda's throat. For a moment she drew up, disoriented, as if waking from a surreal dream. Then she hurried around the foot of the bed and to the other side, checking the floor between it and the wall.

Not a sound from the closet, a mere eight feet away from where Linda stood. Melissa pictured Baxter inside, taut-necked and holding his breath.

"Come on, Linda." Melissa gestured toward the hall, her tone low and patient, as if cajoling a child. "We need to go through the house. What if Baxter's hurt somewhere? We have to go look."

"If he's hurt, let him lie there." Linda's words flattened. "I hope he *is* hurt."

Melissa swallowed. Just what had Baxter drugged Linda with — truth serum? "I hear you. I felt that way about my mom lots of times."

Linda raised her chin and fixed a sickened and weary look upon Melissa. "You have no idea how I feel." She swayed.

"Okay, that's it." Melissa hurried toward her. "I'm getting you back to bed before you fall over. I'll look for Baxter."

Linda's gaze cut left and glued itself on the closet door. Melissa saw the horrifying thought ripple across her face. Melissa reached for her arm, but Linda yanked away from her and veered drunkenly for the closet.

"What are you doing?" Melissa leapt after her, grabbed the back of her pajamas.

Linda whirled around. "Let go of me!"

"You were about to walk into the wall."

"Let *go*!" She slapped both hands on Melissa's chest and pushed. Melissa staggered backward. Linda jumped toward the closet, hand outstretched toward the knob. Melissa fought for her footing, one arm smacking the wall. She cursed and threw herself forward. "Stop!"

Too late. Linda flung the door open. The walk-in gaped black, vague shapes of clothes hanging from long rods on both sides. Her fingers scrabbled around the inside wall, searching for the light switch.

In that split second everything Melissa had built in the last two months, everything she'd fought for blazed before her eyes. Her muscles gathered to spring toward Linda, to *stop* her—and just like that the flame died out. Melissa's limbs slackened. She straightened, hands on her hips, mouth twisting. So Linda wanted to know, did she?

Fine.

Linda's finger found the switch. Light flooded the closet.

FIFTY-TWO

FEBRUARY 2010

A ringing yanked Baxter from toss-driven sleep. He registered the sound of his special cell phone — and his veins flooded with dread. No light shone through the windows. He checked the nightstand clock.

Five-thirty-two a.m.

His hand reached across the mattress, pulled the phone close. "*What* is it?"

"I got Joanne Weeks in my sights."

He blinked a few times. "Right now?"

"Been watching her house. She just got home in her car. I can do her now. That still what you want?"

Baxter thought a minute. "You can break into her house and get to her before she hears anything?" The last thing he needed was for his man to get caught now, before he could kill Melissa.

"I got in there Saturday night, didn't I?"

Baxter sat up on the side of his bed. "So do it."

"I get my money for killing her, right?"

"Sure — after you take care of Melissa."

"The other half for both of them. Ten thousand dollars total."

"*After* you take care of Melissa."

"How we going to meet up?"

"We'll talk about that *after* you take care of Melissa. You lose her, the deal's off."

"I won't lose her."

"Call me when it's done."

"You got it."

Baxter clicked off the line.

FIFTY-THREE

Perched on the edge of my seat, I watched Edgar Trovky pull the cell phone from his ear and punch off the call. The phone was wired up to a recording device that had captured every word. He set the phone on the table with a *clack*. Leaned back in his chair. "Happy now?"

Dan nodded. "I'm happy."

Slater regarded Trovky, his head tilted. "You did good."

Trovky snorted. "Give me a dog biscuit."

My watch read 5:35.

My body felt numb. Coated inside with cold oil.

Perry gripped my hand. "You did it, Joanne. They've got enough to bring Baxter in now."

I did it? I'd sat here for the last few hours feeling absolutely helpless.

Perry shook his head as if reading my thoughts. He leaned close to me. I could see golden flecks in his eyes. How had I never seen them before? "If you hadn't chased down Melissa, if you hadn't thought quick on your feet and taken her to the DA, we wouldn't be here right now."

I held his gaze, then slowly, solemnly nodded. "You helped. We did it together."

Relief and satisfaction, grief and a fulfilled sense of justice swept through me. My head lowered. I wanted to cry.

But I wasn't done yet.

An officer took Trovky away to jail. While Dan made a phone call to Chief Eddington, Perry and I stood like immovable boulders in the hallway. Slater told us to go home—again. It was over.

It wasn't over.

At 6:15 Dan faced Perry and me, hands on his hips. He'd just gotten off the phone with Chief Eddington. Dan and Slater would meet the chief at the small Vonita station, then drive to Baxter Jackson's house, each man in his own car. More police vehicles would follow, carrying a team to search Baxter's house. Slater's vehicle would transport Baxter to the San Jose jail. Dan wanted to be present at the arrest and as Baxter was brought in for questioning. When Baxter learned that his man had squealed, their call had been recorded, and police would be present to intercept Melissa at the drop-off point, maybe, just maybe he'd break.

More likely he'd call an attorney faster than I could reach for a Jelly Belly bag.

"Bet I know why you're still here." Dan looked from Perry to me.

I gave him a slow blink. I knew I looked dead on my feet. No matter, I'd push through. "One more car's not going to hurt anything."

"Chief Eddington wouldn't like it."

"I don't care what Chief Eddington likes."

"Joanne, this is just pure revenge now."

I pulled back my head. "No, Dan. It's pure justice. For my best friend."

They'd almost delayed picking up Baxter. Slater and Dan had discussed the pros and cons of allowing him to make the money drop-off first. They didn't want word of his arrest to somehow reach Melissa. If she didn't visit the drop-off site, she'd be harder to locate, and they'd have to hope she used her cell phone. But they couldn't trust that Baxter wouldn't take matters into his own hands and come after either me or Melissa. In the end Dan and Slater decided a quiet, early morning arrest would be the best choice. Chief Eddington would keep a lid on it as long as possible, giving them a chance to pick up Melissa.

Five minutes after my conversation with Dan, Perry and I headed out in the caravan toward Vonita. My 4Runner would be kept by police as evidence. No telling when I would get it back.

Small price to pay.

My head lolled as Perry drove his SUV away from the San Jose station. "I'm sorry you got pulled into this, Perry." My mouth felt like mush.

"You kiddin'? I got to rescue two women from a killer and kick in a door, all in one night."

I lay back against the headrest. "And you figured out the blackmail part."

He stopped at a red light. "I'm good."

"You and your detective novels."

Perry turned his head and gave me a long, slow smile. "They filled the spaces."

Filled—past tense. I held his meaningful gaze until my courage failed—and I looked away.

We rode the rest of the way in thrumming silence.

At the Vonita station Dan and Slater got out of their cars to greet Eddington. The chief looked none too happy. I wanted to scream and dance. I wanted to fall over and sleep.

Chief Eddington glanced at Perry's car, then pointedly ignored us. My presence surely prickled him, but he would never show it.

We hit the Jackson driveway at 7:15. Two more vehicles, carrying the officers who would search Baxter's house, had joined the procession.

A realization struck me. How few times I'd gone up that drive. Linda had always come to my house, even during the day when Baxter was at work. As if she needed to step out of her life to be with me. Perhaps within her own unhappy walls she knew in my presence her mask would have slipped.

Perry and I were last in the lineup. As the circular drive swept up toward the porch, Perry hung back. We didn't need to be that close. Just close enough. Dan, Slater, and the chief stopped near the steps, the two other cars behind them. All three got out of their cars. Dan stayed by his while Slater and the chief mounted the stairs to the grand porch. Slater rang the bell.

An eternal, heart-stopping moment followed. Had Baxter somehow known we were coming and slipped away?

The front door opened. Baxter appeared, hand on the doorknob.

A rush of air escaped my mouth. I leaned forward, clutching the dashboard, and riveted my eyes upon him.

Baxter Jackson looked nothing like the king of Vonita now. Nothing like the respected head elder at church. His clothes were rumpled, his usually perfect hair out of place. Lines etched his face, as if he hadn't slept.

Slater spoke. I couldn't hear the words, but I knew he was informing Baxter of his arrest.

Baxter's face turned wooden. He looked from his old friend Chief Eddington to Officer Slater. His hand slipped from the door, fell to hang limply at his side.

Slater took hold of Baxter's arm and nudged him outside. Then turned him around and snapped cuffs on him.

In my mind I saw Linda lowering her shirt. *"I didn't get those bruises by running into a door."*

My hand fumbled for the car door. I opened it.

As they escorted Baxter down his own steps to Slater's waiting car, I got out of Perry's SUV and moved to stand by the hood. Arms folded. Like a soldier. Watching.

Baxter caught my movement. His head turned toward me. For a blazing moment our eyes met.

His head jerked away, his mouth twisting.

The last six years rushed over me. In that split second they were all worth it — every day I'd pounded walls because of Baxter, every minute I'd suffered. His expression said, *You win, Joanne. I lose. And I'll hate you to my dying day for it.*

Good, Baxter. That's just fine by me.

Slater put Baxter in his back seat. Shut the door.

The evidence team entered Baxter's house.

I didn't move until the three vehicles circled around the gracious driveway and turned onto the street, headed for the police station.

FIFTY-FOUR

AUGUST 2004

Melissa froze. The sudden light in the closet shown harshly on Baxter, crouched in the back.

Linda stilled, her hands up in front of her, fingers spread. She gaped at her husband as if he were some ghastly apparition.

No one moved. Baxter's mouth opened but no sound came.

A growling cry escaped Linda's throat, full of despair and hatred and rage. At the threshold of the closet she tilted to one side, nearly fell over. Her right hand gripped the door jamb, and she caught herself. Slowly she straightened, her knuckles blanching white.

"I *knew* it!" she screamed, her head tilted back, a throbbing pulse in her neck. "I knew it, I knew it!" She heaved herself backward, fingers dug into her scalp. Her wild, glazed eyes rose toward the ceiling. Abruptly she swiveled and hurtled out the door.

"I'll ruin you both right *now*!" Linda's threat shrieked through the air. Melissa heard her footsteps pound down the stairs.

Baxter jumped up. "Linda, stop!" He ran after her.

A terrifying sequence shot through Melissa's head. Linda would call Joanne Weeks. Or jump in her car and screech over there.

Melissa raced out of the room behind Baxter.

They hit the stairs. Melissa slipped at the top one and crashed into Baxter. He cursed, grabbed the banister. Melissa righted herself, and they tore down the rest of the way.

From the kitchen rolled the sound of Linda's wrenching sobs.

"Linda!" Baxter raced across the hall and around the corner into the kitchen. He skidded to a halt. Melissa nearly ran into him a second time. She swerved to his right and stopped in her tracks.

Linda stood six feet away, both hands pointing a butcher knife toward her husband. Her feet were far apart, her teeth bared like a feral animal. "*Don't* you come near me."

Baxter raised his hands. "What do you think you're doing? Put that down right now." He stepped toward her.

"Don't!" Linda's cheeks flamed. She jabbed at the air, hands shaking.

"Put it down now, Linda. Or I promise you'll be sorry."

Fear stretched her expression. She held on tighter than ever. Melissa took in Baxter's slitted eyes, the rock of his jaw. She'd never seen him so angry. She looked back to Linda, unpredictable and crazed. Melissa knew how sharp that butcher knife was. Many a time she'd watched it glide through meat. Panic bloomed in her head.

Four diagonal feet away from Melissa sat the butcher block of knives on the counter.

"Linda, put it *down*!" Spittle flew from Baxter's teeth.

"I'll cut you, Baxter, so help me." Linda brandished the huge knife. "You and your perfect little Christian self."

Nothing would be the same after this night, nothing. "You're not going to win this, Linda," Melissa spat. "Two against one."

Linda sneered at her husband. "How cute. Now you have a sixteen-year-old protecting you. Were you that helpless in *bed* too?"

Baxter's eyes shot fire. He lunged at his wife.

"No!" Linda carved the knife through the air. Baxter dodged to one side. The blade whooshed inches from his arm.

Melissa darted for the butcher's block and yanked out a carving knife.

Baxter whipped upright and leapt for Linda again. She cringed to her right, fell into the counter. Her clenched hands sank, but she fought to keep hold of the knife. "Stay aw—"

Her husband balled a fist and smashed it into her cheek. Bone crunched. Linda's head ricocheted. Her eyes flattened.

Linda's stubborn hands thrust the butcher knife upward. Baxter swung away.

Melissa darted behind Linda, her own blade raised.

Keening moans spilled from Linda's lips. She staggered a step toward Baxter, knife swinging. Her cries climbed higher, higher, until Melissa's brain would explode with the sound.

Baxter jumped to the side and hit the stove. Linda closed in, screaming like a madwoman sacrificing on the altar. She raised her blade high, pointed down.

Melissa gritted her teeth, jumped behind Linda, and plunged the carving knife deep into her back.

The scream cut off with a gasp. Linda's head rolled to one side, almost in slow motion. The butcher knife clattered to her feet. A strangling sound rose in her throat.

Melissa pulled shaking fingers from the knife handle.

Linda slumped to the hardwood floor.

FIFTY-FIVE

FEBRUARY 2010

Perry offered again to let me sleep in his guest room. He needed to get to his store, so I'd still be alone. "But maybe after all that's happened you'll feel safer at someone else's place," he said.

We'd just driven away from the Jackson house. I'd looked back twice, still seeing that hate-filled expression on Baxter's face.

Justice, Linda. You're finally going to have justice.

"Perry." I squeezed his arm. "Thanks. But now that it's done, I just want to sleep in my own bed—while I can."

Dan and Slater were going to fight against bail for Baxter, but they couldn't guarantee they'd win—especially if plans went awry and they didn't bring in Melissa right away. Until she led them to Linda's body and testified before the grand jury, they couldn't add the charge of Linda's murder to those Baxter currently faced.

If Baxter got out on bail, I would not be spending nights alone in my own house.

Perry gave me a wan smile. He looked tired too. "I understand. Check in with me when you wake up?"

"Count on it."

On the short drive to my house I called Dineen. No answer. She was probably in the shower, getting ready for work. "It's done," I told her message machine. "Everything's okay. I'm going to sleep now. Call you when I wake up."

Perry insisted on coming into the house with me just to make sure all was well. As we walked past Billy Bass in the hall, the stupid thing went off. I nearly jumped to the ceiling. Perry watched Billy's performance, chuckling. "I haven't seen one of these things in years."

I looked from him to Billy Bass, sudden awkwardness floating around in my chest. I rubbed my arms. "It was Tom's."

Perry gave me a long, searching look. Then nodded.

I turned away and made for the Jelly Belly drawer in my office. Popped a handful of myriad flavors onto my tongue and chewed like there was no tomorrow. My jaw seemed to move in slow motion.

"Want some?" I asked Perry, my mouth full.

He shook his head. "It's more fun just watching you."

At the front door I hugged him, and he held me for a moment, chin resting on my head. He smelled slightly of men's lime soap, even though we'd been up all night. His arms around me felt so . . . good. I didn't want to let him go.

"I'll never thank you enough, Perry."

"Nah. It was nothin'. You need me again—'Help Is on Its Way.'" He raised his eyebrows.

My brain wouldn't work. "Chicago?" The tune played through my head. "No. Little River Band."

"What album?"

"Greatest Hits."

"Cheater."

"I gotta get to bed."

Perry smiled. "Next time, no excuse." He stepped outside.

I closed the door and locked it.

On someone else's legs I walked down the hall, into my room. I didn't even take my clothes off. Just fell onto the bed. Vaguely I registered the time on my nightstand clock. Seven-forty in the morning. I'd been up for forty-eight hours.

As much as I needed sleep, my rebellious body fought it. Maybe it just didn't remember how to rest.

I lay on my back, eyes closed, thinking of Melissa and Linda and Baxter. Wondering how all this would play out. Finding Melissa. The hearings, the trial.

So ...

very ...

much ...

to ...

The quicksand pit opened up, inviting. I stepped into it. And sank ...

Sank ...

As it opened its mouth to swallow me, Billy Bass started to sing.

FIFTY-SIX

AUGUST 2004

Melissa couldn't move. She stared at Linda's body, the blood leaking from the wound in her back. Linda lay on her side, fighting to breathe. Her eyes were at half-mast, her twitching hands outstretched. The butcher knife lay on the floor near her fingers.

Did I do that? Did I really stab her?

Baxter pulled himself upright, eyes wide. He gaped at Linda, all color draining from his face. Twice he blinked, as if to erase the nightmare before him. "No. *No.*"

He fell on his knees beside his wife. One of his hands knocked the butcher knife away. It scudded across the floor. Shaking, Baxter reached for Linda's shoulder. "Linda, can you hear me? Linda!"

Her mouth yawed open, creaking in air.

"She's not breathing enough. I have to give her CPR!" Baxter started to roll Linda on her back, but the knife still stuck out of her, angled high and to the left of her spine.

Had it gone all the way to her heart?

Baxter ogled the knife, helpless.

Linda wheezed and gasped. The horrifying sounds shot right through Melissa. She pressed her hands to her temples, trying to *think*.

"Can you do it while she's lying on her side?"

"No!"

"Try it."

"It won't work!"

"*Try* it!"

"Melissa, it *won't work.*" Panic gripped Baxter's face. "We have to breathe hard. If her heart stops we'll have to pump it."

"Then take out the knife."

Baxter's mouth worked, as if the mere thought made him sick. "I—can't. What if it hurts her more?"

Something hard and heavy settled within Melissa. Her mind cleared. "Hold her steady. I'll do it."

"I don't—"

"Baxter, just *do* it!"

Air rattled in and out of Linda's throat. Her eyes were now wide open and fixed, her skin beige.

Baxter crawled on the other side of Linda, facing her. One bracing hand slid behind her shoulder, the other at her lower back. He turned his head to the side, squeezed his eyes shut.

Melissa sank to her knees and grasped the knife handle with both hands. She pulled hard. It slid out with a nauseating, sucking sound.

Linda convulsed. Her throat rattled as if it were her last breath.

Melissa jumped to her feet and out of the way. Baxter eased Linda onto her back. The rattling intensified, then turned to a gurgle.

Melissa still clutched the knife. She edged to the sink and dropped it in. From behind her came the frantic sound of Baxter's CPR. She turned to see his mouth pressed on Linda's, puffing hard breaths. His fingers pinched her nose.

Her hands shot up, desperately clawing the air as if to scrape oxygen from it. Her eyes were wide with terror, the eyes of a dying woman.

Baxter pulled back, chest heaving. Blood bubbled from Linda's mouth.

"No!" He wiped it away with his palm. Surged down and covered her lips again. This time her chest would barely rise, as if the air seeped out of her very pores. Baxter blew like a madman.

Sudden jealousy and anguish surged through Melissa. This was *wrong*. With all of Baxter's shoving Linda around, what right did he have to act like this? Not to mention the man had been in *her* bed just ten minutes ago. Linda had tried to *kill* him. Melissa had just saved Baxter's life, and now look at him. *Look* at him.

Huff, huff. Baxter continued his forced breathing. Melissa wanted to kick him. To scream, *Stop it! She wanted to cut you open. She wanted to ruin you.*

Melissa laced her fingers hard until her skin turned white. This wasn't the first time in her life she'd had to pull herself in tight to protect her own sanity. She closed her eyes and pounded her anger. Beat it down, down into fine sand granules.

In her mind she saw herself sweep the granules away.

She opened her eyes, her jaw set.

Linda's clawing arms slowed ... sank to the floor.

Baxter jerked up again, frantically searching her face. Blood smeared his cheeks. "Linda? Come *on*."

Her windpipe gurgled and choked. One more rasp—and the awful sound cut off. Linda's facial muscles flattened. Her body relaxed.

Her eyes set in a cold, dead glaze.

Melissa's mouth opened, her throat cinched tight.

"Nnnno!" Baxter grabbed his wife's shoulders and shook her until her body bounced off the floor. "Linda. Linda!"

Curses and prayers spewed from his mouth. He slapped both hands against her chest and pumped her heart with fury. He stopped for a second, checked for a reaction. Nothing. Baxter tried again, harder.

Melissa watched him with growing dread. Linda was gone. She wasn't coming back. It was Melissa and Baxter now, and once he gave up trying to revive Linda, who knew what he might do? Silently Melissa screamed to herself that everything would be fine. Not because it looked that way, far from it. Because it had to be.

She reached deep within herself once more and crushed the fear into dust. A pale and chilling wind kicked up in her stomach, blew the dust away

Baxter rocked back on his heels, begging for a breath, a flutter in Linda's chest. She didn't move. He moaned, swiped the back of his hand across his mouth. Started pumping again.

Melissa turned away. The knife lay red and bloodied against the white porcelain sink. Mechanically, she picked it up. Washed and dried it. Slid it back into the butcher's block.

Behind her Baxter was crying. Grunting. Pumping.

Melissa examined her hands, beneath her fingernails, looking for blood. They were unstained.

She rinsed out the sink. Wiped it out with a paper towel. Buffed over the nearby area of granite countertop.

Baxter's weeping increased, his prayers turning off-key and mumbling. Melissa faced him, palms together and pressed against her mouth. His cheeks were splotchy red, tear tracks through the smeared blood.

He raised his hands from Linda's chest. They hovered above her body, helpless and trembling, as his eyes sought Melissa's. "She's dead." His voice pinched. He shook his head, disbelieving. Baxter's body leaned to one side until he slipped off his knees and sat down hard. His chin dropped, a sob wrenching from his throat.

Melissa moved to him and pressed her fingers into his shoulder. "Shhhh. It'll be okay."

His head jerked up. "What do you *mean*, it'll be okay? She's *dead*."

"I know. I'm so sorry."

Anger mottled Baxter's face. "You killed her."

"I — it all happened so fast."

"You *killed* her!"

"She was about to kill *you*."

Baxter's lips twisted. "This is what you wanted, isn't it? Linda out of your way."

"Of course not."

"You planned this all along."

Melissa's back straightened. "No I didn't — it just happened. You're the one who drugged her."

"*I* didn't put a knife in her back!"

"Baxter, she was going to cut you into shreds! What did you want me to do — stand back and let it happen?"

"You did this. You killed my wife!"

Baxter leapt to his feet, greedy hands stretched for Melissa's throat. She stumbled backward, arms before her face, and swung away. He punched her in the kidney. Pain shot through Melissa's lower back. She listed to one side, gagging for air.

He hit her in the spine. Melissa crashed down on all fours, tried to scrabble away, fighting for oxygen. He kicked her in the side.

"Stop it!" She grabbed his leg. Baxter went off balance and caught the counter to stay upright. He jerked his leg to free it, but she hung on tight. Baxter lunged downward, grabbed her hair, and pulled. Melissa yanked his leg. He toppled to the floor onto his side.

The fall seemed to crack him. In seconds all his fight spilled away. He pushed to a sitting position, then slumped against a cabinet, chin nearly touching his chest.

Melissa let go of his leg and scooted beyond his reach. Her open mouth sucked in oxygen. Her whole body burned.

Baxter dropped his face in both hands and moaned.

Melissa watched warily, her muscles tensed to spring away if he turned on her again. A minute passed.

Two . . .

Three.

With caution she crawled to his side. "Baxter. You know I didn't mean this to happen."

He raised his head, nostrils sucking in and out. Sweat trickled down one temple. He would not look at her. Instead he stared across the room for a long time, as if Melissa did not exist. When he finally spoke his tone had thinned to cold steel. "We have to figure out what to do." He raised a shaking hand and wiped at his cheek, further smearing the remnants of Linda's blood. Baxter's gaze raked the floor as if an answer had been cut into the hardwood.

He swallowed. "We need to call the police."

Melissa's head drew back. "No way."

He tilted his head and regarded her with disdain. "Just what do you suggest?"

"What would you tell them?"

"How about the truth? You killed my wife."

Melissa eyed him coolly. "They'll want the whole story. You want to tell them that too?"

He stared back at her, jaw tight. Calculations rippled across his face, as if the two of them had just begun a fatal game of chess.

Melissa's body throbbed.

Baxter forced his eyes to his wife's still form. "We can't claim self-defense. Nobody's going to believe she came at me with a knife."

Melissa's control faltered. For a crazy minute she imagined herself hanging from the corner of the ceiling, looking down at the surreal scene.

She'd done it now. She'd really done it, and there was no going back. Baxter could turn against her in a heartbeat. Say she killed Linda out of jealousy, and he had nothing to do with it. If she told the police he beat his wife, they'd never believe her. Any bruises on Linda's body Baxter could attribute to *her*. She'd attacked Linda, hit her, knifed her. Baxter had heard the noise and come downstairs to find his wife on the floor . . .

Melissa's chin wavered and her lips pulled. She leaned against a cabinet and pressed both hands over her eyes. Drew her knees up to her chest. "I didn't mean to *hurt* her, Baxter. She was going to *kill* you. I *couldn't let her do it*!"

No response from Baxter, not one sound or movement. Melissa played out her crying. After a minute she sniffed and rubbed her eyes, knowing she was smearing her mascara. She fixed him with a dull gaze.

He met her eyes, his mouth curled. "Melissa, the girl who never cries. Not even at her own mother's funeral, so they told me."

Indignation seeped into Melissa's veins. She fought to keep it from her expression.

Wait a minute.

Baxter couldn't put Linda's death all on her. She could cry rape. Linda had caught Baxter in the act and screamed she'd tell the world. He killed her to shut her up. A medical exam of Melissa would prove they'd had sex. Even if Baxter convinced them he hadn't forced her, it would still be statutory rape. His reputation would be in the dirt. The town would turn against him. His real estate business would tank.

He knew this already. He'd thought this through.

Fine then. He wanted to play chess? Bring on the game.

Melissa straightened her shoulders and looked Baxter in the eye. "What do you want from me?"

Baxter's face transformed from grieving husband to the hard ice of a glacial lake. Here was the Baxter Melissa knew. The king of Vonita, master of his castle. The man who could do whatever he thought necessary and get away with it.

He pushed to his feet. "Like it or not—and I *don't*—we're in this together. If one of us goes down, we both fall."

Melissa rose too. She didn't like looking up at him. "Of course we're in this together." She tinged her voice with sincerity—*I'd do anything for you.* Maybe, just maybe she could win him back. "Just tell me what you want me to do."

He ran a hand across his forehead. "Get dressed. In dark clothes. We have to get rid of the evidence."

FIFTY-SEVEN

FEBRUARY 2010

"Don't Worry, Be Happy" called to me through the quicksand. The voice echoed, mocking and full of portent. Abject fear sifted over me, caking my body.

What . . . ?

I swam against the weight pulling me down. Broke the surface.

My eyes pried open.

Melissa Harkoff stood over me, a gun in her hand. Her mouth curled into a vengeful smile. "Hello, Joanne."

No, this was a dream. I'd fallen asleep . . .

"Sit up." Her tone pierced, a shard of glass.

Reality hit. Dull adrenaline prickled my limbs. I struggled to a sitting position and cringed back against the headboard.

I stared at Melissa.

She moved her jaw to one side. "You're going to tell me what I need know."

"What?" My voice shook.

"How to disappear."

My mouth moved. No words formed. My brain, my body refused to function.

Melissa smirked. "Not nice feeling helpless, is it?"

I swallowed. "I'm not helping you get away, Melissa."

"You tell me, you live. You don't help me, you die."

Melissa . . . a liar, a blackmailer. Now a killer?

A heavy rock sank in my stomach. How much had I misread this girl? Could anything she said or did be trusted?

Did she really even know where Linda's body was?

The thoughts sickened me. I'd gone through too much to catch Melissa and ultimately, Baxter Jackson. If there would be any shred of reliability left in Melissa's testimony against him, I couldn't lose her now.

"You kill me, there goes your information."

"I can start with your hand—how'd you like a bullet there? Or maybe your leg."

She'd do it. She really would. Nausea roiled through me. "I don't think well when I'm in pain."

We glared at each other.

Melissa ran her tongue beneath her top lip. "We're going to go to your computer. You're going to type out each step for me. Print it."

"How'd you get in here?"

"Broke the glass to your back garage door. Now get up."

Glass? I hadn't heard a thing. And I hadn't seen a car. How'd she get to my house? She must have parked on a side road and been waiting for my return. Maybe for hours.

"Get *up*, Joanne."

I pushed off the bed. My legs nearly gave way. I clutched the headboard, steadied myself.

"Go to your office."

Melissa backed up, giving me room to walk past her.

I eyed the gun. "That another one of Tony's? Did he bring you here?"

Anger pinched her face. "*I'm* the one wanting information. *Go*."

My chin raised. I walked by her and out the bedroom door.

Up the hall, into my work space. I sat in my swivel chair, flicked on the computer. "It'll take time to boot up. No need to threaten it with a bullet too."

Melissa snarled.

I stared at the monitor, my head still thick. Logic moved through it slowly. As far as Melissa knew, her timing was perfect. From here she'd go to the drop-off location. Get away with the money—for good.

Except that the money would never arrive.

My screen blipped on. Windows came up.

Sudden realization burned my head. What was to keep me from calling the police as soon as Melissa left?

She was lying. Again.

Melissa Harkoff would get her much-needed information. And then she would kill me.

FIFTY-EIGHT

AUGUST 2004

"We have to get rid of the evidence."

Melissa hesitated only a second before hurrying out of the kitchen and up the stairs. When she hit the upper level she stopped, listening. All the TV crime shows she'd watched over the years chugged through her mind. On her left lay the master bedroom, lights on, its door wide open. Way down the hall, past two guest bedrooms and a shared bath, was her suite.

From downstairs rose the faint sound of the door between the kitchen and garage, opening and closing.

Melissa veered left.

Heart clutching, she ran across the master bedroom and into the huge bath area. Her frantic gaze scraped over the counter, taking in lotion bottles, a mirror, hairspray. Linda's stuff.

Heat rose in Melissa's body. If Baxter caught her here, all pretense would be off. No telling what he'd do.

Melissa yanked open a drawer. Inside it lay a man's black comb.

She snatched it up and examined it. A few dark hairs stuck in the teeth. Perfect. She ripped off toilet paper, wrapped the comb in it, and stuck it in the waistband of her shorty pajamas.

Melissa sprinted to her room. She threw on jeans, a dark sweatshirt with zippered pockets. Shoved her feet into a pair of Vans sneakers. The wrapped comb went into her right pocket. Melissa zipped it up and ran downstairs.

In the kitchen Baxter was spreading an old blanket beside Linda's body. The butcher knife was back in its holder.

"Did you wash it?" She pointed to the knife.

"No."

Melissa slid it out, examined it. Looked clean. She rinsed it off anyway before replacing it.

Baxter knelt near Linda's head. "Help me get her onto the blanket."

Melissa sank down by Linda's feet. Together they rolled the body onto the blanket about two feet from the edge. They both took one side of the thick fabric and folded it over Linda. Then they rolled her again, wrapping like a bulky cocoon until all the blanket was used up. Both the top and bottom had six inches of extra material.

A puddle of blood stained the floor where Linda had lain. "I'll clean it." Melissa stood up.

"Use paper towels. We'll need to take them out with us."

Baxter walked over to prop open the door into the garage. Then he disappeared out of the kitchen. Melissa heard the *click* of a car trunk opening.

She fetched a plastic grocery bag and the paper towel holder from the counter. She wiped up the blood, putting the towels in the bag. Then she wet more towels, sprayed the area with a kitchen cleaner, and rubbed and rubbed. Baxter reappeared. He watched as she got down on her knees and examined the baseboards around where Linda had fallen. When Melissa was satisfied, she put the cleaner away and stuffed all the used paper towels into the bag. She returned the paper towel holder to the counter.

They peered around the kitchen. Everything looked in place.

Except for the body on the floor.

Baxter rubbed sweat from his forehead. "She'll be heavy."

Melissa nodded.

Once more she moved to Linda's feet and Baxter to her head. He leaned down, bunched the extra blanket, and picked up his end. Melissa did the same. Together they raised Linda just off the floor, hammock-style. With awkward steps they made for the garage, Baxter traipsing backward and looking over his shoulder. The wrapped body swayed between them. Twice Melissa nearly lost her grip. She gritted her teeth, her body aching where Baxter had punched and kicked her.

They made it over the threshold into the garage. Baxter sidestepped to his right to head down the length of Linda's BMW. He rounded the rear bumper, leaving room for Melissa to make the corner. They lined up even with the trunk.

"Okay." Baxter was breathing hard. "Count of three, we lift. One, two, *three*."

They heaved the body up and over the lip. It fell into the trunk with a thud. The foot end curved up the side of the car too high for the lid to close.

Baxter stood back and stared at it blankly, as if all logic had just drained from his head. Melissa nudged him aside. "Here." She shoved Linda's feet down, bending the body at the knees. Thumped the trunk shut.

She surveyed Baxter. His face had gone pasty. She couldn't let him change his mind now. "We'll need a flashlight. And you need water."

He nodded, no argument left in him.

Melissa headed back into the kitchen. She returned with the flashlight, water bottle, and the plastic bag full of bloody paper towels. Baxter was standing beside his Mercedes, the door open. "We'll take both cars," he said. "Leave Linda's somewhere on the way back."

Great. Melissa got to drive the one full of incriminating evidence. "What's our story?"

"She went out and never came back. I'll work out details on the way."

"You know where you're going?"

"Yeah."

"Should we take cell phones in case we get separated?"

"No. Cell calls leave evidence. Just don't lose me."

"What about a shovel?"

"I put two in your trunk."

Melissa licked her lips, thinking. "Shouldn't we take her cell phone and purse? If she went somewhere, she'd have them with her."

Fear flicked across Baxter's face, as if he gazed down the long gauntlet of the future and knew he could not foresee all the possible dangers. "Go get them. On her dresser."

Melissa gave Baxter the water bottle and put the flashlight and plastic bag in the back seat of the BMW. She scurried out of the garage, through the kitchen, and up the stairs. Spotting Linda's tote Coach handbag in the master bedroom, she ran to it and peered inside. The cell phone sat in a side pocket. Melissa hurried into the bathroom and snatched two washcloths from the floor-to-ceiling cabinet. Back at the dresser, she used one of the washcloths to pull out the cell without touching it. The phone was off. Melissa slid it back into the pocket, then laid the cloth across the handles of the purse to pick it up.

In the garage Baxter was leaning against the hood of his car, deep in thought. Melissa could see his shock had once more passed. Cunning had returned.

She put Linda's purse on the floor of the BMW's passenger seat. Placed the washcloths beside it. She pointed to them. "To wipe down the car."

Baxter grunted.

Melissa took a deep breath. "Anything else we've forgotten?"

"Sanity."

Their eyes locked. Baxter's were flat and dark. Unreadable.

Melissa lifted her hands. "Let's go."

She slid inside the BMW. The keys lay in the center console, where Linda always kept them. Melissa started the engine. The clock read 2:05 a.m. Could that be possible? Only half an hour ago she and Baxter had been in her bed. Linda had been alive.

Dread curled through Melissa's stomach. She turned her head toward Baxter, thinking, *Now what?* Her life here, her plans had just disintegrated. When Linda didn't return, Melissa couldn't imagine social services letting her stay in this house alone with Baxter.

What then?

She couldn't leave Baxter. Couldn't leave her job. And she *sure* wasn't about to go to some other foster home.

Maybe Baxter would find her a place to live in town. She could still work with him. She could steal over at night to be with him ...

The grating sound of Baxter's garage door opening jerked Melissa from her thoughts.

Melissa blinked. She would be okay. She would survive this. Do whatever needed to be done.

She hit the remote button. Her garage door jolted into an upward slide.

Baxter pulled out first. Bearing Linda's body in the trunk, Melissa followed him into the tenuous night.

FIFTY-NINE

FEBRUARY 2010

Five feet away from me, Melissa stood with her feet apart, back straight. Her gun aimed at my head.

My heart skidded. All I could do right now was meet her demand. Buy some time. I would think of ... something.

A voice at the very core of me whispered I was fooling myself.

In grim succession I saw the future play out. Melissa pulling the trigger. Getting away, staying hidden with the information she'd yanked from me. With the loss of both potential victims as witnesses, Baxter's high-priced lawyer would somehow manage to get the solicitation of murder charges dropped.

And Baxter Jackson would never be prosecuted for Linda's death.

I brought up Word. It opened a new document.

Ironic, wasn't it? I had lived to find people. Now I would die helping one disappear.

Melissa's breaths came short and quick. I could feel the angst rolling off her. She wanted to be gone. "Tell me as you type," she demanded.

My throat had run dry. I thought of Perry, wondered how he could work all day without sleep. Of Dineen and Jimmy. Baxter now in jail. Was he talking to Dan and Slater? Or had he already called an attorney?

The world was revolving around me. While I sat with a gun to my head.

Dan's words echoed. *"I'll get a court order for her cell records. If she uses that phone we'll locate her."*

If I did one last thing on this earth, it would be to ensure that Melissa *would* be found.

"You can't maintain a regular address or phone number." I keyed in the words as I spoke. My voice sounded hoarse. "Those are things we use to track people."

"So I move all the time?"

"You keep virtual, even as you live in one place. You leave no correct trail. You leave many false ones. That will send your pursuers looking in all the wrong directions."

I glanced at Melissa—and saw the gleam in her eyes. Already she pictured herself with $300,000, living as she wanted, doing what she wanted. Disgust and revenge bit my nerves. "You love this, don't you?"

She gave me a smile that turned my stomach.

Just wait till you learn that money will never come.

I typed "Bills" as the first heading. "Rent post office boxes in numerous states. Spread your bills out between them. Then call the companies every month for your balances and pay them. Tell each biller they have the wrong Social Security number on file and give them a wrong one. Give them new phone numbers."

"For false trails?"

"Yes."

I labeled another heading "Internet." "Make sure your only email address is a Yahoo or Hotmail. Don't search the Internet from your home computer. Go to an Internet café or library."

I could feel sweat pop out on my forehead. My arms started to shake. Fear and lack of sleep turned my body to wax.

"What else?" Her voice edged, her eyes flicking to my clock.

Long minutes ticked by until I lost track of time. I told Melissa how to open a corporation in the state of her choice, using a certain kind of address. Then open a bank account using the corporation information. Following that, open a corporation in Canada. I typed out the details, my insides churning into jelly. My fingers slipped on keys, and my eyes began to burn.

"Come *on*!" Melissa stomped closer, menacing with her weapon.

I swallowed hard. Tried to collect my melting thoughts.

"Don't continue anything like magazine subscriptions. Pay for all plane tickets with cash. Don't get any type of service, like cable, under your name. Use your foreign corporation."

"What about phone calls?"

"Once you leave don't call people you know from here. Cut your ties."

"I don't have any ties that matter."

Here is where I should tell her about prepaid phones. That she should not make one more call from her current phone. That she should turn it on and leave it somewhere, drawing the police to the wrong location.

Spots began to dance before my eyes. I slumped back against my chair.

"Keep going!"

"I've been up for two days." The words ground like tires over gravel.

"I don't *care*."

What little energy I had left burst into rage. I could feel the surge, the white hotness. But my limbs would not respond. The rage flamed and died, leaving me empty. Too tired to care.

So what if she killed me? So what? I'd be in heaven with Tom.

"Joanne, talk!"

The words bounced off my numb body. Then, from a place unknown, one last remnant of fight seeped into my soul. I opened my mouth to taunt Melissa with the truth. That Baxter had been arrested, and her blackmail plans had burnt to ashes. She would have no money to run with. And nowhere to go.

"Melissa—"

An unseen hand snatched the words from my tongue. If I told her, she wouldn't show up at the drop-off location, wouldn't be caught today.

"*Talk*!" Melissa smashed her gun into the back of my head.

Pain shot through my skull. I cried out. Lurched forward.

Melissa moved behind me. The gun barrel pushed against the base of my head. "How do I use a phone and not be traced?" The words staccatoed from her mouth, hard and acidic.

My brain throbbed. I couldn't see.

"Tell me!"

My fingers gripped the desk, my teeth gritted. This girl was *evil*. "Do you even ... really know where Linda is buried?"

Melissa shoved the gun barrel harder against my head. "*Tell* me about the cell phone!"

My mouth hung open. I dragged in air. "I want Baxter ... to pay."

Melissa yelled a curse. Her left hand grabbed my shoulder and shook until my body rattled in the chair. "Guess what, Miss *Lying Christian*." Her words spat through clenched teeth. "You want to know the truth? Baxter didn't kill Linda. *I* did. She caught us in bed and went after Baxter with a knife. I stabbed her first. And you know what?" Melissa spun my chair around, grasped my jaw, and squeezed hard. She stuck her face into mine. "I didn't *care*." Melissa shoved my head to one side and drew back. "And I won't care when I kill you either."

I stared at her, eyes half mast. I couldn't think, couldn't process what she said ...

Melissa killed Linda?

Melissa jerked my chair around to face the computer. My eyes could barely make out the document.

"Tell me about my cell phone!"

Melissa killed Linda?

"Tell me *now*!"

This girl killed Linda. My best friend.

I licked my dry lips.

"Jo-*anne*—"

"Use your cell ... until your next bill." I didn't even try to type. Couldn't. "Then toss it. Get a ... prepaid phone. Switch to a ... new prepaid ... every month."

"Police can't trace this cell phone?"

Pain spread needle wings, swept through my body. "They can trace ... your number ... to the address on the account ... but you'll ... be gone."

"Can't they trace my location with the cell?"

I forced a sick laugh. "Only in the m-movies."

"You're *lying*."

"No. Not."

"You *are*!"

She hit me again with the butt of her gun. My head exploded. Darkened.

I listed to my right side.

"Print out what you've got, Joanne! Print it now!"

My arms wobbled. Were those my fingers? My failing eyes found Control P. Somehow I hit the keys. My printer whirred into action.

Melissa killed Linda. I couldn't ... let her get away ...

I hit Control S. Had to save the file for evidence. The little box appeared, using the beginning words I'd typed as the file's default name under "My Documents." I clicked *Save*.

Paper rolled out from the printer.

One sheet.

Two.

Melissa leaned around me to snatch them up.

My arm jerked out and smashed into her left wrist.

She cursed and scrabbled for the document. I elbowed her hard in the shoulder. Melissa fell to her right, toward the window. The weapon slipped from her hand. Clattered to the floor.

Dizziness swirled over me in a smothering blanket. *"Run!"* my brain shrieked. *"Hit her again!"* But I could do nothing.

The world dimmed. Melissa snapped down toward the gun. I struggled to raise my arms, fight her away. But the motion sprayed me with nausea.

The office tilted.

Melissa rose, gun aimed at my chest. I collapsed to my left, rolled off the chair into empty space.

A shot cracked the air.

Monster teeth tore through my body, long and sharp and hungry.

I smashed into the floor—and blackness.

SIXTY

AUGUST 2004

Stiff-backed, Melissa hurtled through the night, following the demon-eyed glow of Baxter's taillights. They took back roads out of Vonita and west across 101. Baxter was apparently headed toward the woods that spilled toward the coast.

His comb still lay in Melissa's zipped-up sweatshirt pocket.

Melissa's mind churned through sequences and lies. When would she and Baxter "discover" Linda was missing? What time had they last seen her? Where had she said she was going? Melissa imagined Chief Eddington's narrowed eyes as he grilled her, his suspicious tone.

How good would Baxter be at playing the distraught and worried husband? Could he keep it up day after day? Even now he wavered between emotion and resolve.

Melissa's mouth twisted. Forget whatever weakness Baxter displayed in private. How many years had he played the perfect church man to the world?

Baxter slowed, and his left blinker flicked on. They turned onto a narrow lane leading through a forest. Not a house anywhere nor an ounce of light other than from their cars. Trees crowded the road like menacing sentinels, blocking out the stars, the moon.

How had Baxter known of this place? A possible housing development site? Some Sunday picnic with Linda?

Five minutes later, shortly after they'd passed a lone house on a cleared hill, he turned onto a rutted road. Melissa followed. After a jouncing mile downhill, Baxter stopped. His car head beams flipped off, replaced with the dull yellow of parking lights.

Melissa turned off the BMW and hit the button to pop the trunk.

She stepped from the car into thick, dank air. Silence hung heavy and deep. Accusing. As if the forest *knew*.

Six feet off the road, in the dim illumination of the Mercedes' parking lights, Baxter bent over a bush. "Here." He pointed. "We'll dig it up and replant it on top. We have to hurry."

With enough light from the car, they didn't need the flashlight. They pulled both shovels from the trunk and went to work.

Melissa didn't know how long they dug, except that it seemed like forever. Her arms ached, her back and side ached. They uttered not a word, both racing against time. The smell of dirt filled her nostrils, the *thunk*, *swish* of their shovels reverberating in the pulsing night. Melissa's mind drifted somewhere out in space, detached, unfeeling. She would not think about what she'd done, what they were doing. Nothing mattered at the moment but burying Linda and returning home before dawn.

It wasn't the first time she'd had to put her mind on hold.

The hole grew to a ragged four feet long, the same in depth. Baxter tossed down his shovel. "That's enough."

Melissa dropped her shovel and arched her back. She couldn't have dug much longer.

They hurried to the car and lugged out Linda's body. Carried it to the makeshift grave.

Melissa hesitated. "We need to take her out of the blanket."

"No."

"Yes, Baxter."

"No."

"Why?"

"It'll protect her."

"Protect her from what? She's *dead.*"

Baxter shot Melissa a look so caustic it burned her skin. "I don't want to leave her here without it."

Melissa's arms were about to fall off. She dropped her end of Linda's body to the ground. "And what if she's found, huh? You want her wrapped in a blanket from your garage?"

"Who would know?"

"Someone. Your gardener. Your house cleaner. Or maybe they'd find some telltale fibers or hairs on it, who knows? You want to take that chance?"

Baxter shifted on his feet, still holding his half of the body. Slowly he set it down.

The comb seemed to vibrate in Melissa's pocket.

"Come on, Baxter." Melissa raised her arms. "We have to take her out. We'll throw the blanket in some dumpster on the way back."

For a long moment he stood there, jaw working. In slow motion he bent down over the body.

Silently they unwound Linda. When they were done she lay on her back, her face peaceful, as if she merely slept. Baxter stared at her, fingers flexing.

Melissa squeezed his arm. "I'll do it."

Baxter tipped his head toward the heavens. "It'll be light before we know it."

He turned away.

Melissa squatted down to roll Linda's body into the grave. Again she stopped, thinking.

Her head came up. "There should be blood in her car."

No response.

"Someone will eventually find it, right? We need to make it look like she was killed."

The police had to be able to conclude Linda was dead. So she and Baxter could get on with their lives.

Baxter whirled on her, anger etching his cheeks. "Would you just put her in!"

"There's blood on her back! We need it to smear in the car."

He gave her a long, searing look, as if reading every depraved thought in her heart.

Melissa crossed her arms over her chest.

"You think you're smarter than me?" Baxter's voice growled.

Melissa shoved to her feet. "I'm *not* putting her in there until you tell me how we're getting blood in the car."

"Just *do* it!"

"No!"

In an instant Baxter covered the space between them. He grabbed Melissa's shoulders, squeezing hard enough to rip off her arms. His face pushed into hers, his teeth clenched. "We've got blood on the paper towels." He shoved her. Melissa stumbled back and fell.

She jumped up, mad at herself for forgetting such a detail, madder at him. She shot him a look of pure venom. "Stop shoving me around, Baxter. I'm not Linda."

"You certainly aren't." His tone dropped to cold, flat stone.

He swiveled on his heel and stalked to the Mercedes. "Get her in and shovel the dirt over her."

Melissa cursed him under her breath. Such a macho man. Shoved women around but too weak in the stomach to bury his own wife. Fine then. She'd show him who was stronger.

She knelt beside the slash in the earth and pushed Linda into the grave none too gently. The body landed on its side. Melissa forced the knees to bend up, her chin down to her chest.

Melissa stole a glance over her shoulder. Baxter stood with his back to her, hands dug into his scalp.

The grieving husband.

Quietly Melissa unzipped her sweatshirt pocket, pulled out the comb. Unwound the toilet paper and stuffed the wad back in her pocket. She leaned into the grave, lifted Linda's arm and placed the comb beneath it. She could only hope Baxter's hairs were still stuck in the teeth.

There. Insurance.

Melissa pushed to her feet and picked up a shovel. She thrust its blade into the mound of soil and threw the contents into the grave. Dirt plopped on Linda's side, into her hair. Melissa knew the sight should turn her stomach, but it didn't. She just wanted this over.

She threw a glance at the sky. How long until dawn?

Melissa sent a second shovel-full of dirt into the hole. A third, a fourth, and more. Slowly Linda's face disappeared.

Baxter hadn't moved.

"Hey." Melissa twisted around. "You want us out of here sometime tomorrow, maybe you ought to help."

He turned to her, his face a mask of control, as if one unguarded move would crack it from ear to ear. Was he holding back anger at her or grief over Linda? Or both?

At the moment Melissa didn't care. She was just about ready to push him into the earth with his wife.

Without a word Baxter picked up his shovel and helped refill the grave. When it was nearly all packed into place they replanted the large bush on top. Baxter moved like a robot, tight-jointed and expressionless. He tossed small branches and brush around the edges until the freshly moved earth could not be seen.

They used the blanket to wipe off the shovels without cleaning them completely. Didn't want to arouse any suspicion in the gardeners' minds once the shovels were replaced in the garage. Melissa shook out the blanket, then folded it. She laid it in the BMW trunk, the shovels going on top.

"You know a dumpster where we can leave the blanket?" Melissa closed the trunk.

"I'll handle it."

They stood one foot apart. Baxter wouldn't look at her. His face now screamed blame. "Don't lose me on the way back."

When Melissa started the BMW's engine, the clock read 3:41. So little time.

She followed Baxter out of the woods, her brain sodden and thick. Dully, she gazed at the house on the hill as they passed it back on the road. It looked a-writhe in secrets, like the house in *Psycho*.

When they got back home she'd need to wash and dry their clothes. Check their shoes.

At 4:02 Baxter pulled up to a dumpster behind a small grocery store in a still-sleepy little town. They threw away the blanket. Five minutes later they stopped at the edge of a parking lot behind a strip mall. With the washcloths they wiped down the BWM's front seat, the doors, keys, and dashboard. Baxter then took the bloodiest paper towels from the plastic bag and pressed them around on the front seat and steering wheel. He was careful not to touch anything with his fingers.

"It won't look like drops," Melissa said.

"It'll do. Blood would get smeared in a fight."

They left Linda's purse on its side on the floor of the passenger seat, contents spilled. Baxter hovered at the door, surveying his handiwork. With a small grunt he leaned in, took the money from Linda's wallet, wiped the leather off, and threw the wallet back on the floor. He took her cell phone too. The keys they left in the ignition.

He stood back again, gaze roaming, calculations playing across his tightened mouth. Then he closed the door. "Let's go."

They probably hadn't erased every one of their fingerprints, but it wouldn't matter. Both of them had reason to be in that car plenty of times. Melissa gave the BMW one last glance as she slipped inside Baxter's Mercedes. Too bad they had to sacrifice such a nice car.

Baxter started his engine and headed for Vonita.

Melissa pressed back against the seat, arms folded. Feeling a hundred years old. Baxter believed he'd never be caught because no one would ever suspect him in the first place. Who wouldn't believe the king of Vonita?

Melissa couldn't be so sure.

If things went south, if it came down to her against Baxter, she'd skate free. She'd made sure of that.

Baxter focused on the road, narrow-eyed and stiff. "I'll say Linda left the house around eleven to buy some aspirin at the convenience store. She had a bad headache. I'd just gotten in bed. I fell asleep soon after and slept hard all night. When I woke up, she wasn't there."

"Any aspirin in the house right now?"

"I'll get rid of it."

"What about me?"

"You were in your room and heard nothing. You didn't even know Linda had left."

Baxter's words spit through his teeth, as if he detested Melissa's very presence. As if they were enemies handcuffed together. Melissa's heart twisted. It wasn't supposed to be like this. Now that Linda was dead, why couldn't she and Baxter be together?

Maybe he'd feel differently tomorrow. When he saw how alone he was. How much he needed her.

They entered Vonita as they'd left, through a back road that led to the house. Melissa cast worried glances at connecting streets. "What if someone later says they saw us?"

"You see anyone around?"

"No, but— "

"So shut up."

They turned into the driveway. Baxter pressed the remote button, and they slipped into the garage. The door closed behind them, shutting them off from the rest of the world.

Baxter turned off the car. The engine ticked.

He turned to her, his stare the cold black of cave water. His expression and body were hard, brittle. Melisa gazed into those bottomless eyes and saw a truth that made her heart dry up.

Baxter Jackson would never be the same man again.

She had pushed him over a cliff, and the impact had broken him. This man before her was the glued-together version. Less stable. More volatile.

And he could barely stand to look at her.

"This is what you do, isn't it, Melissa? Turn situations to your best advantage. Play the part, do whatever is necessary to make things come out your way. Now I see it. I see what you really are."

What, Baxter, a deceiver? Just like you?

Baxter's mouth flattened. "How cool you were tonight. Poor little orphan girl, the very picture of control. Almost like you've done this before." His eyes glittered as he read her soul, just as she had read his.

"You killed your mother, didn't you?"

SIXTY-ONE

FEBRUARY 2010

Footsteps shuffled by my head. My eyes dragged half open. Through a warped tunnel I saw shoes. Legs.

I lay on my left side. My right shoulder screamed.

A malevolent presence leaned over me, breathing hard. *What?... Who?*

Melissa.

Killed Linda.

I froze, eyes half mast, in feigned death.

Movement toward me. Something hard pressed against my temple.

My head jerked. I rolled onto my back.

Melissa swept the gun toward my chest.

My right arm wouldn't work. My left arm shot up and grabbed her wrist. Twisted hard.

The gun barrel jerked away from my heart toward the wall. Melissa yelled. I held on, teeth clenched. My nails dug into the tendons of her wrist.

Her hand shimmied, fingers loosening. The gun fell from her grip onto my chest. My flopping right fingers managed to knock it aside.

Something primal and raw rose within me. I yanked her hand to my mouth. Sank my teeth deep into the side flesh.

Melissa cursed and flailed at my face with her other hand. A pit bull, I would not release. I caught her free arm with my left hand and yanked her down. She stumbled and fell. Her forehead hit the arm of my office chair.

She landed on top of me with a grunt, right hand trapped beneath her, still between my teeth. Melissa screamed curses and beat my head with her fist.

My left arm stretched out across the floor, scrabbling for the gun. Melissa hit me in the temple, once, twice. Blackness swarmed in.

My fingers closed on the gun. I clutched its hardness, warmed by Melissa's hand. I raised it high against Melissa's ribs—and pulled the trigger.

A strangling sound wrenched from her throat. Melissa collapsed, her body half on top of me, then rolled to the floor.

My teeth released her hand. My jaw felt like concrete.

I struggled to get up. My legs were mere water. Groaning, I scooted across the floor, weapon still clutched in my left hand. I lifted it up and laid it on my desk. Fumbled for the phone.

Couldn't ... reach.

Somehow I pushed to wobbly knees. Knocked the phone off its base. Picked it up.

Gasps escaped from Melissa. She shifted on the floor.

I hit *talk*. My right hand wouldn't lift. I dropped the phone on the floor and used my left hand to punch in the number.

"911, what's your emergency?"

My tongue thickened.

"911, you there?"

"Yeah. I'm ..."

"What's your emergency?"

"I ... did it."

"Did what?"

My voice hitched. "Stopped her."

"Ma'am, what's happening? Stopped who?"

"Melissa ... Harkoff ... I got her." My eyes filled with tears. "She killed Linda. She killed my best friend."

SIXTY-TWO

The world blurred. I don't know how much time passed. Five minutes? Twenty? The quicksand beckoned, but dull fire lit my veins. My eyes closed, dragged open. Closed, dragged open.

Melissa lay crumpled on her side, unmoving. Blood stained the floor beneath her.

Was she dead?

Somehow I managed to drag myself from the office into the hallway.

In the distance—a keening. It grew louder and louder, then doubled. Tripled. Sirens wailed to a stop outside my house.

I lifted a shaking left hand and unlocked the front door. Then collapsed before it.

Darkness drifted over me.

Then voices. Footsteps.

Someone calling my name.

I was lifted. Rolled. Lights and movement and people touching me.

A siren started up again. So very *loud.* Quicksand shimmied ... rose ... swallowed the horrible noise whole.

I awoke in a hospital room, my right shoulder bandaged. It felt like I'd been asleep for hours. My body swam in a thick and languid sea. An IV tube led to my left arm.

Perry sat by my bed.

I blinked at him. "Wha—?" My voice was little more than a croak.

His face lit. "Hey." He stood up, touched my hair. "She's back in the land of the living."

"That what this is?"

"Yeah. And pain meds."

Oh.

"How do you feel?" Perry's hand lowered to rest gently against my neck.

I swallowed. "Why aren't you at your store?"

He gave me a look. "And miss the excitement?"

Even my sodden brain saw through the tease. Who couldn't see the concern tugging at Perry's brow?

No, not just concern. Something more …

The thought warmed me.

But I couldn't go there now.

I licked my lips and concentrated on breathing.

As if a switch flipped, memories and realizations pierced my mind. For a moment my tongue froze, unable to choose what to ask first.

"Melissa?"

Perry's expression clouded. He shook his head. "She didn't make it."

I ogled him. "She's *dead*?"

He nodded.

My mouth flopped open, but no words formed. Dead. I killed her. I *killed* a person.

"Joanne." Perry stroked my jaw. "She tried to kill you first."

"How … were you there?"

Wait. That made no sense.

"You told 911 and the ambulance attendants."

"I talked in the ambulance?"

Perry smiled. "You downright blathered."

Oh.

"You told them how Melissa came in with a gun. That she shot you." Perry surveyed me, as if not quite sure I was in my right mind. "You said she told you *she* killed Linda."

Melissa's spiteful words washed over me. *"And you know what? I didn't care!"* My eyes closed.

"Joanne. Is that true?"

I wished my mind could think clearly. I tried to see down the tunnel of days, weeks, months. What would happen now with Baxter? Would we ever find Linda? And *where* did I fit? I'd spent six years believing a myth. Even now I didn't know how to let it go.

"Hey." Clearly Perry read my thoughts. I heard a firmness in his tone. "If you hadn't pursued Melissa, the truth would still be hidden. You uncovered it. You got through all the deceit."

"Not all of it. Baxter's still around."

"Yeah, well. Wait till the legal system gets through with him. He'll have a lot to answer for."

If he ever answered at all.

No. Unacceptable.

I wouldn't rest until he did. Now only he could tell us where Linda was buried. My friend deserved to come home. To a real grave where I could visit her, talk to her.

Carefully I shifted a little. My shoulder throbbed at the movement. I winced.

Perry drew back his hand. "I should let you rest."

"I need to talk to Dan."

"He wants to talk to you. Told me to call him when you're ready."

"That would be now."

"Sure you're up to it?"

As if I'd been "up" to any of this.

"If you bring me some Jelly Bellies."

EPILOGUE

MAY 2010

A brilliant sun warmed my head as I leaned over to place fresh flowers at the base of Linda's white headstone. My right shoulder vibrated with pain when I stretched out my arm, but I ignored it. I was making progress in my physical therapy. Some day I'd be back to normal.

I was alone in the small cemetery outside Vonita, which suited me just fine. All the better to talk to Linda. Using my left hand I lowered myself down to sit on the ground, knees to one side.

For a while I said nothing. Just ran my fingers through blades of spring grass, felt the slight breeze on my skin.

In my mind I heard Linda's boisterous laugh.

My eyes fell on her headstone, the etched dates of birth and death. My heart panged, first with sadness, then joyless satisfaction. At least I finally had a grave to visit.

"Well, I did it." I focused on the flowers, pink and white, with sprigs of green. "I visited him yesterday."

In a surprising move, Baxter Jackson had asked me to come see him. I'd never been in the county jail before. Never wanted to go again. The place reeked of dinginess and grim existence, played out in the dull colors of the walls, the lifelessness of inmates' faces. For Baxter this was a holding tank—and a refined one, at that. In a few days he would be transferred to a much harsher and meaner state prison.

Baxter had experienced a "change of heart before God," he'd told me through his attorney. *Yeah, right*, I thought. But a prompting in my own heart nudged me to go.

To that point I could only look at Baxter's actions. After his arrest on that February morning, police had searched his home. They'd found the prepaid cell phone he used to contact Trovky. And they'd found a taped-up box with the name "Ann" written on top. Inside were sheets of blank computer paper.

Even to the last, Baxter had tried to out-deceive the deceiving Melissa.

Eventually, however, he'd broken down and confessed his complicity in Linda's and Cherisse's deaths. And he'd led police to Linda's grave in the forest. But that was after weeks of legal machinations, threats from law enforcement, and promises of lighter sentencing if he cooperated. Even though Baxter didn't kill Linda, due to his conspiracy to kill Melissa and me, a shadow still hung over him regarding his second wife. "What are we going to find if we disinter Cherisse's body?" Dan had pressed. "Some other wound not consistent with falling down the stairs?"

Meanwhile Trovky stood more than ready to testify against Baxter in exchange for his own lighter sentencing.

The further Baxter had been backed into a corner, the better the promise of reduced punishment appeared. *That's* when he agreed to talk. And there was no way to tell his story without including a confession of abusing both his wives.

And so Baxter Jackson finally told the truth — to save his own skin.

His hatred for Melissa Harkoff poured out amid his confession. How manipulative and self-serving she was, feigning sincerity, empathy. "I'm convinced she killed her mother," he told police. "I think she pushed her when the woman was drunk, made her fall and hit her head. Melissa told me she had recurring nightmares about her mother's death. Now I know those dreams were from guilt."

When I heard the accusation, I wasn't surprised. Nothing about Melissa would surprise me anymore. But now the truth of her mother's death would never be known.

Baxter pled guilty to two counts of solicitation to commit murder plus involuntary manslaughter of Cherisse. Charges for his cover-up of Linda's murder were dropped in exchange for his taking authorities to her body. Baxter could have received twenty-five years for his crimes, but the plea bargain reduced his sentence to a mere eight years. For his part in the solicitation scheme, Trovky received three years—also a reduced sentence.

I ran my finger over the pink and white flowers at Linda's grave, feeling their velvety strength. "I didn't know what to expect when I went to that meeting."

At the San Benito county jail check-in, I showed my driver's license and stowed my purse in a locker provided in the lobby. I was not allowed to carry anything with me into the visiting room. Each step of security wound invisible bindings around me until I felt I could hardly breathe. Only then did the dark reality of what Baxter faced hit me. How very far the proud had fallen.

Baxter slumped into a seat opposite me at a table, looking nothing like the man I knew. His hair had been cut short, his eyes were dulled. Gone was that pulsing power, the confident arrogance. In their place hovered shame and brokenness.

I straightened in my chair, arms folded. Remembering his "sincerity" in front of Pastor Steve at my house that fateful day.

Baxter leaned forward, hands laced upon the table. His shoulders were stooped. "Thanks for coming."

I nodded.

Baxter watched his thumbs rub over one another. He cleared his throat. Looked at me. "I just wanted to tell you in person how sorry I am. For … everything. Linda. The fear I put you through. The chase I sent you on. The lying."

The rawness of his expression and tone, of *him*, left me flailing.

Surely he couldn't be telling me the truth. He had to have some angle.

But what would be his reason for now playing the penitent? He was in *jail*, far away from the church and town.

I filled my lungs with dusty air. "Okay."

One side of his mouth curved the slightest bit. "You don't believe me, do you?"

How does one know when a liar stops lying?

"I don't know what to believe."

Baxter dipped his chin. "That's understandable. It may take a long time for people to believe I've changed."

"*Why*, Baxter?" The words burst from me. "What happened to you and Linda? She was so happy when she married you."

He swallowed and looked away, as if wanting to turn from the memories. I waited him out. He wanted forgiveness? I wanted answers.

"I never hit Linda until after we were married." His voice ran low, pained. "I grew up watching my dad hit my mom. Thought I'd never be that way. Especially as a Christian. But one day this rage just welled up. And I lashed out. I was horrified. I apologized all over the place. Promised it would never happen again. And then it did." He paused. Sighed at the table. "After awhile I couldn't control it. Fear built up inside me. Of who I was becoming. That Linda would tell someone. That I'd lose my reputation. The more fearful I became, the more I lashed out. Then the more I had to hide. Around and around we went. Linda …" Baxter's voice caught. "… was a saint."

My own throat tightened. Yes, she was.

If only I'd reacted differently the day she came to me. Once I missed that opportunity, Melissa arrived, and Linda and I had no more private time together.

Baxter shifted in his chair. Blinked a couple of times. "The ironic thing is, Linda wanted a foster child because she believed having a third person in the home would stop me." He shook his head. "She had me believing it too. And I tried. I really did."

"You obviously didn't try hard enough." I couldn't keep the accusation from my voice.

He lowered his eyes. "No."

"You could have prevented all of it, you know." My anger spilled out. "That very first time you hit Linda—did you ask anyone for help? Confess to our pastor, go for counseling? Did you ever ask *God* to forgive you? To *help* you change?"

Baxter could not raise his eyes to my face. "I was too ashamed to pray."

I made a disgusted sound in my throat. "Too ashamed, that makes a lot of sense. Like God didn't know the truth."

Baxter raised a hand, palm out. "Don't you think I know that? Don't you think I've been over this a thousand, million times? I stepped off the path. It wasn't that far to step right back on, with God's help. But I didn't. And then I just got farther and farther away . . ."

I couldn't stand to look at Baxter a moment longer. My head snapped to the side, my eyes glaring at the wall. Emotions raged through my veins like floodwaters. I wanted to strangle the man for his arrogance. I wanted to rage and cry. Turn back time, like Superman. Everything that happened—it was all so *avoidable*. So totally, completely *stupid*.

Why hadn't I forced Linda to tell our pastor, the police? *Why* did I let her get away with her silence?

"I'm sorry, Joanne." Baxter's words were a mere whisper. "I wish I could change everything."

"Me too, Baxter. Me too."

My eyes burned, and the tears fell.

Now at Linda's grave I reached out to slide my palm over the smooth top of her headstone. "I still don't know if Baxter's 'change of heart' is real. I know God can change people. He can. But I just ..."

Out of nowhere, Melissa's sneering voice surfaced in my head. *"Miss Lying Christian ..."*

I closed my eyes.

"God's changing *me*, Linda. That I do know." I aimed a wan smile at her flowers. "I have some things to sort out."

Like willing myself to forgive Baxter—whether he was still lying or not. I hadn't been able to say the words yesterday as we parted. But I needed to get to that point, or bitterness would overwhelm me.

And I needed to look within myself, through God's eyes, and root out any deceit that lingered in *me*. I didn't know what that would do to my work. How do you skip trace without pretexting once in a while? (Pretexting—such a benign word for lying.) Perry said I was "catching the bad guys," so it shouldn't bother me. "Cops lie during interrogations," he told me. "Sometimes they *have* to—to see justice done. You saw that happen with Trovky."

But was God okay with that?

One thing I did know. If I opened my heart to God's leading, he would show me any deceit he wanted me to shed.

For fifteen more minutes I sat at Linda's grave. Praying silently. Talking aloud to her. Telling her how much I missed her.

"Well." I took a deep breath. Tilted my head toward blue sky. "I should be going. I'll be back soon." I struggled to my feet. Brushed off my clothing. "Perry's coming over for dinner."

A regular occurrence these days—at least twice a week. Perry had hired new help at the store. So he could spend more time with me, he said.

Not such a bad thing, I thought as I walked away from my best friend's resting place.

Besides, the smart man always brought Jelly Bellies.

AUTHOR'S NOTE

Dear Reader:

Thank you for taking yet another Seatbelt Suspense® ride with me. I hope I've entertained you as well as raised some provocative questions in your mind about man's natural tendency toward deceit. Some willfully dwell in it; some dabble. Others allow themselves to be pulled in, then can't seem to escape. Thank God that he is able to deliver us from all manner of deception, if only we will allow him to do so.

And now I must thank some very helpful folks.

First, the usual suspects. The Zondervan team, ranging from editor Sue Brower to copy editor Bob Hudson, and all the assistants and proofreaders and marketing people along the way. Julee Schwarzburg, freelance editor, made this a far better book than its original draft. Thank you, Julee!

In my research for the field of skip tracing, I ran across Robert Scott's *Skiptrace Seminar.com— The e-Book*. Scott, owner of Inter-Agency Investigations in Los Angeles, deserves credit for his detailed work, from which I drew much information. Tips on how to disappear were culled from skip tracer Frank M. Ahearn's site.

Mike Carlson, retired ER doctor, was a great sport in answering my medical questions. Doc, thanks for allowing me to interrupt a very nice dinner party for a visual lesson in how to fatally stab someone in the back.

KANNER LAKE SERIES

Coral Moon

Brandilyn Collins

The figure remained still as stone. Leslie couldn't even detect a breath.

Spider fingers teased the back of her neck.

Leslie's feet rooted to the pavement. She dropped her gaze to the driveway, seeking ... what? Spatters of blood? Footprints? She saw nothing. Honed through her recent coverage of crime scene evidence, the testimony at last month's trial, the reporter in Leslie spewed warnings: Notice everything, touch nothing.

Leslie Williams hurries out to her car on a typical workday morning—and discovers a dead body inside. Why was the corpse left for her to find? And what is the meaning of the message pinned to its chest?

In *Coral Moon*, the senseless murder of a beloved Kanner Lake citizen spirals the small Idaho town into a terrifying glimpse of spiritual forces beyond our world. What appears true seems impossible.

Or is it?

KANNER LAKE SERIES

Violet Dawn

Brandilyn Collins

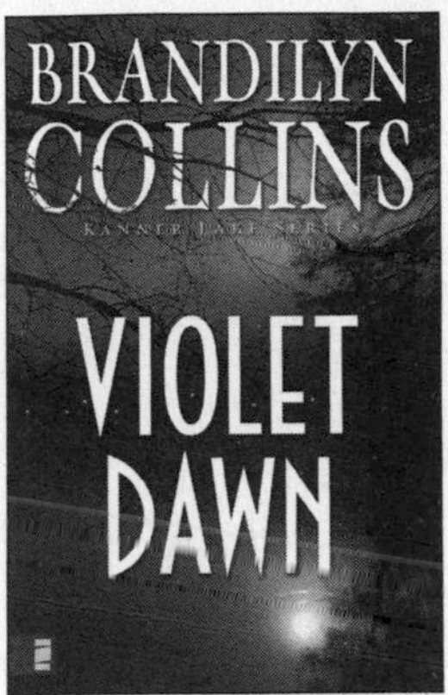

Something sinuous in the water brushed against Paige's knee. She jerked her leg away.

What was that? *She rose to a sitting position, groped around with her left hand.*

Fine wisps wound themselves around her fingers.

Hair?

She yanked backward, but the tendrils clung. Something solid bumped her wrist.

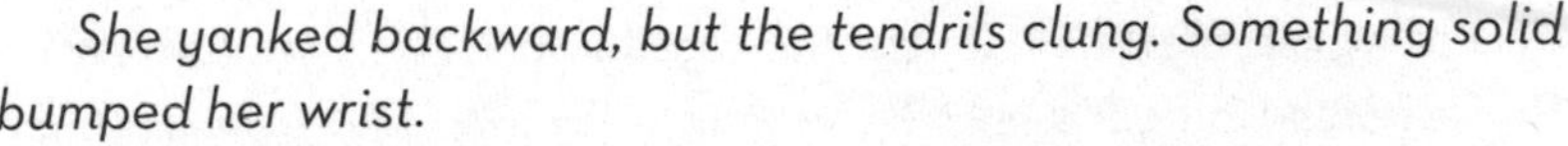

Paige gasped. With one frantic motion she shook her arm free, grabbed the side of the hot tub, and heaved herself out.

Paige Williams slips into her hot tub in the blackness of night—and finds herself face to face with death.

Alone, terrified, fleeing a dark past, Paige must make an unthinkable choice.

In *Violet Dawn*, hurtling events and richly drawn characters collide in a breathless story of murder, the need to belong, and faith's first glimmer. One woman's secrets unleash an entire town's pursuit, and the truth proves as elusive as the killer in their midst.

Available in stores and online!

Dark Pursuit

Brandilyn Collins,
Bestselling Author

"Ever hear the dead knocking?"

Novelist Darell Brooke lived for his title as King of Suspense—until an auto accident left him unable to concentrate. Two years later, reclusive and bitter, he wants one thing: to plot a new novel and regain his reputation.

Kaitlan Sering, his twenty-two-year-old granddaughter, once lived for drugs. After she stole from Darell, he cut her off. Now she's rebuilding her life. But in Kaitlan's town two women have been murdered, and she is about to discover a third. She's even more shocked to realize the culprit is her boyfriend, Craig, the police chief's son.

Desperate, Kaitlan flees to her estranged grandfather. For over forty years, Darell Brooke has lived suspense. Surely he'll devise a plan to trap the cunning Craig.

But can Darell's muddled mind do it? And—if he tries—with what motivation? For Kaitlan's plight may be the stunning answer to the elusive plot he seeks ...

Share Your Thoughts

With the Author: Your comments will be forwarded to the author when you send them to *zauthor@zondervan.com*.

With Zondervan: Submit your review of this book by writing to *zreview@zondervan.com*.

Free Online Resources at www.zondervan.com

Zondervan AuthorTracker: Be notified whenever your favorite authors publish new books, go on tour, or post an update about what's happening in their lives at www.zondervan.com/authortracker.

Daily Bible Verses and Devotions: Enrich your life with daily Bible verses or devotions that help you start every morning focused on God. Visit www.zondervan.com/newsletters.

Free Email Publications: Sign up for newsletters on Christian living, academic resources, church ministry, fiction, children's resources, and more. Visit www.zondervan.com/newsletters.

Zondervan Bible Search: Find and compare Bible passages in a variety of translations at www.zondervanbiblesearch.com.

Other Benefits: Register yourself to receive online benefits like coupons and special offers, or to participate in research.

PRAISE FOR NOVELS BY BRANDILYN COLLINS

EXPOSURE

... a hefty dose of action and suspense with a superb conclusion.

RT Bookreviews

Brandilyn Collins, the queen of Seatbelt Suspense®, certainly lives up to her well-deserved reputation. *Exposure* has more twists and turns than a Coney Island roller coaster ... Intertwining storylines collide in this action-packed drama of suspense and intrigue. Highly recommended.

CBA Retailers + Resources

Captivating ... the alternating plot lines and compelling characters in *Exposure* will capture the reader's attention, but the twist of events at the end is most rewarding.

Christian Retailing

Mesmerizing mystery ... a fast-paced, twisting tale of desperate choices.

TitleTrakk.com

[Collins is] a master of her craft ... intensity, tension, high-caliber suspense, and engaging mystery.

The Christian Manifesto

DARK PURSUIT

Lean style and absorbing plot ... Brandilyn Collins is a master of suspense.

CBA Retailers + Resources

Intense ... engaging ... whiplash-inducing plot twists ... the concepts of forgiveness, restoration, selflessness, and sacrifice made this book not only enjoyable, but a worthwhile read.

Thrill Writer

Moves from fast to fierce.

TitleTrakk.com

Thrilling ... characters practically leap off the page with their quirks and inclinations.

Tennessee Christian Reader

AMBER MORN

... a harrowing hostage drama ... essential reading.

Library Journal

The queen of seatbelt suspense delivers as promised. Her short sentences and strong word choices create a "here and now" reading experience like no other.

TitleTrakk.com

Heart-pounding ... the satisfying and meaningful ending comes as a relief after the breakneck pace of the story.

RT Bookreviews

High octane suspense ... a powerful ensemble performance.

BookshelfReview.com

CRIMSON EVE

One of the Best Books of 2007 ... Top Christian suspense of the year.

Library Journal, starred review

The excitement starts on page one and doesn't stop until the shocking end ... [*Crimson Eve*] is fast-paced and thrilling.

Romantic Times

The action starts with a bang ... and the pace doesn't let up until this fabulous racehorse of a story crosses the finish line.

Christian Retailing

An unparalleled cat and mouse game wrought with mystery and surprise.

TitleTrakk.com

CORAL MOON

A chilling mystery. Not one to be read alone at night.

RT Bookclub

Thrilling ... one of those rare books you hurry through, almost breathlessly, to find out what happens.

Spokane Living

... a fascinating tale laced with supernatural chills and gut wrenching suspense.

Christian Library Journal

VIOLET DAWN

... fast-paced ... interesting details of police procedure and crime scene investigation ... beautifully developed [characters] ...

Publishers Weekly

A sympathetic heroine ... effective flashbacks ... Collins knows how to weave faith into a rich tale.

Library Journal

Collins expertly melds flashbacks with present-day events to provide a smooth yet deliciously intense flow ... quirky townsfolk will help drive the next books in the series.

RT Bookclub

Skillfully written ... Imaginative style and exquisite suspense.

1340mag.com

WEB OF LIES

A master storyteller ... Collins deftly finesses the accelerator on this knuckle-chomping ride.

RT Bookclub

... fast-paced ... mentally challenging and genuinely entertaining.

Christian Book Previews

DEAD OF NIGHT

Collins' polished plotting sparkles ... unique word twists on the psychotic serial killer mentality. Lock your doors, pull your shades—and read this book at noon.

RT Bookclub, Top Pick

... this one is up there in the stratosphere ... Collins has it in her to give an author like Patricia Cornwell a run for her money.

Faithfulreader.com

... spine-tingling, hair-raising, edge-of-the-seat suspense.

Wordsmith Review

A page-turner I couldn't put down, except to check the locks on my doors.

Authors Choice Reviews

STAIN OF GUILT

Collins keeps the reader gasping and guessing ... artistic prose paints vivid pictures ... High marks for original plotting and superb pacing.

RT Bookclub

... a sinister, tense story with twists and turns that will keep you on the edge of your seat.

Wordsmith Shoppe

BRINK OF DEATH

... an abundance of real-life faith as well as real-life fear, betrayal and evil. This one kept me gripped from beginning to end.

Contemporary Christian Music magazine

Collins' deft hand for suspense brings on the shivers.

RT Bookclub

Gripping ... thrills from page one.

christianbookpreviews.com

DREAD CHAMPION

Compelling ... plenty of intrigue and false trails.

Publisher's Weekly

Finely-crafted ... vivid ... another masterpiece that keeps the reader utterly engrossed.

RT Bookclub

... riveting mystery and courtroom drama.

Library Journal

The cleverly complex plot, realistic courtroom drama, well-sketched secondary characters, and strong pacing make this book a fascinating read.

dancingword.com

EYES OF ELISHA

Chilling ... a confusing, twisting trail that keeps pages turning.

Publisher's Weekly

A thriller that keeps the reader guessing until the end.

Library Journal

Unique and intriguing ... filled with more turns than a winding mountain highway.

RT Bookclub

One of the top ten Christian novels of 2001.

christianbook.com

Captivating ... An imaginative plot, rounded characters, and workmanlike prose.

Moody Magazine

Also by Brandilyn Collins

Exposure

Dark Pursuit

Rayne Tour Series

(Cowritten with Amberly Collins)

1 *Always Watching*

2 *Last Breath*

3 *Final Touch*

Kanner Lake Series

1 *Violet Dawn*

2 *Coral Moon*

3 *Crimson Eve*

4 *Amber Morn*

Hidden Faces Series

1 *Brink of Death*

2 *Stain of Guilt*

3 *Dead of Night*

4 *Web of Lies*

Bradleyville Series

1 *Cast a Road Before Me*

2 *Color the Sidewalk for Me*

3 *Capture the Wind for Me*

Chelsea Adams Series

1 *Eyes of Elisha*

2 *Dread Champion*